Best of 2024 Volume Two

WELL READ Magazine

Edited by Mandy Haynes

WELL READ Magazine
Best of 2024
Volume Two

Copyright © 2024 Mandy Haynes

Cover art by Lindsay Carraway

Book & Cover design by Mandy Haynes

ISBN 978-1-7334675-6-8 (paperback)
ISBN 978-1-7334675-8-2 (e-book)

Published by three dogs write press

Dedicated to storytellers, poets, and artists who make the world a better place.

Also by WELL READ Magazine:

WELL READ Magazine's Best of 2023 Volume One
WELL READ Magazine's Best of 2023 Volume Two

In January of 2023, *WELL READ Magazine* began accepting submissions for prose, poetry, and visual art. I was blown away by all of the talented poets, authors, and artists that first year. I can't explain the thrill I felt sharing them with readers every month through the online journal, and the excitement of opening up another new submission.

That feeling is still strong today and I'm just as excited to share the submissions from 2024 with you. They are too good not to share again – in print – to give readers another chance to find them. There are no prompts or themes for the submissions so I never know what I'm getting into until I dive in. Every submission is a surprise and each one hits you in a different way. I love the emotional rollercoaster each new entry takes me on, so I've broken the traditional rules for publishing collections and kept the anthologies in the same format as what you find in the online journal. You never know what's coming next so get ready for a fun ride!

In the *Best of 2024 Volume Two*, you'll find fifty-one submissions written by a fantastic mix of award-winning authors and poets plus new ones to the scene. Three submissions in this volume were nominated for a Pushcart Prize: *Hanging Pictures* by Micah Ward, *The Lone and Level Sands* by James Wade, and *American Chestnut* by Candace Marley Connor. The cover art is by artist, Lindsay Carraway, who had several pieces published in February of 2023. You can find that issue and all past issues here www.issuu.com/wellreadmagazine.

If you have a story, essay, poem, or some artwork you would like to submit for consideration in upcoming issues of *WELL READ Magazine*, I would love to hear from you. You can find the submission guidelines at wellreadmagazine.com. If you have any questions, reach out to me at wellreadmagazine@gmail.com.

Thanks for reading!

Sincerely,
Mandy Haynes
Editor-in-Chief of *WELL READ Magazine*

Table of Contents

American Chestnut

Candice Marley Conner

Cate was born on this table.

No, that wasn't right.

Cate had borne many things at this table.

***

The largest existing stand of American Chestnut trees grows in Wisconsin, descendants of twelve chestnuts planted by an early settler in the late 1800s. A single American Chestnut was discovered in 2005 in the Talladega National Forest in Alabama. Three years later, a rare adult tree was discovered in a marsh off Lake Erie. The exact location is a carefully guarded secret.

These hundred-foot-tall trees were once an economically important hardwood timber, a staple fall food for wildlife, but were devastated by a stowaway blight in 1904. In a course of eighty years, the toxin infected over three billion trees, killing tissue and spreading sores across their trunks.

Entire forests now only contain the massive trunks of the dead, shorn of bark and once reaching limbs.

Ghosts standing in for the living.

***

Cate set the table with the fancy mock-silver candlesticks she had unearthed at Dirt Cheap. Those were followed by cloth napkins from the clearance bin at Wal-Mart and a properly placed knife and fork on either side. A gardenia plucked from the apartment complex's entrance and placed in a champagne flute was the finishing touch. Today was her birthday.

She really was too old to still believe in birthday wishes, at the ripe old age of twenty-seven, but she was optimistic that tonight her boyfriend, Kev, would give her good news. There would be a change.

Adjusting the volume on the radio, she daydreamed of different scenarios: he'd repaid all his gambling debts so she wouldn't have to choose whether to pay their bills or pay toward his debt each month. Or, he'd finally gotten that job with benefits at the shipyard so he could pitch in towards rent or her car note. Better yet, both of those were true and he'd gotten a sign-on bonus at the shipyard so he bought her a ring and would propose to her tonight.

Cate gasped in shocked delight at her ring finger and twirled around the table, showing off the bare hand to her cat, who dozed in one of the chairs.

"See that sparkle, Tiger?"

The cat, as cats do, looked at her with a peeved expression and stalked off toward the bedroom.

Unperturbed, Cate imagined showing it off to the girls at the salon tomorrow. Especially Jen who always had a lemon-sucking duckface any time Cate mentioned Kev. This ring would show her who was wrong.

Cate looked at the clock—almost dinner time!—and dashed off to the bathroom for a spritz of perfume. She smoothed her pink dress as she watched herself in the mirror. She looked nice. A golden tan from working at the salon, thick chestnut hair she'd inherited from her mama, sparkling green eyes fringed with long lashes she'd gotten from her daddy.

Her reflection took on an underwater sheen. She sniffed and quickly turned her thoughts away before that deep ache made her mascara run. She wouldn't have time to retouch her makeup if she remembered how this was the second birthday she'd spent without her mama and daddy. And the fact that, besides her looks and the money she got every year from their estate for her birthday, all that she had left of her family was her dining room table.

The kitchen timer beeped. She hurried back to the kitchen to turn off the burner under the rice. She checked the roast in the crock pot, and watched the clock again.

She'd tried to replicate her mama's famous spice cake but wound up having to buy one from Wal-Mart. The cream cheese frosting slid off on the car ride home so she'd had to prop it back on with toothpicks.

Kev should be here any minute. Traffic on Airport Boulevard was notoriously snarly so he was probably stuck at a red light. Or maybe he had a hard time finding a ride to the jewelers so he had to take the bus. She knew he hated taking the bus.

The front windows rattled. She glanced skyward as she ran to look outside, wondering if Miss Doris in 203 would bang on the floor with her cane. Peeking through the blinds, she watched Kev get out of a friend's truck. He tossed his bag over one shoulder and tucked his other hand in his tight jeans pocket as he walked up the sidewalk. Cate smiled, thinking he looked like a modern James Dean.

Grabbing his glass of wine, she stepped into her heels and smoothed her dress again. Then she waited for him to open the door.

"Whoa, Babe! Lookin' good." He tossed his bag to the floor and twirled her around.

Cate giggled happily. "You're going to make me spill your wine."

"Wine? Nah, I need a beer. Man, it smells good. What's the occasion?"

Cate's smile slid off her face. "My birthday?" she said to his back as he leaned into the fridge.

He popped the top and took a gulp. "Right, just kidding. I got you something. But not until after we eat. I'm starving."

He sat down at the family table. She made his plate then hurried to make hers as he attacked his with gusto before she had a chance to sit down.

"Wanna hear my news?"

Cate beamed. She knew it! "You got the job at the shipyard?"

"Nah, even better."

"You paid off your debts?"

Kev frowned. "How would that be fun?"

Cate did a little happy dance in her chair. The ring was in her near future—

"No, I met a guy who knows a guy at the Greyhound Park and I got..." Kev leaned closer, his eyes sparkling. "... insider's tips!"

"Oh." Cate couldn't taste the roast she'd just put in her mouth.

"So T's picking me up after I eat and we're going to check it out." He shoveled another bite, then looked at Cate in confusion. "What? That means I can win thousands, maybe millions. So I don't need a job." He said the last slowly, deliberately, as if Cate had suddenly developed a hearing problem.

"No, that's... it's just that—" Something caught in her throat. The gravy somehow soured, the meat suddenly rancid. She loved that about him—his optimism, how the world was his oyster just waiting for him to pluck out the pearl. Though sometimes it was simply a grain of sand. She shook her head. "It's my birthday. I got a bottle of champagne and thought we could rent a movie for us to watch together."

"Champagne? Ain't that expensive?"

"It can be, but not the one I— "

"And is that a new dress?"

He noticed. That was something else she loved about him. He noticed the small things. "Yes, but I bought it at Tar— "

"So you're looking at me like I done something wrong when I'm trying to make money and you're spending it on shit we don't need?"

"It's money my parents left me."

"And we couldn't use it to pay our cable bill? Really, babe, I thought we decided to use the money toward our bills and our debt. Instead you spend it on new clothes, champagne, and wine? A little selfish, don't ya think. You know I don't drink that frou-frou crap."

Your debt, Cate corrected. Not ours. But she didn't want to start an argument so she chewed on her top lip, her appetite gone.

Kev dropped his fork to his empty plate with a clatter. "Hey cheer up. It's your birthday. Wanna see what I got ya?"

Cate nodded.

Kev got his bag. "Close your eyes."

Squeezing them tight, she held out her hand, fingers splayed, and palm down.

"Turn your hand over."

Cate did and felt a cold cylinder drop into her hand. Confused, she opened her eyes. A flashlight.

Kev laughed. " 'Cause the power's been going out so much with all those tornadoes."

Cate couldn't hide the disappointment.

Kev's eyes lost the gleeful sparkle. "What? You don't like practical gifts? Should I've spray painted it pink and glued frickin' rhinestones all over it?"

"No, it's fine. Thank you. Practical. We need a flashlight." Kev snapped his fingers. "Ah, you're mopey because you want a birthday cake? So you can make your wish, that it? I told you I didn't forget."

"No, I already…"

He dug in his bag. She cringed at the thought of eating anything that had been inside that dirty, crumbled thing. He triumphantly withdrew and unwrapped a Little Debbie cake, reformed its spongy corners, and pulled a burning candle out of its fake silver candlestick holder.

"Ta-da!" He stuck the candle in the middle. It leaned precariously to the side, dripping wax onto the carpet. "Make a wish."

Cate squeezed her eyes shut and wished birthday wishes could stitch families back together. Knowing the impossibility of that, instead, she wished to be stronger.

Kev's pocket buzzed. He gave Cate a peck on the forehead. "Great dinner. And don't worry. The next time you see me, I'll have more money than you can wish for."

Cate nodded, but kept her eyes shut as she heard the door open then close with a bang as the wind from the breezeway slammed it shut behind him.

Miss Doris in 203 thumped her floor with her cane.

She sat, clutching that stupid flashlight until she felt Tiger weave in and out of her ankles. Tears leaked down her face as she cleaned the kitchen and wiped the dining room table. Using a baggie of ice and her blow drier, she picked melted wax out of the carpet with a butter knife. Then she popped the cork out of the champagne and sat back down at the table, absently tracing the old quilt tracks like a mysterious connect-the-dots.

The table was the only thing in their apartment not from a thrift store. It still matched the—as Cate optimistically called it—shabby chic décor of their home. Her great- grandfather had made it and counting herself, four generations had gathered around it, sharing love and hope and dreams. But now with her parents gone, and Kev at the tracks, it was just Cate, Tiger, and a bottle of bubbly that tasted bitterer with each sip.

She didn't know if there was anything in the world sadder than drinking champagne alone. She dipped a finger in and watched the bubbles viciously, or enthusiastically, depending on how she looked at it, cover her fingertip. She flicked the bubbles off.

She refilled her glass. Cate was born on this table. No, that wasn't right.

Cate had borne many things at this table.

Like the news her parents' vacation had come to an abrupt end.

A semi was in their lane, an eyewitness said. There was a hill so neither driver could stop in time.

Cate suspected at least one of the chickens had seen something. She made it to the scene in record time, though did pull over to breathe when she almost caused a wreck herself. And when she couldn't catch her breath, Kev had sent a friend to drive her the rest of the way.

The aftermath looked like a middle school sleepover. There were feathers everywhere. Like warm snow or wispy cotton, idyllic except for the dead chickens and parents. It seemed unnaturally quiet apart from the odd murmurings of survivor chickens and creaking metal. The feathers muffled Cate's footsteps, soft mounds of who knows—the chickens who didn't make it, parts of her parents. She didn't eat chicken anymore. She was afraid of what she might bite into. Deep-fried, a chicken tender resembled Mama's biceps.

The table had borne many things here. Kev's boots, his greasy satchel. It had been a tree once! An exceptional tree, though its table-ness had saved it from extinction. Had changed it. Given it new life. Formed from scraps her great- grandfather salvaged before the blight hit.

What had Cate done to give something new life? Because isn't that what folks do if they've borne something? You endure to make it new, better? Gather the scraps of your life and hammer and nail them into something sturdy. All that Cate had accepted was good things sour.

She gulped down the bubbles, viciously.

No, she hadn't accepted the pessimism. She knew it was a truth but not the truth.

The dinner table was born here. It had been a tree in the forest. Then it was a sewing table. Then it was a burrow when Cate was five.

She was a rabbit when she was five. The table had borne a burrow.

The rabbit, chestnut hair in pigtails like long bunny ears, covered the table with a scratchy blanket. Mama would bring her carrot sticks and the rabbit would watch, nose twitching, for trouble.

Daddy would roar, talons outstretched, and the bunny would shriek in excitement as she bounded back to safety.

Once, he snatched a pompom off her sock. The rabbit sat down and cried.

"What's wrong?" the eagle asked. "Mama can sew it back on."

She wrung an ear. "But it's my tail. How can I be a bunny without my cotton-tail?"

The table had borne a burrow to a rabbit with no cotton-tail. Mama brought the rabbit a carrot and the carrot was bitter.

***

At work the next day, Jen stared pointedly at Cate's empty ring finger but thankfully didn't comment. Commission was nonexistent as Cate couldn't muster the enthusiasm needed to push a sale. All she could think about was the fact that Kev never made it home last night. Even Tiger had left her to chase geckos.

She had slept alone on her birthday.

Well, not completely alone. She woke with a hangover snuggled tight.

***

When she got back to her apartment, Kev surprised her at the door with fistfuls of money.

"You won?" Cate worried all day for nothing. Everything was okay.

"Even better! That guy who knew the insider guy? He's into antiques. When he dropped me off, he saw our table—" Heart dropping, Cate pushed past him and gasped at the empty room. Four ghostly furroughs in the carpet were the only things left.

"Yeah, who knew that creaky old table was worth something? He said it was from a tree that got wiped out in the 1900s and was valuable. Pretty much extinct. Uhh…"

"American Chestnut," Cate whispered, sinking to her knees.

"That's it! Ain't it awesome? Six hundred dollars!" He fanned the bills over her head.

Shell-shocked, Cate stared at him. "That table was all I had left of my entire family. You knew that." She was a rabbit again, her cotton-tail snatched off.

"Babe, I'm your family now. So stop being selfish and think of how I can turn this money into thousands at the track. Hell, I'll even drink some of your champagne if you wanna celebrate."

The same part inside Cate that cracked like a chicken's wishbone when she found out about her parents split again as she traced a finger into the flattened patch of carpet. "It's my money," she said through gritted teeth.

Kev laughed. "Like you know a damn thing about dog racing. How about you come with me for good luck, we take your car, and I'll place the bets."

Cate picked up Tiger and stood. "Where does your friend work?"

"That pawn shop on Cody. You wanna go to the tracks now?"

Cate stepped between Kev and the door. She still had her purse on. With Tiger in her arms and the family table gone, there wasn't anything else in the apartment Cate worried about Kev destroying, so she might as well do it. His name wasn't on the lease.

"No. I'm leaving. When I come back, I want you and all your stuff gone. I'll bring the cops if you make me."

He snorted. Undeterred, Cate snatched the money he was still waving.

"What's gotten into you?" he sputtered.

Cate had borne many things at that table. "I'm getting my table back."

Picnics with Aunt Kathryn

Kaye Wilkinson Barley

Several years ago, my Great Aunt Kathryn and I decided to start a tradition all our own. We decided to get together for a picnic one Sunday a month, agreeing that picnics help keep you young. Further agreeing that sharing our bounty, however small and simple, with Mother Nature, along with the ants and the bees via picnics, was a fine, selfless and virtuous tradition we could proudly champion.

There were, of course, occasional exceptions to that rule. There were those cold or rainy Sundays when we would giggle like little girls as we plopped the picnic basket down on Aunt Kathryn's mahogany dining table in her oh-so-formal dining room, but it wasn't quite the same without the ants and the bees.

Our tradition began the day we found our beloved old picnic basket, the one we always filled to brimming with treats we both love. Simple fare, like picnics are meant to be. But also a nod to the whimsical and fancy that Kathryn and I have always been prone to.

It was one of those fortuitous little accidents that started a chain of events. A fun and lovely journey with an undefined ending or estimated time of arrival.

I was visiting Aunt Kathryn in Savannah that day, and we were in one of those frou-frou antique shops that I love to browse in but where I'm rarely able to buy anything. The dumpy places on the roadside are much more my style and where I'm usually able to find a treasure I can afford – like dusty old white ironstone pitchers back before Martha Stewart and Country Living Magazine started displaying them on every surface from a window sill to a toilet tank.

When "The Basket," as it became known, fell off a shelf,

landing at my feet, it was love at first sight. I knew better than to let the shop owner know that I was already coveting this old thing—a faded old red wicker picnic basket.

The owner raced toward me squealing "Ooh, ooh, ooh. Is it hurt? Is it broken?" I wasn't sure if she was concerned about the basket or my foot. All the while, she was waving her hands and fluttering her fingers like she was feeling moved by spirits usually encountered in a revival tent while I just stood there waiting to see what was going to happen next.

Aunt Kathryn nudged me from behind and whispered. "Do not say one word, sugar. Not one."

When the shop owner stopped in front of us and finally stopped waving her hands and fluttering her fingers, she noticed my aunt.

"Oh. Kathryn. Um. How lovely to see you!"

"Hello, Marguerite."

"Where have you been keeping yourself, I haven't seen you in the shop in just an age."

Aunt Kathryn looked around, "Actually, I don't believe I've been here before. Lovely things you have here, dear. But tell me, do things often come tumbling off the shelves barely missing giving your patrons a concussion?"

I could have sworn I heard a quiet little "tut-tut" from Kathryn as she continued looking around, never letting her eyes fall to the picnic basket on the floor between us.

Marguerite pulled her shoulders back, put her nose another inch in the air. "Certainly not. And that old picnic basket is light as a feather. It wouldn't have even dented a hair on your head, Kathryn. Why it's even in this shop, I have no idea. It's just a cheap ol' piece made overseas somewhere. And you know how those things are, no substance. Light as a feather. Here, I'll get it out of your way."

Kathryn gracefully leaned forward and snatched up that basket as quick as I could blink my eyes.

"Oh, here, Marguerite dear, I'll take care of it for you. My grandson's sister-in-law's little girl would love to play with this. And you know, with it being so cheap and all, no need to worry when it falls apart the first day she tries to get her cats to take a nap in it. I'll be more than happy to take it off your hands. How much?"

We watched Marguerite turn to stone in front of our very eyes. She knew she had been found out. This beauty was no cheap piece of nothing from somewhere overseas as she had described it

"Oh, why, good heavens, I couldn't take your money for this old thing. I'll just toss it in the trash can right over there."

"Oh my no. I'm quite excited by the very thought of that adorable little girl tucking her kitties into this old thing. If you won't accept my money, I'll just toss it in the back of the car. You go along, Katy, take your time and look around. I'll be right back."

And that's how we came to own our beautiful 19th century Heywood-Wakefield wicker picnic basket with metal hinges and peg nails, its original color faded to a soft warm red. The woven wicker in surprisingly fine shape. This old basket had been lovingly cared for. Score one for the home team. That would be me and Aunt Kathryn since there was no little girl with kittens belonging to Kathryn's grandson's sister-in-law. Indeed, not even a grandson.

My aunt had known Marguerite Harald Alberta Woolsey all her life and knew she was one of those women who would just rather tell a lie than tell the truth, and Aunt Katherine loved taking advantage of that little lifelong trait.

We immediately planned a picnic to take place the very next day.

And it was so much fun, we decided to work a monthly Sunday picnic into our busy schedules.

We now had the perfect reason, allowing no excuses, to get together once a month—for me to make the trip to Savannah from my home a couple hours away.

Picnics became a tradition for the two of us, and something we both looked forward to. Our phone conversations now included picnic menus and locations.

It was early on that Aunt Kathryn spoke up and made it clear that eating on paper plates, even for a picnic, was unacceptable. Not even acceptable to Mother Nature, the ants, or the bees.

She wanted china. And silver.

And crystal. Oh, my.

All these things would join the linen table cloth and napkins she was donating to the cause of a well-stocked picnic basket

With that in mind, Aunt Kathryn decided we needed to choose a china pattern. And a silver pattern. And, yes, a crystal pattern.

When I reminded her we weren't planning a wedding, only outfitting an old picnic basket she did that "tut-tut" thing she does.

So, of course, we did it her way.

Which gave us the perfect excuse to start scouring antique and junk shops for the things we would keep stored in our basket.

Anyone who loves to antique or junk knows the hunt is part of the fun, and our hunt was a hoot.

When we had our first china-related disagreement over exactly which pattern we should choose, we agreed we would each pick out a piece, or two, of china to suit ourselves. One that appealed to us individually rather than as a collective.

As it turned out, we both chose Limoges luncheon plates. They were different patterns, but close enough in design that they made quite a lovely aesthetically pleasing mismatch. We both chose white with small pink flowers, Kathryn's with a pink rose and white daisy border, mine with a random scattering of tiny pink roses. At some point, a slightly chipped Limoges creamer and sugar bowl of yet another pink and white floral pattern found residence in "The Basket." As did a couple of teacups, small bowls, and one larger covered dish. We had a veritable mash-up of Limoges before we finally had to say "enough!" Or there'd be no room for food.

While hitting a few yard sales on a pretty spring Saturday, we both knew we'd found our perfect silverware which turned out not to be silver at all, but stainless. With the most darling little bumble bee embossed on the handles. Perfect! We swooped in and scooped up the few odds and ends available—enough that we both had our own fork and a spoon each, but would have to share a knife.

Our crystal needs were met when we stopped at an old falling down shack of a place on a back road between Savannah and Tybee Island. There was a sign stuck in the ground with "Old Stuff" and an arrow drawn on it pointing to the shack where an elderly couple were sitting in rockers on the front lawn. Both were smoking pipes, and both were dressed in well-worn overalls and work boots.

We introduced ourselves as we approached and were offered our choice of drinks from an old Coca-Cola cooler and a bit of tobacco in case we had pipes of our own. We passed on the tobacco, but took them up on their offer of a cold drink and sat of the steps for a visit.

By the time we left, we knew quite a bit about Henry and Harriett, and we had a few pieces of delicately etched antique Rose Point crystal by Cambridge. Henry and Harriett were quite well suited to their choice of livelihood in sales seeing as how we intended to buy two pieces of crystal and ended up with, well, never mind. A lot of crystal—some only slightly chipped. I still have quite a few pieces at my house, Aunt Katherine ended up with quite a few pieces, and friends and family who have admired it might arrive home with a piece of two. Still not sure how that happened. But. It's a lovely, lovely pattern, and because we had so much to choose from, the pieces that resided in "The Basket: were on rotation.

I arrived at the spot chosen for our picnic—a serene spot in Bonaventure Cemetery, on a bluff overlooking the Wilmington River. Bonaventure is hauntingly beautiful, and if you're one who enjoys the mysteries and peacefulness of a walk through a cemetery, this is one not to be missed. If you read John Berendt's book "Midnight in the Garden of Good and Evil," you've seen one of the Bonaventure statues—the "Bird Girl" which was featured on the book cover. It's no longer there, however, due to over-zealous visitors who perhaps weren't as respectful to "Bird Girl" as they could have been. She now resides in Savannah's Telfair Museum.

As I put down our linen tablecloth, our much loved, long used picnic finery along with today's repast of country pâté and crusty French bread, plump strawberries, a salad of crunchy fresh lettuces topped with slices of cucumber, mushrooms and local tomatoes, I noticed a line of ants headed our way, and a few bees hovering around the azaleas. I poured some of Aunt Kathryn's favorite champagne,

Krug Grande Cuvée, into our glasses and leaned back on my elbows, enjoying the quiet laced with birdsong.

"Yes, Aunt Kathryn, I know, I know. I did splurge on the champagne. But, well, we couldn't let your birthday go by without a bit of celebration. I mean, I think your old pal Conrad Aiken started a Bonaventure tradition of drinking with the dearly departed by having his headstone constructed as a bench, declaring it to be a place for his friends to sit and enjoy a martini while conversing with his spirit, right? Do you suppose he didn't like champagne? Heaven forbid. Well, with apologies to Mr. Aiken, we'll forgo the martini and enjoy the Krug, what say?"

After wiping away a few errant tears, I raised my glass to the headstone that read "Kathryn, a woman who loved picnics. She always did the best she could, and lived her life with enormous joy. Much loved and greatly missed."

Then, as I felt a soft breeze whispering in my ear I got up, whispered, "I love you too, Aunt Kathryn," and walked away, leaving behind "The Basket" and all the treasures it had held safely for so many years. Leaving the now threadbare tablecloth and all that rested on it. All to be shared with Mother Nature, the ants and the bees. As it should be.

The Berlin Flower Shop

Mike Ross

"When the bombs began to fall, that was the worst. We'd hear a whistling, then an explosion and the floors shook, like an earthquake. Windows shattered and the walls rattled," her hands mimicked the motion. The Great Depression was terrible but the bombs were the worst!" I'm talking with Frau Rosen in Rosen's Floral Shop inside the Friedrich Street Train Station in central Berlin, Germany.

This unlovely structure in the center of the city is unlike any other. It has a soul, a heart, a living presence. The streams of humanity flowing through it for 150 years gives it life. If you stand in the middle and close your eyes you can feel the vibrations of the past, and the relief of the present. You hear the screeching trains from the 1880s to the 2000s, smell the ever present simmering bratwursts, the tang of coffee and the woody aroma of the bookstalls. This is the here and now, this is the wave and thunder of life as it sweeps over a great city, this place is the "now", no matter when that "now" is or was, past, present, future in the same instant. Open your eyes and the soaring cantilevered roof spreads for acres up and down the tracks, sunlight streams through the glass walls.

I have a couple of hours between trains and wander into the floral shop to get a closer look at a black and white photo in the display window. The photo shows a smiling young man, hands on hips, in an old fashioned cap standing in front of this store, flowers spilling out of buckets arranged on the pavement near him, old-type lettering, 'Rosen's Fine Florals', stenciled in an arc across the plate glass. Inside, the shop is filled with customers and the front door stands open. Under the photo is written, '1887'. Frau Rosen, seeing my interest, comes over to explain the picture.

"That's my grandfather," she points to the man in the photo, "he founded the business in 1887, shortly after the station opened. My father took it over when Opa died and Papa ran it through World War I, the Depression and the start of World War II. I was 15 or 16 when he left for the Russian front." She pauses, glances at the photo and back to me. "He never came back so I took over the shop." She says this as a matter of fact, just routine for a girl in her mid teens to take on running a family store. She tells me about the bombs, Hitler's suicide and the Russian occupation.

She is now in her mid 90s, small and smartly dressed. "And I'm still here." I congratulate her on her success but she waves away the compliment. "That's what we all did. If you wanted to eat, to live, you worked. No one told me I was too young or that a woman couldn't run a business. But I did dress like a boy for a few years, in the late 1940s." I ask her why.

"The Russians. This part of the station was in the Soviet Zone. I was a young woman so to protect myself, I dressed in pants, wore my Papa's cap, cut my hair short and wore no makeup. Sometimes I'd smear a bit of dirt on my face. It worked. I was never raped. The soldiers didn't want flowers. All they wanted was vodka so they never bothered me. The Reds were awful but, oh, the bombing was worse. I was one of the lucky ones. I survived both."

Her two young employees wait on the constant stream of customers, the bell above the door tinkling each time it opens. I apologize for taking her time but she only smiles. I ask her what the Friedrich Street Station was like during the years of Soviet occupation and the now vanished German Democratic Republic, known in America as East Germany.

"The Soviet years were a quiet nightmare," she says, "with so many soldiers and the harsh regulations. The Russians left sometime in the 1950s, I think. In 1961 the East German government divided the station and set up barriers to stop us from fleeing to the West. This station became the main border crossing between East and West Berlin. I was in the East but the other end of this building," she points, "was sort of in the West, or at least it was used by Westerners to change trains."

All of Friedrich Station was in the East but the zigzagged routes of two subway lines that served West Berlin converged here. The few stops of those lines that were in the East were bricked up by the government. The Berliners called the stops Ghost Stations, where no one could get on or off except ghosts. Westerners passed through the Friedrich Station but couldn't leave the building.

She sighs and shakes her head. "When we looked over the barriers, we could see the Westerners getting on and off their trains, well dressed, well fed, reading real newspapers, but we weren't allowed over to that side, nor they over here. So all we did was watch." She stops to answer a question and turns back to me.

"Life on this side was hard. Not much food and what we had was terrible. Often no heat or electricity, but they told us we lived in a workers' paradise! What lies! Thank goodness for the government employees who worked near here. They still bought flowers, thank God. Kept my shop alive."

I thought back to the late 1960s, when I changed subway lines at the Friedrich Station. While I waited for my connection, I peered over the barricades and passport booths into the East. The place was grimy and smelled of urine, the windows thick with dust. When I returned 22 years later in the summer of 1990, just weeks after the Berlin Wall had come down, the station was much the same but the atmosphere had undergone a sea change. I walked down the platform from what had been the West into the former East, past barriers I would have been shot at just 6 months earlier had I tried to flee, past the relics and detritus of collapsed passport booths. East Germany had died, a piece of trash on the dustbin of history, a ghost in the station among a carnival of other ghosts.

I ask her if she had ever read the spy novels like *The Spy Who Came in From the Cold* by John le Carre that had made Friedrich Street Station famous. Yes, she had, but the intrigue in those books was exaggerated.

"I remember spies being exchanged. Soldiers marched a guy in and stood at the barricades. Another guy between soldiers was on the other side. The passport gates opened and the two fellows switched. It was usually a pretty quiet affair. Once a guy who owned a bratwurst kiosk," she points to a spot where a coffee shop stands, "was arrested. He tried to run but they got him. He worked for the West, passed messages somehow. I don't recall anyone making it across. The guards were everywhere so life was routine, quiet."

Was she here in the 1930s when 10,000 Jewish children were evacuated through Friedrich Station to London? "I was only 7 or 8 when that happened," she says. "My best friend, Sarah Goldschmidt, was a little Jewish girl who lived near us, just 3 blocks from here. We went to the same school and I was always at her house. Her mother, Anna, was a wonderful baker. I remember eating loaves of her chocolate babka. She always sent a big hunk of it with me as a gift for my mother. One day Sarah was here, the next day she was gone. The family disappeared, too. Their shoe shop closed. My mother told me never to talk of it, never to mention my friendship with Sarah to anyone. I didn't but I never forgot her." Frau Rosen stares out the window a long moment before she continues.

"I found out after the war, Sarah had survived but her family perished in Auschwitz. That was life—and death—with the Nazis. Worse than the Soviets." I glance at my watch and know I have to get to my train. I buy some flowers, thank her for her time and walk toward my platform.

In 1990 the Berlin Wall fell and the station began its long escape from the cold war. In June of that year, I was on the first train from the West to the East that stopped at the ghost stations. Tearful Berliners crowded the platforms, holding balloons and wearing party hats. They boarded the train and sang songs of freedom, of relief, sang to their beloved Friedrich Street Station.

I walk to platform 9 for my train to Hamburg. The Gothic-like ceiling vaults above me, light pours in through the glass walls, trains screech and passengers bustle. With eyes closed, I sense the vibrations of the past, hear the bombs falling, the jack boots of Soviet soldiers, the silent scream of a long dead regime realizing it's a corpse, the joy in the voices at the ghost stations when the springtime of freedom dawns, the relief of the new era. My train rushes in, stirring the smell of bratwurst and coffee with the aroma of the past and the sounds of the present.

1968

Will Maguire

1968 is buried like a bruise in my memory. It was long ago. But I still feel it. Amputees say they still feel a missing leg. A phantom pain that remains long after what's taken is gone. 1968 is the year part of me was taken. I still feel it.

That year brought terrible collisions between old virtues and new verities. Truths taken of faith were tested and sometimes failed. The nation but also families were shaken to the bone by wars declared fought in jungles but also undeclared wars fought over kitchen tables.

It was the year I discovered loss. And the kind of heartache that climbs down and in and stays. Forever.

And this year, 2024, has begun to feel like then. I recognize something in it. Something coming.

1968 began when a kid I knew was expelled from my Catholic grammar school for the grave sin of wearing Beatle boots. We both wore white shirts and clip on ties but the nuns explained he was a heretic. His hair was over his ears. And though we learned to read together and memorized the commandments and confessed our sins each Friday that year, they said, he was different. One morning, hands over hearts pledging our allegiance in the parking lot, the principal dragged him out of line.

She sent out a mimeograph sheet home to all the parents reminding them of the dress code. When his parents resisted, the principal sent him packing. Off to the heathens of public school.

I listened as my teachers whispered he was a bad seed, sure to become a thug. All the while I practiced my own private heresy.

Stealing cartons of Lucky Strikes, dreaming of my escape into puberty and learning to inhale behind the school.

Beatle boots and anything but crew cuts were, as it turned out, just the beginning. By 1968 a war that had started in a faraway jungle a few years earlier had begun to find its way home. It crept into our living room each night through the television screen. After supper the TV showed jungle firefights and riots. American soldiers crying calling for medical and protesters, just kids like me, beaten bloody in city streets.

And every night the black and white flicker of the slow roll of the names of American boys that died fighting for something almost none of us could explain in class.

The night LBJ decided he would not run again I found my mother, face in her hands weeping at the kitchen table. Not for him I can see now, but instead for what she sensed was coming. Something as certain as a freight train with all we still believed waiting on its tracks.

There was an old man down the street whose oldest son had gone into the marines. Killed in combat that year. A widower and regular at the American Legion, he had a bad ticker. The doctors told him he wouldn't last the year without a transplant.

As he began to fail, the parish ladies, unsure of how to help, started a school bake sale. They believed I suppose that everything bitter, even the world, could be made sweet with confectionery sugar. So they made cakes that we sold after Mass on Sunday.

I was elected to bring him the envelope. I rang his bell then earnestly told him that we raised $47. . . to help with the medical bills. As I handed it to him he began to soundlessly cry, then without a word slowly closed the door.

That spring some kid one town over wrapped his daddy's Buick around a tree. I overheard my father tell a neighbor the kid was a hippie. Wore bell bottoms. Hair was over his ears.

The old man was terribly sick and they decided to give him the kid's heart. After the operation he almost died a couple times. The doctors said that his body kept rejecting the heart.

I suppose he felt every beat was both his only chance at survival and a betrayal of his soldier son. But by summer he had recovered enough to walk around the block with a cane. As the year deepened draft cards were burned, Nixon secretly bombed Cambodia, rioting broke out at the Democratic Convention in Chicago.

Kids, not much more than teenagers, sensed they were being lied to, that every thing they had been told was good and true was merely a mask for power and avarice.

And soon the entire country started to seem just like the old man, clinging to a tired and worn out heart. Unable to do anything but reject the very thing that could save it.

In my house my oldest brother, all of 19, was called to the draft board. Like everyone I knew then, he was impossibly young, certain of what was right. True in the way only the innocent can afford.

He said he didn't want to fight in a war on the other side of the world. He said it felt wrong.

And my father, an immigrant and World War II Veteran, told him that this country had been good to us. That the United States stood for right and that our family owed a debt that he had been called to pay.

And so there were fights.

The quiet kind. The kind that no longer used fists or even words but instead collided in sharpened silence at the dinner table each night. The wreckage was hidden, but no less severe. And love, its nightly casualty, began to roll away like the names of the dead each night on the news.

My brother finally agreed to go to the draft board and was rejected. 4F, asthma.

But no matter. The war, between my father's faith and my brother's growing distrust continued at home. Finally my father, with tears in his eyes, told my brother to pack and leave.

Hemingway famously wrote that the world can break just about anything, but that some become stronger in the broken places. But 1968, it's fractured families and broken faith, did not feel strong to me. Some boys I suppose, are strong at 19. Many leave much younger. I myself, an unrepentant fool, left at 16. But my brother, was not strong.

I watched him pack and listened to him lie to me that everything would be all right. And, just a boy, I felt the wrong in it all. Some kind of sin like stealing or lying or not standing up when everything in you whispers you must...or be lost forever

I went to my father and told him that he was making a mistake. I pleaded with him. Something's wrong, I said. This is some kind of sin there isn't a commandment for. The kind you can't forgive yourself for. The kind you carry all your days.

He gazed at me in silence with a look I did not recognize and finally said, "You don't understand. You're too young to know."

I understand that look now. It was grief.

The day my brother left I stood at the front door watching. The old man, slowly limping down the street, stopped by him. They talked for a moment. And I watched as the old man, put a hand on his scarred and unsteady heart, then tenderly touched my brother's arm. He whispered something and my brother bowed his head like it was some kind of absolution passed only between the wounded. Then my brother turned away forever.

That year, 1968, was long ago but I still feel its fracture. My family, my country, my heart. I still feel the phantom pain of the part cut away from me, gone these many years. And I became stained by the memory of the way things were supposed to fit, but never would again.

Nixon resigned, the war ended, and the country, like the old man's heart, eventually grew stronger. And, though it took some few years, my brother died alone. Of that year's wounds.

But 1968, its quiet wars and rejected hearts, its riots and o unforgotten sins became a bruise on my memory. Its self inflicted wounds crawled into my 12 year old eyes then down until they finally reached my heart that now, like the old man's, sometimes feels worn out and tired of beating against this world.

And now 2024, has begun to feel to me like 1968.

I can feel it coming like a freight train. And once again all we believe lay in it's tracks. I feel that it's dark shape rushing toward us and feel it's coming collision begin to cast a shadow of undeclared war.

All around a kind of mass hysteria has taken hold. A toxic mix of grievance and outrage fills airwaves and phone screens whispering that democracy has failed. It bellows that we must free this one man from law and accountability to do what he will, because he and only he can restore our fractured hope.

Talk of poisoned immigrant blood and dictators, vast deportation camps and retribution are now cheered by millions. Never mind that many of these rabid ideas were defeated in 1946. Today they are coated in a fresh veneer of patriotism and called righteous.

Fathers and uncles, brothers and neighbors have been convinced. These misguided people want to cut out the heart of democracy and replace it with something smaller. Something meaner.

They tell us again and again that the only way to save America, as they demand it should become, is to destroy America as it is.

And like 1968, I am beginning to feel that rending of families. Of country. I have seen this before. I know where it leads.

I have watched its flicker and slow roll of loss. I have seen its mournful demands, calling still from long ago, in my father's eyes.

We...each of us...have to decide. Will we honor the kind of people we still aspire to be or will we surrender to this other colder America.

I am Irish, which is another way of saying that I know in my bones that the world is meant to break your heart.

But I am American too. Which is another way of saying I believe...pray really...that Hemingway was right. That the broken I feel barreling toward us will somehow...please God..., in the end, make us stronger.

Recent Events

AJ Concannon

I'm wondering if I should risk a shower, but I can't decide, see it's the people next door, this dog outside, barking, they keep it tied up outside and it barks just keeps barking morning noon and night, rowf rowf rowf, drive you absolutely mental. I would say something but one look at you and they panic, bloody foreigner at the door, saying something about the dog in his mangled Japanese, I think he wants to take it for a walk or something and I probably would, you know, take the thing for a walk, I'm that much of a pushover. Walking with the yapping Shiba, it would become a regular event, you know, I would go round to shoot the bloody thing and end up taking it for a walk and picking up its poo.

I put the TV on to drown out the dog and Hiroshi Kume is in full flow, incredulous, something about the little boy, the head on the school gates, and after the sarin gas and the earthquake these recent events have him stunned.

And I am getting wound up by the barking as well as thinking about recent events with herself and the phone goes. I don't snatch at it because then you're too keen, and she knows, you see, she can tell you've been sitting by the phone waiting for her to call. So I let it ring a couple times and answer very nonchalant, you know, very me answering the phone as a regular event, you know, which it certainly is not, not in this house.

It's a woman but not her. I can't hear who it is over the yapping and Kume's outraged tones but I know it's not her. And I'm really wound up now. Then I realize it's this company who phone me up now and again, to check their English tests, all these tests they send out to hundreds of kids, thousands of kids, to rearrange these bizarre sentences; 'You're right, we don't have enough tangerines', and they pay me seriously daft money to tell them it's grammatically correct but nobody would say it. And they hate when I tell them that, but it's true. They tell me I should comment only on structure, but I just happen to come from a land where we speak English, you know, they want to ask real teachers about that. And even if I could tell them they wouldn't get it, they are all History and Literature graduates and stuff, you know, except the one who is on the phone just now competing with the Shiba and Kume for my attention, she graduated in Life & Culture or some such nonsense. They did have one who spoke good English for a while, but they moved her to Domestic Science.

And we've done the preliminaries and she's asking me about 'acceptable.' I love this acceptable, I argued for hours about it once with them, 'Acceptable to who?' I kept asking but they just agreed and kept repeating my own questions to me. "'She is honest' is acceptable?" she says. And I'm wondering if this is some kind of ironic comment on my private life and recent events but I let it pass, my persecution complex acting up again.

"Acceptable."

"And 'She is honesty' is acceptable?"

"Not acceptable."

"But honesty is a noun," she says.

And I'm thinking to tell her that shite is brown but what's that got to do with the price of mince? But she never met my granny and probably wouldn't comprehend her profound sense of irony. "It is," I tell her, confident. The nouns I am good at, the doing words and describers I tend to struggle on.

And there is a silence. Even the dog. But Kume's still talking. He's going on about the age of the boy, the fact that he was only fourteen. I thought he was eight, but no.

"So, 'She is just' is acceptable?"

And again the reply 'not in my book' forms in my head, based on recent events.

"Okay," I tell her.

"So 'She is justice.' Acceptable?"

"Only in a kind of abstract, superhero sense, you know, like if she is Wonder Woman, you know?"

I'm feeling quite proud of that answer. The mutt disagrees and starts up again.

"Sorry?"

"Not acceptable," I tell her. And again, there is a silence.

"Thank you," she says, and thanks me three or four more times, and apologizes for bothering me, and by the time we hang up the Shiba is in lung-bursting form, really howling at the heavens now, and I want a shower, but it would be my luck for her to ring while I'm in there. The flex is long but when I try taking the phone to the shower it doesn't stretch anywhere close to the bathroom door. And it's cold, I'm not wanting to be on the phone in the hall wet from the shower, and freezing cold, you know.

But I really need a shower, it's been four days, and I put the hot water on so the shower fills up with steam and it's not so cold when you go in. And I'm in, but the towel is outside so I open the door to get it and the blast of cold air cuts right through you. I hang the towel up and start soaping up. The water pressure is not great, it's an old building and the shower head holder is level with my shoulder, put in when even the natives were smaller, although they sit down in the shower, so perhaps not. And I've got a plastic holder glued on the tiles above. I had to get my brother to send over the superglue specially. "All they hi-fis and computers and they can't make superglue?" he said. "A mystery right enough."

See I shave in the shower but there is no mirror in there. I had a great wee disposable razor, single blade, shaved with it for three months. It's great how that happens sometimes, you'll go months using razors that cut you to pieces, then you'll get one you can just keep on using. I had to stop because I let the growth go for three days, and it was too blunt to handle it, hurt like hell. I had to go half-shaved to the convenience store at Sannomiya Center Gai for a new packet. And they only had these twin blades, I'm not keen on them, but it worked fine. I threw the other one out but that was stupid I should have kept it and went back to it after the twin blade handled the three-day stuff.

Standing there naked with the hot water coming down, you get all worked up, you know, and I'm thinking of her naked in here beside me, it's been a while, but the recent events come to mind and I calm down a wee bit and start shaving. Like I say I don't like the twin blade, and they are worse the second day. And the only thing worse than a second day twin blade is a second day twin blade on a swivel head. Whoever thought that up should be shot. Fits the contours of your face? Only if your face looks like the side of a cliff, and if it doesn't it soon will after the swivel head has a go at it. Before you know it, I've cut my throat. Pretty bad. The blood running down the razor onto my fingers and dripping onto the floor. Bloodshed and recent events. I am seeing signs everywhere. The facecloth is red so the stains don't show up. But the bleeding won't stop. And I've got grazes and cuts on my legs from recent events that start to hurt now they are being washed, and the bleeding won't stop, and I'm thinking about what I'm going to say to her on this bloody phone, she won't meet me, she loves that phone, and we talk, and what do we say we talk about this and we talk about that we just talk talk talk and we get nothing, it leads nowhere.

So I dry off but I forget the blood and the white towel has got blotches of red, it's streaked through with it, and it's a good one, the big fluffy Sailor Moon job. And with the water off I can hear the yapping Shiba and something else, I'm pulling the t-shirt over my head, trying to keep it away from the blood on my neck, and the towel tied round the waist, and I can hear, under the dog, the phone going, and I'm out and across the kitchen floor, but the answering machine is on and it's my voice followed by another, and Kume is saying that the killer was fourteen, I thought it was the victim, but no, my Japanese isn't great but I'm sure he's saying they've arrested a 14-year-old boy, the head on the school gates, he was only eight right enough, and Kume's outraged, going on about children killing children, trembling earth, sarin gas attacks and children killing children, what have we come to he asks, and I'm thinking about this as I'm running past the fridge and the fridge cartwheels into the air, but then I realize it's me, and I land on my backside but my leg shoots out and my ankle cracks the corner of the door jamb, crushes the bloody thing, the wood splinters, and there is a wee blank in time and then pain, the leg broken, lying there, wanting to touch it, but scared to, and my throat bleeding on the tatami now, and I pick up the phone, she hasn't hung up, she's still talking. And she realizes the machine is gone and it's me now, a person, she's talking to a real person.

"'She is right' is acceptable?" she says.

I'm on my back and the leg, dear God, twitching now, the damp towel in the cold, the blood streaking the towel, throat like a butcher's dustbin, and the yapping Shiba going bananas next door, and Kume is, I think, crying, sobbing on live TV, but I'm elsewhere, on recent events, and I want to say "She's always right, that's the problem." And then I think I have, you know, said it, kind of spoken the words out loud.

And there is a silence.

She Would if She Could

Patricia Feinberg Stoner

Why was it, Dora wondered, that it was always the nerdy, the needy or the downright nasty who got in touch?

The gorgeous boyfriends so light-heartedly discarded. The very special girlfriends who had somehow drifted away. *Their* names never turned up on Facebook or What's App. *Their* emails never dropped into her in-box with the inevitable 'Don't know if you remember me but . . .'

That's how the message on her computer today began, of course. She re-read it with a faint sense of despair.

'I remember you so well, with your lovely blonde hair, and always laughing. Where are you now? It would be so good to meet up . . .'

'I'm so sorry,' she emailed back kindly. 'It's lovely to hear from you, but I live in West Sussex now and hardly ever go up to London.'

What a monstrous fib! 'I'll never get to heaven, Ben,' she said. Hearing his name,

Ben looked up at her and thumped his plumy tail. 'Time for a walk?' said his hopeful grin.

Ben and she were agreed in their love for their tiny Sussex bungalow with its small, pretty garden. It was less than two minutes' walk to the Greensward, a swathe of unspoilt, grassy walk stretching from Littlehampton to East Preston, with the beach below.

It was a million miles away from their second-floor flat in London, slap bang on the Edgware Road—one of the main roads leading to the M1, and noisy twenty-four hours a day. The flat itself had been lovely, but the building hadn't had an enclosed garden, so walking Ben had been a daily chore: either a trudge round the streets with the retriever straining at the lead, or a ten-minute drive north to the park at Dollis Hill.

The break-up of her marriage had been sudden and devastating; once the dust had settled and she and Martin had achieved a shaky truce, her first thought had been to get away from London.

She was a Sussex girl at heart. Born in Brighton, she had gradually moved west, as her parents relocated first to Shoreham and then, in retirement, to Rustington. By that time, of course she had flown the nest, thankful to be away. Uni had provided an escape, and then her career as a successful publicist took over.

Now, older, her loyalties were divided. Coming back to live by the sea felt right, but London had wound its tentacles into her heart.

'I'm a Londoner now,' she used to tell her friends. 'I own an Oyster card. I Mind the Gap! This is my city.'

And so her friends were astonished when she fetched up in Rustington. Astonished, and highly amused.

'It won't last,' they told each other. 'Not Dora. You can take the girl out of London but you'll never take London out of the girl.'

'But then, they didn't know about my Cunning Plan, did they, Ben?'

She had done her research carefully, poring over maps and train timetables before settling on this part of the South Coast. Anywhere along here, Littlehampton, Rustington, Angmering, Worthing, was within easy reach of an excellent train service to London–and the theatre. Dora's passion was the theatre. And two or three times a month she would travel to the city—her best friend Maggie lived conveniently close to Victoria station-and together they would go to a matinee.

Which brought her back to the monstrous fib—and the troublesome email.

She smoothed back the "lovely blonde hair" that Swithin remembered so fondly. The years hadn't been too unkind. So often a natural blonde would fade into dispirited mouse, but with a little help from nature—and a lot from her salon—it was now a shining silver-gilt.

She remembered him too, from her University days. He wasn't one of the nasty ones. Needy, yes, a little. He was one of those boys who, with an ounce of confidence, could have been devastating: tall, slightly craggy, with a perpetually untidy thatch of russet hair. But at twenty-one he had been uncertain, shy, hiding behind thick-lensed glasses and a hesitant smile, and the nineteen-year-old Dora, pretty and popular, had had better fish to fry.

She could just imagine him as he would be now. Stooped, peering through even thicker lenses, his hair a flyaway of white wool from a bald and shining pate.

Nerdy he certainly was. Today we would call him geeky, she thought. Terrifyingly brainy, he was on course for a first- class physics degree and a high-flying career in astrophysics. Dora would never have met him—as a first-year languages student her path would never have crossed his—but that she had shared a room, briefly, with his sister during Freshers' Week.

She and Freya had become friends and eventually ended up sharing a flat. Swithin was a frequent, though silent, visitor. Over the years Dora and Freya had kept up an intermittent email correspondence but they had not met for a long time. Swithin had disappeared unnoticed off the radar. She pushed back from the computer, stretching the ache out of her back. Ben leapt to his feet with an excited bark. This was his best time of day, the moment when Dora finally agreed it was time for a walk. There were five points in his doggy compass, she thought fondly, tugging at the silky ears. Walks, food, cuddles, play and sleep.

'It won't be a long one today, Ben,' she told him. She was still limping slightly: Maggie had given her a balloon ride for her birthday, a treat she had always longed for. The flight was glorious but the bumpy landing had caught her unprepared and she had twisted her knee.

As soon as they got to the Greensward Ben disappeared as usual, snooping and snuffling through the bushes, always hopeful of flushing out a rabbit.

She too was hoping for an encounter, though she preferred not to admit it to herself. To begin with, she had called the man "Mr Purdey" in her mind. Dog owners always know the names of other dogs long before they get to know their owners, and so people become dubbed with whimsical names such as "Mrs Fluffy" and "Mr Gizmo".

When he had first appeared on the Greensward some months ago, Dora—and a lot of other lady dog walkers—had noticed him at once. Although clearly in his sixties, he had an erect, almost military bearing. His strong features, thick white hair and rather forbidding aspect discouraged instant familiarity. A nod and the occasional "lovely day" or "dreadful weather," which was the common currency of this little community, was all she could hope for.

Ben, though, had other ideas. Dogs don't know about British reserve—thank heavens!—thought Dora the day Ben and Purdey made friends. "Mr Purdey" turned out to be Sam, she discovered as they chatted. At first it was all doggy talk—Purdey was another golden retriever and she and Ben made a handsome couple.

'Why Purdey?' Dora once asked teasingly. 'I'll bet you fancied Joanna Lumley in The Avengers!'

It was a mistake. Sam's face changed and she was afraid she had offended him.

'No, actually, not at all. It's an appropriate and not uncommon name for a gun dog. Purdey, as you may know, is a maker of exceptionally fine shotguns.' He paused, then, as if aware that he was being pompous, continued rather diffidently: 'Of course, that wasn't the original reason we called her Purdey. She had been lost, and we adopted her. My wife decided to call her Perdita, which became Purdey.'

Damn! There it was. "My wife." The good ones were always married.

Many hopeful walks later, Dora learned more. Yes, there had been a Mrs Sam, but she had died of cancer some 18 months ago. She could tell from his face, and the tone of voice in which he spoke of her, that the loss had hurt Sam deeply. A doggy friendship, it seemed, was all that was on the cards. Sam was reticent about his background, but from things he let slip from time to time she deduced that he was a well-respected scientist.

***

Over the next few weeks, Dora exchanged a few more polite emails with Swithin and then the correspondence tailed off. She dismissed him from her mind: she was busy with other things. She went to the theatre twice and concentrated on her French lessons. Since Ben had acquired a passport they had made several trips across the Channel together.

Summer turned, and the days got shorter. After a glorious golden October, the weather deteriorated sharply. Battling across the Greensward one morning, her umbrella held shield-like before her against the biting rain, Dora ran slap bang into Sam coming the other way. After the flurry of apologies they stood a moment to chat.

'Have you got any plans for Christmas?' he asked.

'Oh, yes, I've got a real treat planned: I'm going to Paris for the big Christmas fair in La Défense. I've been wanting to go for ages.'

A look of something like dismay crossed his face. 'What's the matter, you don't like Christmas?' Dora asked quickly.

'Let's just say it doesn't have the best of memories for me. I plan to be away for most of December.'

A whole month without meeting him! Dora struggled to conceal her disappointment.

'So when are you going to Paris?' he added casually. 'The market opens at the end of November this year, and I'm planning to go on December 5th. I'll travel up to London and spend the night with my friend Maggie, then we'll take the train from St Pancras the following day. I'll be back on the 8th.'

'Oh, that's all right, then,' Sam muttered. Dora looked at him quizzically but he didn't elaborate.

'But what about Ben? Surely you aren't taking him with you? I could have him, if you like. I'm not going away till the 10th.'

Dora's heart did a flip: what a missed opportunity. 'That's very good of you,' she said regretfully, 'but my neighbour Jessie is going to take him. They adore each other and she spoils him rotten.

***

Dora came back from Pars to find a new email from Swithin awaiting her.

'I don't want to pester you,' he wrote, 'but I know how you love the theatre.' Dora paused. How did he know she loved theatre? That had come later in life, after she had left Uni.

'It's just that I happen to have a couple of tickets for She Would if She Could at the Old Vic,' the email went on.

'I was going to go with my colleague, Jim, but his sister has been taken ill and he is going to go and stay with her to look after her. It's next Wednesday, frightfully short notice, I know, but I wondered if you would be interested. I'm afraid it's only a matinee, though.'

It was a dilemma. She Would was the hot ticket of the Christmas season. Half pantomime, half farce, it had audiences on their feet cheering at every performance. Seats in the stalls were eye-wateringly expensive, but even so they went like the proverbial hot cakes. By the time Dora tried to book, the show was completely sold out.

'No, Dora!' she admonished herself. 'That would just be using the poor man. But it's She Would if She Could, and I so wanted to see it.'

'Dear Swithin,' she wrote back, rather guiltily. 'It so happens that I am free next Wednesday, and I would love to go to the Vic with you.' Was that too gushing? Never mind. 'As a matter of fact,' she continued, 'a matinee would suit me well. I have a large, soppy dog these days, and he gets rather disapproving if I am away overnight.'

Neatly put, she congratulated herself. Using Ben as an excuse she had quashed before it arose any possibility of her remaining in London with Swithin for the evening.

The following Wednesday she walked into the foyer of the Old Vic with a certain amount of trepidation and some curiosity. Swithin had suggested they meet at two o'clock—the performance was at 2:30—so they could have a drink and a sandwich in the bar first. But the first person who met Dora's eye was not Swithin, but his sister.

She was unmistakeable. The copper curls had become a soft white cap, but the determined chin and humorous mouth hadn't changed. Although they hadn't seen each other for almost ten years, Dora knew her at once.

'Freya!' she exclaimed, and her real delight was tinged with an element of relief. If Swithin had had the tact to include Freya in the party, the whole enterprise wouldn't be so awkward after all.

After the hugs and kisses and exclamations, Freya suggested they go downstairs to the bar, where Swithin was waiting. She stood back to let her friend precede her, so that Dora had a clear view of the tiny bar area. And there, tucked into a corner, was someone she recognised. Coincidence? Serendipity? Or a set-up? She glanced sternly over her shoulder at Freya, who seemed to be choking back a giggle.

In two strides, Dora crossed the room.

'Sam! What are you doing here?' she demanded.

'Er, it's Swithin, actually,' he said, standing up. 'I'm afraid I've rather deceived you, Dora. I don't live in London anymore—in fact I'm almost a neighbour of yours. I'd always wanted to live by the sea, so when my wife died Purdey and I moved to East Preston.

'Freya has been keeping me up to date with your news. I knew you lived in Rustington and that you had a dog too, so it was a pretty good bet that we'd meet sooner or later. You haven't changed a bit. You're just the same shameless little liar you always were. "I hardly ever come up to London" my foot!'

Dora had the good manners to blush. Then a thought struck her.

'What about you?' she demanded. 'You called yourself Sam, didn't you? And we've been chatting on the Greensward for months. Wouldn't it have been simpler just to tell me it was you?'

'It was a lot more fun this way, and it gave us a chance to get to know each other again. It was Freya who came up with She Would. She knew you wouldn't be able to resist that. Oh, and by the way, I'm not going away this month. Purdey and I both agree that the best place to celebrate Christmas is in your own home. So perhaps we'll see each other over the festive season.'

***

Christmas lunch was a success. The goose was golden and succulent, the obligatory sprouts were crisp and well larded with chestnuts, the pudding had flamed most satisfactorily. Dora sighed happily and settled back against Swithin's shoulder.

'That's the best Christmas I've had for years,' she said. 'And I'm fairly sure Ben enjoyed himself too.'

'Purdey certainly did,' said Swithin. 'I think she's fallen for your Ben big time. It's a pity she can't tell us how she really feels.'

They looked across at the hearth, where two warm bodies merged in a golden fluffy heap of dog. Purdey raised a sleepy head and her tail thumped twice.

'She would if she could,' said Dora.

WILDFIRES

Gregg Norman

to think that fires in our Canadian woods could send smoke to choke
a Manhattan cabbie a Jersey gangster
a Georgia peach

tumbling gouts of flame fly along a long fiery front ravaging our
green sward
belching a mantra OUT OF CONTROL

from around the world they come in yellow suits and hard hats
to dance a haka in the fire's face

pundits chat about cycles and change but does anyone listen to the
fire?

GRIEF

Robin Prince Monroe

She walked through fire.
The flames licked her tender skin
pieces of her singed, then sizzling, fell to the ground. Pain
screeched deep into the hollows of her heart where love lived
She wanted to give in to the heat.
To stop.
Stop trying to breathe.
Hands reached for her through thick, dark smoke.
She tried to grab hold.
She couldn't.
There was nothing left but raw, empty hurt.

Until

His big hand stretched down to scoop her up,
and lift her out of the haze. He gently set her on a rock.
Where living water tumbled over her weary head and into her
mouth,
and over her charred skin--
that cooled and healed   then toughened with scars.
The ache in her soul moved to the background of living
becoming bearable,
but never gone.
A reminder of how much love it took to die, and how much
love it takes to live.

Gordy's Poem: The Cornerstone
(a poem written for my father after his death)

Ramey Channell

"Then what is the meaning of that which is written: The stone the builders rejected has become the cornerstone?"

Beneath the birding sky, cold blue and safe,
bricks laid one to another, timeless bond and true,
by hands long learned and destined to this trade,
a world of walls and beauty, shelters made.

Unlost, unvanished, close beneath blue skies,
and yet somewhere a'wandered, biding still,
he built a hearth within our hearts laid strong
in patterns laid of mortar, brick, and song.

THE GODDESS OF BOOKS AND THE SINGER-SONGWRITER

(for Dale)

April Mae M. Berza

I am but a goddess of books
welcoming you with my loveliest chapters,
the soul of eternal words and finite worlds.

You are a mortal, a singer-songwriter,
who crafts poetic kisses and embraces
to my lips, mellifluous, mellifluous.

Music embraces the two of us
and I sing paeans for you
as you immortalize me with songs.

Open up the library of my wounds
and a vast kingdom of lexicons
will show you a way to my heart.

The gates to a secret Paradise
are enchanted pages to my skin,
leaf through the pages and own me.

My divine bones and sinews
are passages to a beautiful realm,
read me up until the breaking dawn.

We both drink the sweetest wine
from an immortal cup,
immortal cup making you a deity, an equal.

We meet in bookshelves of dreams,
the sweetest Philomels serenading.
Worship me with welcoming worlds.

A Little Feud

Anne Leigh Parrish

It happened sometimes between husband and wife, a little feud over something small and simple that became huge and complex. They'd been married long enough to have had many of these. In the early days, they could really go at it. Yelling down the night until the neighbors called the cops. Frank always got the evil eye then. Tammy was inspected for shiners. These tiffs were verbal, not physical, unless Tammy pitched a plate at the wall, which she didn't do anymore. Plates cost money, and the set they had now was quite nice, though Frank didn't care for the daisy pattern.

They owned a shop that sold stone monuments for gardens. Not for cemeteries. That was its own specialty, and required you to deal with the bereaved, which Tammy would be no good at. Misery made her uneasy, her sympathy ran out fast. Get a grip, she'd be tempted to say, which wouldn't be helpful, and would probably lose her a sale. Frank got along well with the customers, and she generally let him do the talking.

One wet Tuesday, when everything else so far had gone wrong—the milk for their coffee had spoiled and the truck wouldn't start—they received a shipment of statues they didn't order. They'd asked for Buddhas and Japanese pagodas because Tammy loved them, and they sold well. What they got were St. Francis (four), the Virgin Mary (six), and a flock of small, fat cherubs. Tammy was raised a Catholic and despised the whole rigamarole almost as much as she hated Republicans, though she tried to keep politics out of the workplace. She learned the hard way about that. Ben, their employee, was a staunch MAGA and regarded Donald Trump as the

56

new Messiah and Joe Biden as the anti-Christ. Oh, that discussion got heated as hell. Tammy came close to firing him and knew she couldn't because Ben was her sister's boy and had trouble holding a job, so she let it go. Frank told her she'd done the right thing. Who cared what that dumb kid thought, anyway? Tammy didn't care, not really, except for the fact that a sizable percentage of the country thought the same way.

Frank thought the new pieces were cute and put them on prominent display. He wasn't raised in any particular faith. His parents had been hippies and believed in auras and astral signs and that kind of b.s. They lived in Florida now, a long way from Western Washington. In truth, Frank missed them, especially his father, whom he'd come to appreciate more as he entered middle age. Life was full of unexpected challenges and insurmountable problems, and though they never spoke of it, Frank felt his father would understand.

Tammy said they weren't keeping the crap they got by mistake. Frank said yeah, they were, and that it would sell fast enough. At home, Tammy made dinner without a word. Frank said it was important to try new things, to shake things up. Maybe the universe was trying to tell them something. Then he complimented her casserole. She raised her eyes and looked at him dead on. She said she didn't need to remind him that Christianity was founded on the concept of patriarchy. He said most religions were, unless you wanted to talk about the Vikings or ancient Romans and their panoply of gods, though they tended to put men first, too. He understood how often she'd been smacked across the hand by a nasty cane-wielding nun, but she couldn't blame all Christians everywhere for that. She said just try and stop her. As if Fate were mocking her, five of the six Virgin Mary's sold by the end of that week.

The order of Japanese pagodas and Buddhas arrived. Tammy set them up right in front, where they'd always been, and Frank later moved the Buddhas to the far end of the yard. They were hollow and easy to lift, which was a blessing, given how much trouble his back gave him these days. She told him to put them where she'd had them and he said he wouldn't, so she moved them herself and stood them at regular intervals, in a nice, gentle arc.

She needn't have bothered. Ben got snockered, came in after hours, and kicked them over. Then he went at them with a hammer, destroying two. He hated them, he said, with their fat grinning air of superiority. He didn't care how much customers liked them, or that they represented good luck. To him it was all garbage, Chinese interference. Hadn't those people done enough by giving us COVID? When he sobered up his remorse was hard to take. He cried as he picked up the pieces. His girlfriend had kicked him out, Tammy and Frank learned, a girlfriend with a particular fascination for Eastern mysticism. He told Tammy to take the cost of replacing the Buddhas he'd wrecked out of his paycheck. She said she most certainly would.

Frank saw his doctor about his back and was told not to lift anything over ten pounds for at least two weeks. He had a disk that was calcifying. One day, it might require surgery. That evening, they discussed the implications of his limited duty at the statuary yard. Tammy told him he might as well stay home.

Tammy arrived at work in the morning to find things in chaos. A St. Francis had fallen over into a Buddha's lap. The cherubs were all over the place, even in their showcase fountain which stood five feet tall. The remaining Virgin Mary stood close to a gnome whose cap concealed his eyes, as if ashamed of his idiotic appearance. Tammy was furious and called Ben only to be told his number was no longer in service. Ben showed up, in worse shape than usual, and Tammy accused him of getting drunk again, using his key to open the padlock that secured the chained gate, then having a fine old time ruining her set-up. Ben looked at her with red-rimmed eyes that reminded Tammy of her sister, who bawled a lot as a child, and said he'd done that once and once was enough. Oddly, Tammy believed him. Maybe some local kids jumped the fence, he said. Tammy called Frank to fill him in and he said they should install cameras in prominent locations as a deterrent. He'd read this discouraged theft more than an alarm system on the property, which they also lacked.

Tammy told Ben to help her move everything back the way it

was. It didn't take them long. She asked what happened to his phone. He said he forgot to pay the bill, but that was okay, he didn't need it right now because he'd only look at it to see if his girlfriend had texted him. She asked where he was staying, and he said he'd gone back home. Tammy was surprised her sister hadn't mentioned that, but they weren't close, and her sister wouldn't have thought it necessary.

On Thursday, the supplier called again about the pieces he'd sent by mistake. He hoped Tammy was still okay with the arrangement they'd come to, about crediting her next shipment. She said she was. He asked if she happened to have a spare Virgin Mary left. He had a customer, well his uncle actually, who wanted one for his aunt as a surprise. Tammy said yeah, she had one, and his uncle could come by anytime. The supplier thanked her and apologized again for the earlier mix-up. He'd been having problems with their new inventory software and more than one order had gotten scrambled. Computers were supposed to be time savers, but they just seemed to complicate everything, right?

Tammy hustled him off the phone. She had to drive Frank to another appointment for his back and Ben was supposed to come in early to cover for her.

Ben didn't show, so Tammy locked the place up and left. When she returned, more mischief had been done. The Virgin Mary, which Tammy had put by the front window for the supplier's uncle to see easily, had her back turned. So did the Buddha she stood next to. Maybe they'd been put that way in the first place, and she just forgot. She'd been so distracted lately by everything, but when she tried to think of exactly what, she couldn't for the life of her come up with anything other than the usual irritations and disappointments of the human condition. Well, sometimes those were enough to drive a saint to sin as her mother used to say, her mother, a hard-drinking, smoking, card-playing Irish housewife without a drop of kindness.

Tammy turned Virgin Mary around. Then she did the same to Buddha. Poor Buddha was half Mary's height, but he didn't seem to mind. He was suffused with inner peace, pure tranquility, but then so was Mary, judging from the gentle tilt of her head as she gazed lovingly into empty space.

Ben arrived with two coffees he'd picked up on the way in. He apologized for being late. He'd had to help his mom around the house that morning. They'd painted the whole downstairs over the weekend and today the curtains needed to be rehung. Tammy accepted her coffee and tried to remember what color the walls at her sister's house had been. She hadn't been there for a couple of years. Holidays weren't celebrated together. The sister's husband and Frank didn't get along, not because they had different world views, but because they could both be opinionated and loud after a few drinks and their bombast became a competition between them around the dinner table. The sister's husband had threatened Frank one year with a fork, holding the tines perilously close to his face. Ben had been the one to break up that fight.

The supplier's uncle came by. He was a small, timid-looking man, with neatly combed white hair. He walked with a cane. He said his wife was ill, quite ill, in fact, and he'd hired someone to redo their garden and she, the wife, wanted a statue of the Virgin Mary placed so that it would bless the roses in spring and summer. At this the little man's face tensed up and for an awful moment Tammy thought he might be about to burst into tears. But he pulled himself together and said he thought it might be a good idea to buy the statue now, before the roses bloomed, so his wife could see it there whenever the window beckoned. Tammy understood that she was being told that the wife wasn't going to make it to next spring. Her throat tightened.

Tammy told the little man the Virgin Mary was on the house. He said he couldn't possibly take it for free. Tammy said he'd be doing her a favor. She'd been trying to get rid of it and didn't have high hopes, given how long all the others had taken to sell. At this, Ben started to correct her and she glared at him. She asked him to please put the statue in the gentleman's car, but to wrap it in plastic, first. After a few more feeble protests, the little man accepted and shook Tammy's hand.

"Bless you," he said.

Tammy sat in her office and watched him drive slowly out of the yard. Ben watched him go too, then went back to work. He was moving the water features closer to the building so they could be connected to a hose for people to see them in operation when the weather improved, which it wouldn't for several months, but Tammy appreciated his initiative.

Frank called up, bored, restless, and asked if she needed him to go the grocery store because he might as well be useful while he was on furlough. He didn't like being dead weight. Tammy told him to take that pork roast out of the fridge and let it come to room temperature before putting it in the oven. Did he want her to walk him through it? He said he'd seen her do it often enough and he should be fine. When she hung up, she watched the rain fall gently. She wondered if the little man had someone at home to help him put Mary where he wanted her to go. It was such a nice idea, getting it for his wife to comfort her in her final days. That's what religion was all about at its best, wasn't it?

Comfort and kindness. People should stick to that and stop using it as a weapon.

One day, maybe.

For now, she had to call the supplier back and place the order that slipped her mind before when he wouldn't shut up about his uncle, this time for tortoises, rabbits, and grazing deer. A woman just the other day asked why they weren't stocking animals anymore. Tammy had forgotten about the animals. They were part of everything, too, for the gentle kindness they could show one another. She'd be glad to have them back, yet wondered if they'd move themselves around when she wasn't looking. It bothered her that there was still no explanation for what had happened. It was. . . what was the word Frank used?

Unfathomable. There was nothing to do but take it as a handy reminder that sometimes you had to accept things you didn't understand, and never would.

The Arts and 'Bad' Words

B. A. Brittingham

During the 2018 Halloween season, NBC's Megyn Kelly naively made some remarks on blackface as it pertained to costumes. Due to its racial insensitivity, it cost her a well-paying news job. It is now a moot point but should bring into question the concept of political correctness vs. reality. As a nation we have all learned (or are learning as Megyn said in her apology) that ethnic slurs are no longer tolerable in the modern world. It is one of the good things that seems to be coming out (belatedly) from the Civil Rights Movement of sixty years ago, from the anti-bullying movement of today, the #MeToo movement (words, not just groping, can be a form of sexual harassment), the politically correct movement (which occasionally goes a bit overboard in its good intentions), and even the stated consciousness of another person's physical differences (Internet trolls and body-shaming.)

We are stumbling, and occasionally falling flat on our faces, in the search for judicious ways not to be hurtful, first in our words and then, by extension, in our attitudes. And that is a positive path to an improved society.

But why is the road so rocky? Why is it taking so long? Because like most change, the negative aspects of our joint thinking must be undone before the positive seeds can take root. Less than a hundred years ago, one of America's most remarkable presidents, Franklin Delano Roosevelt sat in the White House. Scion of an upper-crust family, recipient of a sterling education, a man of wealth and ideas, FDR was nonetheless known to exchange anti-Semitic jokes. As did others. (It should be noted that he was not averse to the appointing of Jews to important posts, witness Secretary of the Treasury Henry Morgenthau, Jr. who later, during the Truman administration, became the first Jewish individual to be first in line for presidential succession.)

It is unpleasant to contemplate this high-level anti-Semitism, particularly in view of subsequent world events with respect to Hitler's treatment of the Jewish people. But we should always remember that, at the beginning of the 21st century, we cannot in conscience judge the past by today's standards. Not only did the president and other politicians exchange Jewish jokes, but most people did likewise. Along with Irish drinking jokes, Polish stupidity jokes, German toilet jokes, and Scottish cheap jokes. It was the way of the then-world.

Humanity has moved forward since, but we still have ground to cover. Let us give ourselves and our society a brief pat on the back for our somewhat evolved thinking.

And then go on to making other needed adjustments in matters of semantics.

As a fiction creator, I consider the phrase "suspension of disbelief" as Nearly Canonical in its necessity; if an author does not make a scene so real that the reader is compelled to accept it, then the story will collapse. It holds a chief position in the writing process of most authors.

This is about fabricated lying and the role it plays in story construction. The writer is basically telling a tale that didn't happen about people that have never lived—other than in his or her imagination—and he wants you to believe it so that he may get across his point or message. To do this, she/he must create a landscape that is so real, the reader buys into it even though, under it all, the reader knows that it is basically a falsehood. Reader and writer thus become cohorts in chicanery.

A significant part of this belief suspension is the manner in which characters are drawn. We can tell a great deal about the birthplace, education, social status, occupation, or trade, and even garner some insight into the ways these "persons" think when we listen to how they speak. Are they from New York and speaking with a Brooklyn accent or from East London and talking old fashioned Cockney?

(Which is very much in decline I am told.)

This also fits the way a character gets emotional and the words he might use in its expression.

A scene set in a Southern state such as Virginia or Georgia in the 1920s or 30s and involving the racial disparity so viciously prevalent there, must contain the word "nigger." Now before you pick up your phone or keyboard to crucify me for using a word with such a horrific history, stop and think: can the brutality of the attitude and the people involved be appropriately conveyed to persons living eighty years later?

Like the 1970s cigarette commercial said, "You've come a long way, baby." We have. We've learned that words and unfair generalizations can bring pain, extreme dissent, and even innocent deaths. So, the use of expressions like N-*word* heralds an important change in our society—even if there are those who still enjoy using it. Thirty years ago, it was the *F-Word* that was taboo; for Brits it was *bloody*. Now such designations are largely passé.

What we need to remember is how to differentiate between the words themselves and their context and delivery.

Going back to the South of the above example, the need for that word is implicit in allowing the reader to begin understanding what African Americans felt upon hearing it fall—with snarling vehemence—from the lips of people who believed that white skin made them superior. I'm not certain that those of us who are Caucasian can even begin to experience the fear, denigration, or immediate panic that poured forth from the collective racial memory of a Black man faced with an angry mob of whites. Somehow, "Get a rope and let's hang that N-word bastard" does not carry quite the same horror as what was actually meant.

When writers are trying to recreate a time and place, it is imperative that they be allowed to use the verbiage that is part of it. It is not our intention to promote the continuation of *bad* words and the political incorrectness of them; but rather to demonstrate how hideous and vulgar they can be and what the consequences are.

Their true badness rests with those who should know better and still use them offensively anyway. All in the name of Free Speech.

A Sliver of Peace

Robin Prince Monroe

The summer sun was hot, white, blinding. The kind of sun that leaves light squiggles in the aqueous humor of your eyes. It was so humid I felt like I needed scuba gear to breathe. Occasionally a dandelion fluff of cloud would pass over the sun and for a brief moment I'd anticipate relief only to feel the blaze heat up again.

People were milling everywhere around the field, watching, waiting, eye-protective glasses at the ready. Dark shields to keep them from being hurt by the very thing that they can't live without. Afraid to be blinded by the very thing that enables them to see.

Blankets were scattered across the dry, crisp grass like the bright patches of a quilt. The grass crunched as I walked carrying my soft, red blanket. My small, burlap pack patted my back with each step. I needed to find a secret place away from the people chattering, the kid's laughing, and the smell of lunches, growing too hot in the sun. A hidden place that was open enough to see the sky.

I couldn't find it. I couldn't find the right place to experience this once-in-a-lifetime event, until I noticed a large oak at the edge of the field. It stood there ready to greet me. I ran over, threw my blanket in its shadow, then reached up to climb into its arms. Maybe, just maybe, I could find a spot high enough that I could see a big swatch of sky.

I climbed hand-foot-hand, higher and higher, the warm, rough bark kept my sweaty palms from slipping. The leaves brushed my skin soothing the anxiety that we all felt. Anxiety? Somewhere deep inside of me, was the primordial feeling that light meant safety. And that without it, even for only a few moments, I was somehow vulnerable.

Do the others feel this? Do the children? Does this tree? Finally, I found it, open sky above a branch large enough to hold my weight. I braced my right foot on a sturdy branch below. I dangled the other foot, and had a flash of how much I had loved climbing when I was a child. Do kids do that anymore? I hoped so.

Secure then, I gently pulled my backpack off and opened it, looking for the certified dark glasses I had put there. I had packed two pair. I put one on, then to test it, I looked up at the spotlight sun. When I looked back down to find my power bar the backpack was a dark abyss. I had to remove the glasses to retrieve my snack. I munched on the bar and checked my watch. I had made it just in time. In a few more minutes it would start. The anxiety changed to excitement, the kind that makes a minute seem like forever.

Then it happened. The moon's shadow took a tiny nip out of the sun. A baby nip, like the ones I would sneak when Grandma made her best chocolate cookies. The nip slowly turned into a bite, then the bite changed into a soft gray blanket that was pulled slowly over the sun's bright face. Everything went still. The wind stopped, the birds quieted, even the bug's high pitched hum hushed. The bright, busy light became a silky twilight, then a silent night.

And with the grayness came the whispered hush I so desperately needed. A few quiet moments without artificial lights, and graphics screaming at me on too many screens.

When the shadow was at its deepest the people cheered, but the quietness owned me now.

Then the moon stopped hugging the sun, and slowly slipped away. The wind, the birds, and the bugs, started up their busy life songs. I climbed down onto the field of chattering people, giggling children, and smelly lunches, to go back to my life, carrying with me the soft peace I had found.

Waiting for Coffee as a Measurement of Time

Mike Austin

You wake at midnight and again at one. It's been three months since you've slept the whole night through. The pain in your hip has only gotten worse in that time. Now it's New Year's Morning and you have another seven weeks of waiting until your hip gets replaced.

But whether it's seven weeks or seven months doesn't matter any longer. Time has lost any meaning so that you barely recognize morning from evening. Like now. It's one in the morning but you want to make coffee. That would be a good way to ring in the New Year, with a cup of coffee in the wee small hours.

Instead you get dressed. You move just a little easier after those few hours of sleep. But it's still a grindingly slow and groaning process of moving, of bending your leg to pull on pants, socks and shoes. In between each item of clothing you sit and stare and wonder if the effort is worth it. It isn't, but you get dressed anyway.

You pull on your heavy parka. It feels like a comforter. Maybe you can curl up on a park bench and take a nap. All you have to do is close your eyes to drift off again.

The taverns nearby are still busy. The sidewalk here is cluttered with people, individuals and groups walking between bars or to their cars or just walking for air. One couple is arguing about driving or calling a cab. They stop when you limp past. When you smile and nod, they look away. They're arguing again as soon as you pass.

It hurts to walk. It hurts to lie in bed. It hurts to stand and it hurts to sit. It hurts in your short hours of sleep and keeps hurting when you wake. Seven more weeks. There is no meaning to those words. Time is immeasurable. The only time that matters right now is coffee time.

You don't know why you keep going. It's not even a proper walk. You give up on using your left leg to walk with. It's more of a prop to hold you upright while your right foot propels you forward.

It seems that people look away when they see you coming. Nobody wants to watch the show of a broken man, a man who looks like he might ask for money.

On the next block you're alone under the scant scattering of streetlights. You're further away from the New Year's celebrations. It's quiet here, and the only thing moving is your shadow as it lurches and drags before you, growing longer, then fading as the street light recedes behind you.

When you turn to look down the block, it looks like a dark forever distance. You're in a walking waking dream in which the terrain and the neighborhood and even the city are strange. You wonder if there's a place nearby that serves coffee at this hour.

There's a saxophone being played somewhere up ahead and brings you awake in your own neighborhood where nobody is serving coffee. The music sounds like it's up by the river. The sax runs up and down the scales and then does a few slow jazzy riffs. You smile at the cliché of a sad sax in the darkness. You turn up your collar and pull down your hat. You shamble to the river and the footpath that leads along the narrow river to the lake a mile away. You can picture the lake at night, rolling into blackness beyond the small reflections of homes along the shore. You won't be able to walk there tonight.

The path is well lit. The light from overhead dances yellow in the ripples of the dark slow river. There are traffic noises up ahead but the night feels quiet, as if the noise is more a sensation than sound. It's background to the sax that's growing louder with each step you take.

The musician is a woman. She's playing under the heavy concrete bridge of a busy thoroughfare. She's across the river from you, between the feet of two concrete arches. She's flanked by a couple of musicians, two guys who stare at her adoringly. One is slapping on his bongos. The other is plucking an upright bass. They're both being drowned out by the sax, but don't seem to care.

She's their star while she makes the sax wail "Harlem Nocturne" slow and sad. It echoes past you and off the concrete abutment behind you, then back across the river.

The musicians notice you standing across the river from them. The men stop playing. Their gaze seems hostile. The woman's playing falters as if she's suddenly self-conscious of her audience of one.

You turn away toward a bench that's under a light. "Harlem Nocturn" slides into "Oh Little Town of Bethlehem." It's a sad and sleepy lullaby that makes your eyelids even heavier.

You pull up your hood and the music is muffled, along with the traffic noise, in the pillowed quilting of the parka. If you can just get to the bench you could close your eyes. Ten minutes of sleep under the dim stars will clear your mind. It's good to have a goal. Sit. Nap. Limp home, a few yards at a time. Why did you come this far? If you ever get home, you'll make coffee. You'll make it as strong as you want. A thick black cup of coffee to greet the New Year. While everyone else is going to bed, you'll be waiting for daylight, so many hours away.

While you look at the bench under the light, a sudden thump and rustle beside you makes you realize how alone you are here at night. Alone and vulnerable and almost too tired to care. You barely move at the sight of something tumbling like a black sack of garbage down the concrete stairs from the street above. It stops beside you at the foot of the steps. It's a young man. His face is chipped and bloodied from the fall. His head is backwards, looking at you from over his coat collar. There's a spark in his eyes. Fear? Warning? Whatever it is, it's fading fast.

You look up and see a shadow standing at the top of the stairs. A shadow wearing a heavy parka, the hood up and drawn tight looks down at you before it steps from view.

You look down again. There's no spark left in the eyes of the man at your feet. Maybe it had never been there.

The thing at your feet is suddenly not worth your attention. It has nothing to offer you. It didn't bring coffee. It didn't bring relief from this sleepless incomprehensible world you're in. It might not even be real. You look at the park bench. The bench is real. You

70

desperately want to sit there with your hood pulled up and drawn tightly. Just ten minutes. But when you reach the bench, it doesn't feel right. It doesn't feel safe. There's something nearby that you don't want near you. You'll be better off at home. You shamble back toward the underpass, keeping your eyes on the river, away from the untidy bundle at the foot of the stairs.

You don't look at the musicians either. You keep walking, dragging your bad leg along and moaning softly. If you could only twist things in the right way it might pop back to where it belongs. It might stop hurting. But it doesn't.

You try to keep track of the music, to listen as you get further away and closer to home until the music fades far away, comes back lightly on a breeze like a distant siren and then is gone for good.

You're back among people again. You're the only one who's alone. You feel like a ghost limping a few steps at a time and sometimes groaning among the living until you finally reach your stairs. You drag yourself up onto the porch, good leg first, bad leg dragging behind until you're inside the house. You lock the door and draw the quilted insulated curtain across the doorway. It's safe to talk out loud to yourself now.

"Let's get this coat off. There we go. That wasn't so bad. How about those shoes? Come on, it won't be so bad. Oh. No, no. It is bad. We can do this. Holy hell that hurts. So much. There we go. Now for some sweat pants. Oh. You're already wearing them, aren't you? Don't you know only losers wear sweat pants in public? Get those slippers on, loser. You want some coffee? Oh yes, coffee would be lovely. Let's ring in the New Year with a cup of coffee. Maybe we could whiskey it up a little. Yes, whiskey can be a verb. Don't be pedantic, just make the damn coffee and whiskey it up. Let's do this. Can you make it? Well, I guess I have to, don't I? Then maybe we can sit. Maybe. If the old leg will bend. Yeah. A little coffee, a little whiskey, a little nap. It's all so far away."

You forget whether it's morning or evening. It's dark out. It could be either. The clock on the stove says it's three o'clock. It must be morning. Ray Bradbury wrote, "...three in the morn, full wide-eyed and staring, is living death!" Yeah, ol' Ray knew.

You grind the coffee beans and set up the coffee maker. While the coffee drips, you hum to match the pitch of the compressor of your old refrigerator. The harmonics clash when you change your pitch. It's a small joy, but you take what you can get. You carry a coffee mug and a bottle of Jim Beam to the living room and set them on the table beside your easy chair. Then you drag yourself back for the coffee. You pour it into a thermos. You're practically falling when you reach your chair again. You turn to sit, but your hip won't bend. You start to crouch just a little, sweating while your hip grinds and pops until something breaks loose and drags you groaning to finally sit. You laugh/sob at the sudden relief. The long walk has faded like a dream.

You're finally able to reach over and pour your coffee. Only half a mug full, topped with whiskey. You breathe in the warm sweet aroma of evaporating whiskey. You take a long swallow and close your eyes. In an instant you're back beside the river, looking up the stairs while the shadow above you limps and drags itself out of sight.

FOREST OF LOST DREAMS

Sara Evelyne

Yesterday the mirror told me who I was,
today I don't agree
the fracture of identity birthed seasons of change.

Change. Loss. Moving On.
Transformation.
Is that what lost dreams are?
Where do they go — this collection of the hope of tomorrow?

the loss of self
the loss of control and autonomy
the transformation of power and voice
the soft change of my story
the new narratives, new beginnings, new desires.

Does the new replace the old, smothering and stomping
it down until it is no more?
Or does loss coexist with the love of today to forge a new
kind of dream?
I wish someone would tell me the answer, but then who
would I be?

As wisps of dandelions crossing the sky, I, too,
float through time. Some dreams go with me and some,
like the dandelion seeds, float away to somewhere else.
The dreams I hold in my heart
my hand, my mind, and in my breath
are mine to love, grieve,
to transform, and to outgrow.

I just wish someone had told me sooner.

Loretta's Gift

Jennifer Smith

Loretta weaves baskets from willow,
on a screened in porch at Lost Creek Church Camp;
hands adorned in Appalachian artistry,
not opals or pearls.

Fingers kindred with forest fibers,
landscape sourcing the vessels deep;
form and function entwined, designed
in crisscross flair.

Loretta bakes in farmhouse kitchen,
cinnamon swirls through sourdough raisin,
suppleness sifts, palms knead dough,
shaping loaves—and life.

Knowing that idleness lures devil's work,
artisan fingertips form angel biscuits,
and pick blueberries ripened by summer
to dot lemon scones.

When autumn comes, weathered hands tuck
honey wheat bread inside a sunflower tea towel,
nestling loaf into willow basket,
with handcrafted recipe cards
for great niece Juniper.

HERE

Loretta Fairley

Here on this mountain
gazing at such blue beauty
I want for nothing

First Walks

J.L. Oakley

Hazy blue sky, treeless hills sleeping like beached tan seals with their eyes closed. The wind tickles the patches of bunch grass at my feet so they tremble just at their seeded heads. There is almost total silence except for the distant sound of farm machinery somewhere deep in the Methow Valley below and a crow calling from far off. I'm here for a nature-writing course in Eastern Washington and I'm working on my assignment, but I am distracted, lost in memory and nature.

A couple walks by on the dusty trail below.

How many times did I do that? One thousand? Ten Thousand? How many times in thirty-one years?

I walked with you first on a trail up in the Ko'olau's in Hawaii, a jungle tangle on the way to Manoa Falls. It smelled of *plumeria* and overripe *lilikoi*, yellow and as smooth as chili peppers. The trail was muddy from its daily wash of rain, catching boot and sandals from a score of others. The caretaker hut as we passed was like a woodcutter's cabin from a Grimm's fairy tale. It was made of recycled windows and old floorboards. Honey jars and bean sprouts sat in the window.

I didn't know you well then, but I learned to love your back as it went ahead, strong and powerful and your shaggy golden hair rebelling from your tour of duty in a deep jungle far away in Vietnam. Your feet were eager on the trail.

This place where I sit is like the mountains and hills behind Kailua-Kona several months ahead where we scrambled through *a'a* and *pahoehoe*. The lava rocks cut at our boots and we slipped on the straw brown grasses I cannot name. We found `*ohelo* berries sacred to the Goddess Pele and learned the local joke of "Oh, Hell," berries.

We stuffed them in our pockets and ate them one by one as we sought out *Nene* and *heiau* and the goatherd hut where we spent the night at twenty degrees above zero.

I knew I loved you then. You were golden, my serendipity.

I met you by chance. I was living in Honolulu and going to art school at the University of Hawaii. Just off campus there was a bungalow run by a local woman who rented only to girls. There was a strict policy: *No gentleman callers.* But you called. A friend of one of the girls in the house introduced you to us by letter, and after much discussion, we decided that you and your friend could stay until you found something suitable to rent. We didn't dare tell Mrs. Ho.

The day you arrived, you kept calling from the airport, but no one wanted to go pick you up. That was your problem. When I came home from my class, the phone was ringing off the hook.

"Oh, those guys," someone groaned from the hall.

"I'll get it." I picked up the phone.

"Hello, beautiful," the voice said on the other end.

It was you. Providence was calling. It was as close to love at first sound as you could get. I felt I'd known you all my life.

We rose at dawn for our hike on the Big Island. My roommate drove us down to the Honolulu airport where twenty people hung outside the airport lounge dressed in various degrees of hiker funk and Aloha wear. A chilly morning breeze stirred in the coconut trees silhouetted against a mango pink sky like loopy black swizzle sticks. Nervous about flying, I struck up a conversation with some of our unknown companions.

One of them was Bob, a *malihini* from Boston who had come out as a sailor during World War II and never left. He was married to a local woman and spoke pidgin as his second language with a Yankee accent. He worked in some sort of industry and he loved to hike. Another one was a young, skinny man with tousled dark hair and a Houston accent that stretched Hawaiian words out in a soft drawl. He had been in the islands only one month. But he was game. By the time we boarded the plane they were making plans with us.

After a lurching ride up into the mountains behind Kona-Kailua, we unloaded inside the gate to a private cattle ranch covered with bleached grass, trees, brush and *panini*, a type of cactus. The air was chilly and fog loitered in some of the groves and rocks.

Our little foursome stayed together and walking two by two we trudged along with the whole group for a couple of hours. The morning sun beat back the mist exposing a ragged land full of lichen-covered boulders and `ohelo bushes as high as our calves. Far off, white-headed Mauna Loa and Mauna Kea rose against a bright blue sky. Houston and I laughed as Bob told stories of World Two and life in the islands then. You talked about the cool, deep forests of the Pacific Northwest and where you liked to fish.

At one point you went ahead of me with your tee shirt tied around your head and climbed up a hill of grass and rock. Your chest and shoulders were brown and hard. You're Sinbad, I thought. I love you.

Once we came upon an expansive area where fifty-foot cinder cones dotted our way like black upside down teacups. The land around them rolled and dipped. It was filled with *keawe* trees and sunken holes where giant lava bubbles burst a long time ago. From deep in one of the holes two *Nene* flew out. Mated for life, they looked like miniature Canadian geese with their black caps and buff-colored cheeks. They were as rare as blue moons. Their calls echoed in the late morning air as they flew across our path to a spot further away. We stopped to watch them and drank water from a goatskin bag.

Could I be like that? I thought. Could I love forever?

At about four-thirty in the afternoon, when the sun was slanting in the western sky, we stopped at the remains of ancient *heiau*. All that was left of the temple was its stone platform. Once there had been carved wooden statues, perhaps to the god of war.

Some of the hikers walked around it. Others gathered around a map. The group was breaking up for the night. Bob decided to take us to a goatherd hut he heard about. It was going to get cold at night.

What is it about love and nature? Why, many years hence, when I smell some pungent dirt, see a trembling frond of a fern along a shady hiking path or feel the breeze of wide open sky and hills, why can I so clearly remember this single day in my life and think of you?

Is love bound to nature or does nature just frame the setting of love?

Using only the map and some notes about the surrounding area, we found the goatherd hut forty minutes later. Set on a long grassy ridge, it was formed of old boards, a rusty tin roof and stood on stilts at its back. It was locked, but you found a way in through a Chinese puzzle key to the window. There were bunks inside, multi-paned windows at the back and a butane stove.

The hut was narrow, but had all the comforts of home. Bob got the stove going. You fried steaks and potatoes we had carried in plastic bags from Honolulu. When the food was cooked, we sat around the small table at the back and ate. Outside the trees turned black against the twilight sky. The steam on the window began to freeze.

Before we crawled into our sleeping bags, you stepped outside with me. There in the mountains on the Big Island of Hawaii in the South Pacific the night was as cold as a New England winter, the sky black, and its massive field of proud stars unyielding. We moved close together and you warmed me with a kiss. Then holding hands we watched a shooting star cross the sky. I never felt so close to love or nature. It was the first night of our first long hike together.

***

The sun is hot where I sit. It is turning westward and towards winter, but it still makes sharp shadows on my jeans and on the grass.

Too soon, you have passed on before me. My walks with you are over. I listen for birds. You taught me about pheasant, chukker, and turkey and how they hide. You taught me about early mornings and shooting stars at the breath of dawn.

You taught me to listen, to wait and to see. Without you I never would have seen.

High above a jet plane tails across the sky, leaving a ghostly white line.

A crow calls.

I am missing you.

Aunt Mattie Goes to the Dentist

Celia Miles

"I'd rather be a knot on a hickory log than to have to go to the dentist," Aunt Mattie said. She adjusted her black hat and made a face at her image in the mirror. Her left jaw was so swollen that she couldn't really pull much of a frown, and when she let her guard down, I could see the pain in her eyes.

"Can't I go with you?" I'd never been inside a dentist's office, The kids at school called it the torture chamber.

"No. Addie and her brother's coming by to get me. She's getting a permanent wave while I'm at the dentist's."

I thought I'd like to see a permanent wave being given plus see the teeth-puller's torture room. Aunt Mattie thought I shouldn't waste my time.

"You've got schoolwork to do, young lady. And the other chores you've been laying off to get done."

It was true I had been so busy reading Lorna Doone lately that I'd neglected a few things around the house. Aunt Mattie didn't expect me to do a whole lot, but I'd promised to split kindling and to re-stack the fallen-down woodpile. "I'll have supper ready," I promised. Aunt Mattie couldn't smile without hurting, but I saw the little gleam in her eyes. Cooking was not something that came naturally to me.

"Just some soup beans, June. I won't be able to chew anything anyway."

It was dark when Addie and her brother brought Aunt Mattie home. Luckily I had fixed a big pot of beans and the cornbread was in the warming oven. When all three came in the front door, I knew we'd have company for supper.

Brad Schuler put his hat on the peg and settled himself in front of the fireplace. The women looked exhausted. They came in the kitchen, and Aunt Mattie said, "Run get some kraut, June, and I'll fry us some potatoes."

"Are you all right?" The swelling had gone down some in Aunt Mattie's jaw, but her lips were drawn to the left. I had some trouble understanding her instructions.

"Yes. Minus not one but two teeth." She was already picking potatoes out of the bin and fumbling for a paring knife.

"Sit down, Aunt Mattie," I said. "You look done in. I'll get the potatoes started in just a minute. Everything else is ready."

It surprised me that my aunt left off what she was doing and joined Addie at the kitchen table. As I hurried past her in the semi-darkness, I saw Addie's hair.

"What in the world happ—?" I didn't finished, knowing what I was about to say was uncomplimentary. Addie's gray hair was frizzled up in little tight kinks that made her head look like nothing I'd ever seen.

In record time, we were seated at the table and I poured buttermilk for all of us. I was proud of my first "cooking for company" supper, even if it was just ordinary fare, no chicken or ham. Brad Schuler set right in to eating. He looked up only once to say, "Good potatoes, June. You'll make some man a good cook one of these days."

After that one comment, like he'd uncorked a bottle, both women started talking.

"Lord, Mattie, don't talk to me about the tooth-puller!" Addie crumbled bread into her beans. "If you want your head fried, and your brains just about jolted out of your head, go to Thelma's. If I'd a-knowed what I was in for—"

"Well, I'd risk that any day, compared to that dentist chair." Aunt Mattie's voice quivered just a little. I couldn't believe it. I'd seen her deal with burns and cuts and stonebruises and bad headaches without more than a word or two of complaint.

"What happened?" I asked. Aunt Mattie got a head start.

"He set me down in this cold as cream chair, I was surrounded by these little instruments, picks and tweezers, and before I knew—"

"Thelma's got this contraption with wires coming down in all directions—," Addie chimed in.

"'This ain't going to hurt much, Miz Geer' is what he said. 'But I've got to look in there. Open up.'"

"And Thelma took these chemicals out of this bottle and that bottle, smelling to high heaven—"

"I'd put my glasses on this little tray beside the chair, so I couldn't see right clearly, but I saw that big needle in his hand. 'Lord, Doc,' I said, 'is that meant for me?' I could see that needle sharp enough and that dentist's teeth. Now he's got the prettiest teeth I've ever seen on a man. True pearly whites. I started to tell him just give me a pill or two—"

"Thelma's got a washing chair, and she had my neck bent backwards and my head in that wash basin before I could say more'n that I wanted a permanent wave, fine as she give Miz Duffey last month. Long as I can remember this was the first time anybody's fingers have been scrubbing my head besides mine. The shampoo just foamed up. She's got a way with washing hair, I'll tell you. My head won't recover till a month of Sundays."

"'Bad luck, Miz Geer. There are two molars that will have to come out, truth be told, I ought to delay on one of them, a little abscess there. You do want them out, don't you? This will sting a little.' How was I supposed to answer, me with my head in these little padded cushions and a big white cloth clipped to me. He kept on a-talking, mumbling this and that and waving that needle around. I had both eyes wide open, but I couldn't say a thing. Now, that needle part was the scariest part. When it scrunched right on into my gums, I thought I'd die."

"And the minute Thelma pushed me back straight up after a-rinsing and a-rinsing, she started in with them wires, just a-twisting this way and that. Then she started attaching me to that machine, clamping me tight as a drum. Lordy, all I could think about was that electric chair in Raleigh."

"Funny thing, after I thought I'd die, I kind of lost track of what was going on. Then all of a sudden, I thought my face was gonna come apart from my head! I could hear this scrunching and wrenching and pulling and tearing, and I had to hold on to the chair or I believe he'd have pulled us both right out of that chair and through the wall and down Main Street, it was that bad. There was a sucking sound—"

"My hair was all twisted up and Thelma was a-humming to herself, halfway talking, things like 'your hair's right coarse, it'll take a wave just fine, am I hurting you,' and all the time my eyeballs are being pulled back to China. They'll never be the same—"

I kept looking back and forth from one to the other.

"This sucking sound, and he said 'Ah, that's the worst one. Might as well go ahead while you're here. You feel anything?' What could I say, blood gushing out as it was and me with my head over that little sink. I was spitting like crazy and feeling this big hole in my mouth, and—"

"Well, she turned on the power and I swear I heard my head a-sizzlin. I smelled something burning too and I said—"

"You know I couldn't say a word, my lips wouldn't work right. Now that's a funny feeling. You got something to say, though I don't know if it would have been 'stop' or 'get the other one,' and not a word come out. In a flash he was back in my mouth. I held on to the chair while he pulled and twisted. I was sweating by then. What a blessed relief when he held up the tooth, and I started spitting blood again. Now I hope that's the last time I ever darken the door of that or any other dentist."

I shivered and put my hand on Aunt Mattie's arm.

"'Thelma,' I hollered, 'you're a-burning my head up!' I was getting pig-sick of that smell and all them potions she used aforehand. If I'd been out of doors I'd have puked right there."

Addie covered her mouth with her hand. She realized she'd said a word that wasn't for the supper table.

"I mean it, Mattie. Still Thelma just come over and untwisted one of the curls and said I'd need a few more minutes."

"That smell's enough to turn a man's stomach," her brother said. "Good thing your man's working in Yancey County."

"You shut your mouth, Brad Schuler. Don't talk like that in front of June."

"Do you hurt now, Aunt Mattie?"

"I'm feeling better, just got what feels like two of them—what did you tell me about last week, June? Two big craters in my jaw. But never again will I darken his door."

"And that Thelma charged me extra for some fine spray she used. That's likely what you're talking about, brother. You don't know a fancy smell when you smell one."

Aunt Mattie must have gotten her lips under control. She smiled and said, "Of the two of us, Addie, it's a toss-up as to who got the worst deal. But my ordeal don't show!"

HIBISCUS

Kris Faatz

The boy at the garden shop could be the son Jeannie doesn't have. His lean build and serious eyes hint at her own reflection. Most of all, his smile shields him like sepals around a furled bloom. Jeannie's job has never demanded much except the wits to count out customers' change, but she knows how it feels to furl her own colors and hide them in the dark: so he matters to her.

He's not really a boy—he's a manager, technically her boss—and the two of them aren't friends. Workdays on the crowded sales floor, they trade a scatter of words. How's it going? Can't complain. His job seems like a suit of armor, its overlapped plates dragging at his young shoulders. Now and then, a chink between them lets through a flare of vibrance, there and gone.

She sends the words she can't say through the air. Are you okay? Is this life right for you? Absurd to think he'd tell her, or show her what he shows no one. She's a stranger. Each day, though, she does something rare for her: she holds up and waves a corner of her own colors, not caring who else might see.

One afternoon, he passes her station behind a straggle of customers. Rushed as always, needed somewhere.

"Jeannie." He holds something out on his palm. "This is for you."

She takes it, aware that it's soft against her fingertips, but her eyes are on his face. His smile, this time, is a visor lifted. One glimpse at the light behind; then he's gone.

The gift in her hand is a single hibiscus bloom, flame-orange petals with a wine-red heart. The colors reach out for her.

Thank you. She sends the words to him on the air. I see you.

PLOWING

Ed Nichols

Time stood still sometimes when Sam worked his mule. Sometimes they would stop plowing and stand in the field. One day when they were stopped, Amy, Sam's wife walked to the edge of the field and hollered, "How come y'all stopped plowing?" "Oh, we do that to rest now and then," he said. "Well, I come to tell you that the elected official's wife over on Sardis Road has gone missing again," she said. "Well they say she's done that before," he said. "I know," she said. "This afternoon is scorching," he said. He could smell the tobacco leaves and he wanted a chew, but his arms were wet with sweat and plumb limp. He wanted to fly away. But it was too hot, and the sun was too bright. He said, "I may go blind soon." She said, "Quit talking like a silly mouse and go back to plowing." "Okay. You sure are hard on me. Git up Maude," he said. "I'm going back to the house," she said. "You look out for that elected official's wife if she were to come traipsing through here." Sam nodded and held the reins tight as Mauda plowed hard. After an hour or so he felt dizzy. At the end of a row, he stopped Maude and walked over to the big oak tree where he kept his jug of water. He sat down in the shade, drank water and relaxed his arms. A woman's voice from the woods said, "Can I have a drink of water?" "Sure," he said. When she stepped in front of him he recognized she was the elected official's wife. He handed her his little gourd dipper full of water. "Thank you so much," she said.

She drank all the water in the dipper and he refilled it for her. "I think I'll sit a minute if you don't mind," she said. "That's okay by me," he said. "Thank you," she said. "Where you headed?" he said. "I'm not sure now but I've got an idea. A place where everyone is treated nicely. A place where each day is like a day in paradise." She finally arose, and said, "Thank you for the water, I am leaving now." Sam watched the elected official's wife walk into the woods. He unhooked the plow from Maude, picked up his water jug, and led Maude into the woods.

WHAT NEED FOR PITY?

Linda Imbler

There's no remnant of life
where we linger,
we who feel bitter cold
and enjoy it.

We started as an anxious crew,
the meek buried with the arrogant,
doubtful in the grave,
superstitious about bones.

But over time,
our troubles decayed along with us.
There's things here familiar to us all,
and we share an indifference about death,
inside the sepulchers,
below the monuments.

We dread those who strive
to console all who have died,
attempting bizarre ceremonies
to send us back.

Here, there are no wretched prisoners
afflicted with melancholy.
We meet new friends with joy,
so, what need for pity?

I KNOW THIS TRAIN

Annie McDonnell

My nerves were like a series of railways,
Once upon a time they all communicated with my brain
as if it was led by the smartest of conductors.
like you find at Grand Central Station.

My body, my brain, my movements
were once this glorious series of veins
with free-flowing blood nourishing my body.
and nerve pathways making it all happen.

I remember that feeling.
walking into Grand Central Station.
That's the very moment I'd wake up
when I worked in New York City.

Everything felt electric,
Pulsating with the sensation of my blood flow.
Electronic misfirings all trying to make sense.

I felt like I was in a movie,
Each step to a playlist of my life's songs.

Which made my body feel so alive.

Like I was waiting for a flash mob to start
singing and dancing at any given moment.

I was always waiting for something
to happen here at Grand Central Station. Excitement
was waiting around each corner.

When we would go down to the train tracks each train
would be running on time.
If a train was off even by a minute Everybody gets lost.
dazed.
confused.

Just like my brain,
confusing my body.
zero messages making sense.

My brain feels like it's turning gray.
Just like this train.

Slowly shutting down.
It has lost communication with my organs.

My body was once so alive,
Now everything's neurogenic.

My brain, like the train,
No longer the conductor.
It is just sitting there alone.

Dying and there's nothing anyone can do.

Like the train,
my brain
feels put out in the graveyard.

Did you know that exists?

If you're on the Long Island Railroad,
You see it every day
On your way into the city.
That train graveyard.

It's so very sad

Oh, the stories we could both tell.

The train,
people were there every day,
Sometimes there were parties,
before people got to New York City.

They celebrated weddings,
divorces, birthdays!!

Exactly how my body felt!

I was a constant party.
I was always traveling.
and enjoying each moment!

The best train trips were
going in twice to watch the ball drop-in Times Square
on New Years Eve,
or to see the St. Patrick's Day parade.

Those trains brought good things to life.
My brain used to do the same thing.

When it becomes useless or
begins to slow down,
You could throw all the medicine at it.

You can eat all the right foods, do all the right exercises,

But just like this old train
It gets put out to pasture.

It gets lonely.
It's hard to feel happy.
The skies always feel gray
and definitely stormy.

Feeling like I always need to run for cover.
Only I don't ever have an umbrella.

My body used to feel so alive.

I'll never forget that feeling at Grand Central Station.

I wish my brain would go back to running
as smoothly as it did there.

My brain.

It doesn't want to be that train.

Left all by itself to wither and die,
with no one visiting or showing it love.

Just think of all the possibilities if
they could just fix it up, and get it moving again
just by attaching it to another train.

Even if they just pulled it along
so it felt like it belonged.

My organs are crying out
to belong!

For brain to lead the way

I see the train in this picture.
And my heart bleeds for it

I know how alone it feels,
without its conductor
its passengers
its travels.

I know this train,
For you see,
it's me.

Both of us trying to never forget
Our beautiful memories.

THIS, I SHALL NEVER FORGET

Mike Turner

Faint murmurs in quiet rooms
Dust motes settling on unused furniture
Cast down, thus abandoned
Yet remaining
Cloaking scene with muffled scorn
This, I shall never forget

Intended slights and sorrows
Muddied waters flowing 'cross untrod lanes
Eroding, and moving on
Yet leaving sediment
Damning with faint praise
This, too, I shall never forget

Songs unsung, plays un-staged
Unspoken scripted lines and sonnets
Delivered to absent audiences
Thus unheard
A lifetime's passion, muted
This, too, I shall never forget

Gentle whispers
A balm upon disturbed reverie
Breathing life, and hope
A slender ray of sunlight between grey clouds
Renewing faith amidst despair
A zephyr, blowing old haunts clean

This, I shall always remember

HANGING PICTURES

Micah Ward

Two men sit in a basement bar in downtown Savannah. It is the basement of an old building on an historical square and is a frequent stop on the local ghost tours. The old man serves as sort of a mentor to the young one. Listen to what they say.

"Shit, boy. They're all just pictures," says the old man. "Now, some of 'em are gonna look bigger than the others. But they're all just pictures."

He sits on a sofa. His legs stretched out. Feet propped on a long low table. The young fellow sits in a chair facing the old man. He props his feet on the selfsame table. They drink bourbon in the early afternoon while the working folk of Savannah scurry from one meeting to the next.

This building hails from the early 1800's and the underground bar was, in those years, one of the cooler places in the city where gentlemen could escape Savannah summers to drink and conduct meaningful conversation. It has the look of a dim study with lamps on side tables and paintings in dark frames hung with a carefully planned randomness.

The young man sips and says nothing. His eyes partly closed. The elder sage continues.

"Everything that happens in your life is just like a picture in your memory. Some are like these big old paintings here in their fancy frames. But some are just little snap shots left in a drawer. You can't throw 'em away either. They're always there. They're like a private museum in your brain." The young man shifts in his chair and looks at the old man. "And what if I don't like them pictures?

What if I don't want 'em in a goddamned museum in my brain?"

"You ain't got that choice. You lived the life you lived son. You can't go back in time and not live it. All you can do is choose how to hang the pictures. Hang the best in the main hall and take the worst down to the root cellar and lock 'em behind a door. If somebody else takes 'em out, then just put 'em back. It's your choice."

The young man says nothing and the old man raises his hand to the bartender and signals for another round. The bartenders know the old man. He graces the bar often, drinking bourbon every day except Sunday. Even though liquor is now legal on Sundays in most parts of the south, the old man chooses not to partake on the Sabbath. A hold on him from his days as a Baptist minister. Days before his proclivity for sin took him from the clergy. But this is not Sunday, thus, the bartender brings two more bourbons.

"I heard an old boy up around Statesboro put it this way," says the old man. "Sometimes life serves you a great big shit pie. But you choose how big of a piece to eat."

The young man smiles and raises his glass in toast, "An eloquent truth."

The old man lifts his glass in return and continues. Of course.

"Look here, I don't know what's goin' on in your head. I don't know what kind of demons you're fightin'. But even though they belong to you alone, other people been fightin' demons just like 'em for all the history of the world. Ever since that day Cain killed Abel, we've been paintin' some ugly and nasty pictures for each other's museums."

"Yeah, and I reckon we've been servin' up them shit pies to one another too. Ain't we?"

The old man laughs low. Looks around the room. Two young women converse in a quite conversation with their heads almost touching. A well dressed, bored man sits with them and is obviously not included in the conversation. He stares into space. Perhaps he strolls through the galleries in his own mind.

"If they're all just pictures, why can't I build a big assed fire in my mind and burn the ones I don't like," asks the young man.

"It'd be nice if it was that easy. A lot of people go to all kinds of therapies tryin' to burn 'em up. But the damned old pictures are fire proof. They're always gonna be there."

"But I don't have to look at 'em if I don't want to?"

"Nope. You sure don't. In fact, you don't have to give 'em any more than a passin' glance. Every day that you live you paint new pictures. So, pay attention to what you're paintin' today. Don't worry 'bout where to hang them pictures from yesterday. They ain't got to be any more important than you want 'em to be. Now, we can sit here and talk it to death but the real question is, what are you gonna do?"

"I guess you'd just tell me to paint new pictures and lock them others down in that cellar in my brain. Then go on just like nothin' ever happened."

The old man planted his feet on the floor and leaned with solemn authority toward the young man.

"You can't go about as if nothin' happened. It did. Those demons are always gonna be there. But you gotta be the one who controls 'em. What do you want to do? Go on through life with some kind of thing that ain't never gonna leave. A thing that shadows ever' decision and ever' feelin' and ever' day of your life?"

The young man turns a pained gaze toward the window.

As the bar squats in a basement room all the young man sees are legs and feet. This person hurrying in one direction and that one in another. The old man leans back on the sofa. Returns his feet to the long low table.

"It didn't happen to you," the young man flatly states.

"No, I reckon it didn't. And if I could have prevented it from happenin' to you, I would have. But it doesn't do a damn bit of good to wallow around in that patch of mud. Somethin' happens to all of us. I never knew those people but I've damn sure known others like 'em. I just want you to understand that they ain't got a hold on you no more."

The young man turns back from the window. Fixes the old man with accusing eyes. "You'll be tellin' me to forgive 'em next, won't you?"

"Can you?"

"Could you?"

"It's the best way of loosenin' that hold they got on you."

"But could you?"

"Well now, that ain't my decision to make. You—"

"Of course not," the young man almost shouts. "You just sit there and drink your whiskey and talk all fancy like and then you still leave me to eat the shit pie."

The young man settles back into his chair. The bartender, unaccustomed to anyone speaking with such passion toward his regular patron, walks to the table and places a bowl of nuts between the two sets of propped feet. He receives a reassuring smile. The bored man with the whispering women looks in their direction but it is difficult to tell if he is interested in the outburst or simply needs a place to gaze while he inwardly examines the pictures in his gallery. Pictures of boredom or pictures of passion? Pictures that inspire pride or pictures to hurl into the fiery pit to be consumed in eternal flames of regret?

A week later our pair have descended into the below to resume discussion. Bourbon in hand, reclined in the same positions, feet propped on the same low table.

"Is this becomin' some kind of therapy," asks the young man.

"Well, it could be; analysis by corn mash."

"It makes as much sense as some of the therapies I've had."

The old man smiles. "Ah yes. I imagine that one or more of those preacher therapists told you that what happened was for some kind of grand or profound reason. But unfortunately, things rarely happen for a reason. They just happen. God set this here world in motion and made us with the ability to do good or to do evil. And we choose to do what we will. Most things that happen in our life happen because of our own decisions. And to a lesser extent the decisions of others. It ain't the finger of God orchestratin' some master plan that we don't understand like some people want you to believe."

"So, what happened to me had no purpose. It didn't mean a damned thing. Why'd I have to go through it then?"

"You didn't have to in the sense that there's some master plan for the universe that requires you to suffer in order to achieve some greater purpose in life. Or some plan that requires your pain for someone else to benefit. No, sometimes we just suffer."

Silence as the old man watches the eyes of the young one dissolve into a blank stare. In his mind, the young man feels the crumbling of his concept of a universal master plan. And his thoughts turn to something darker as his eyes focus and roam the paintings on the walls.

"How much of a purpose do you want to give it," asks the old man.

"You mean it's my choice?"

"It's completely your choice."

"And where does God or maybe no God at all fit into this?"

"No God? You mean like, how can there be a God with all the sufferin' in the world? If there really is a God why does He allow plague, pestilence, war, disease and so forth and so on? And specifically, if there is a God why did He allow what happened to me to happen? Is that where we're headed now?"

The young man stares with silence. And the silence compels the old man to attempt theological wisdom.

"In the beginnin',' to quote Genesis, God created it all. And when I say all, I mean every bit of it. God created evil as well as good because you can't have one without the other. In Asia they talk about yin and yang, the complementary opposites. When God created love, he had to create evil too. And when God created man, he gave us free choice. That's why all the evil exists. We choose it. We also choose how we respond to it."

The young man catches the eye of the bartender and signals for another round. The old man raises his eyebrows and asks, "Are we gettin' somewhere?"

The old man knows that the ultimate question must be dealt with. He sits silently and waits on the young man to broach the subject. He does.

"My first counselor said that God had a reason for everything that happened to me. Said that I wouldn't understand it. But someday God's plan would be revealed and I would understand the meanin' behind it all. That's a piece of shit pie ain't it?"

"That's the counseling from somebody who can't explain or comprehend the choice of evil. So, he blames God by sayin' that God has a reason for it. Some people get more comfort by believin' that God inflicts the evil for a greater good. They just can't accept the idea that certain people choose to do great evil and God doesn't stop 'em."

"Well hell, if God loves us, why doesn't he stop 'em?"

"Because that would violate the law of free will. Our entire existence wouldn't be any more important than two mules fightin' over a turnip. Why, we'd just be like checkers that God moves around on a checker board. I won't believe that. Our existence doesn't mean shit if we ain't free to choose our own actions and our own beliefs. And the greatest decision is whether we follow God or not."

"Do you still follow God?"

The old man faces the question that he struggles with daily. In silence he looks around the room and stops on a painting of a nude couple. Then, as if facing a sad revelation, he turns his attention back to the table and drains the glass of bourbon. He is slightly unsteady on his feet as he stands.

"I've chosen to follow God on some days. I've made other choices on others."

He sways slightly as he climbs the steps to the sidewalk outside of the bar. He joins the anonymous legs that pass the window. The young man is left alone. He thinks of free choice and pictures in the gallery of his mind. He smiles at the beginnings of an idea.

Two weeks pass. We find them again in their therapeutic postures awaiting their usual libations. The young man is different. The old man notices. "You seem different today, boy."

"Well I should. You see, I took a little trip. And when I got there, I painted some new pictures and hung 'em over those old ones. The ones that keep me up at night."

"Well, now, you feel better about it then?"

"I control the demons now."

"Where did you go?"

"Now, you used to be a Baptist preacher. If I tell you a secret, are you like one of them Roman Catholics? Do you have to keep it a secret from everybody?"

"What have you done?"

"I went to the graveyard."

A silence settles on the two as the old ex-preacher worries about the next question and the young one waits on him to ask it. The bartender puts two bourbons on the table. "Your silence disappoints me," the young man finally says. "I thought you'd want to know what I've been up to." The old man sits and stares. The young one is eager to tell his story so he continues before the old man can summon a question.

"You ever been out to that graveyard? It's at the end of the road on the edge of some swamp land. Ain't nothin' out there but live oaks and alligators. Anyway, the road ain't paved and it's barely wide enough for two cars. It ain't an easy place to get to on a good day and I didn't expect anybody to try it on a rainy one. I watched the weather forecasts and when we hit that cold spell and the rain turned to sleet, I knew it was time to go. It was the perfect weather to keep anybody else from being there and interruptin' me." The old man sits in stillness and fear and fascination.

"I left before daylight and when I got there it was just light enough to drive that little path right up to the graves. It wasn't as hard to dig as you might think. It's mostly sandy out there and when you got the proper motivation, the work ain't that hard. The vaults and caskets weren't really that much of a problem either. I only needed to open it enough to slide the bodies out."

The old man's breathing becomes shallow and fast and he starts to regret the counseling that he thought was so needed and so brilliant.

"When I got the first one out, I just let it lie there in the dirt with the rain and sleet fallin' right on the face and hands and that damned nice funeral suit. He didn't seem to mind. I left him there while I dug the dirt out of the second grave. The rain and sleet were getting' harder all the time. But I finally got that one out and I laid it right beside the first one. Side by side, just like I see 'em in the pictures in that make-believe gallery you told me about."

The old man sits. Waits for what may come next.

"I decided to take a break and just look at 'em. A hell of a lot different than when they's alive. I sat on the tailgate of the truck and drank out of a pint of whiskey that I had brought for the occasion. I looked at the pictures in my mind that they were responsible for; the ones in the big frames hangin' up there where I got to see them every damned day. The fog started rollin' in and pretty soon I couldn't even see the tops of the trees. The sleet was harder than it had been all mornin'."

The young man stops talking long enough to order two more bourbons. The old man has gone still and silent and has drunk nothing from the glass he already has.

"I didn't talk to the sumbitches, I just stared. I drank the whiskey and every time I swallowed, I thought about them things they did to me when I was a little boy. When I finished, I threw that empty bottle into one of the graves. I didn't bring a chainsaw even though it would have been easier. I wanted to use my own strength. I wanted it to feel personal. I used a broad headed axe and I chopped those bodies into as many pieces as I could."

The young man drains the glass before him. He stands with proud countenance peering down at a now stunned shell of wisdom. "Well, it was fun but, I think it's time to leave before the law starts lookin' for me. Mexico maybe. Switch to tequila and paint some better pictures."

As he walks away the old man stares at his untouched glasses on the table and can think of only one response.

"Forgive me Father, for I have sinned."

THE LONE AND LEVEL SANDS

James Wade

1

On weekend nights the town calls to it a procession of pilgrims in rattletrap buggies and mud-covered coupes and trucks with wooden beds. They come in vehicles or they come, entire families, by the wagonload. They come bundled in moth-pillaged coats and hand-me-down trousers too big or too small. They come with their quarters and their flasks, and they come in the heat and the cold alike. They haunt the sidewalks and board porches like clochards too proud to beg. And they huddle about streetcorners as soapbox prophets speak of the world's end. The hillbilly hucksters peddle their cheap or stolen wares, and the back alley molls lure their shameless suitors to the edge of a pimp's knife.

But on they come, in hopes that whatever is missing might be found, and whatever is broken within them might be mended. They have an inclination towards seeking. They are, like you, American.

He is among them on this night, our hero. Forefather. He watches the lights from their cars reflect off the wet road and the lights of the businesses and the streetlamps lit and burning, but none so magnificent as the luster of the full moon. It rises out over the black river and the battalion of stars at its back. Pale lights. Pale blue dark. Across the face of this moon are craters and shadows of craters. Footprints of giants. He does not look. He does not see.

He goes instead into the hotel and through the lobby and into the cafe. There are iron sconces affixed to wooden columns and each giving glow to the tables near the center of the room. In the corner it is darker and in the corner sits Walters, the man our hero has come to see.

2

What say there, Walters, our man stands next to the table and there are two others seated and these others look up at him peculiar-like.

It is not without reason, their looking, as our man does have a ragged and woebegone appearance to him. Black matted hair hanging over his ears and down just past the arch of the brows. Patches of facial hair that grow unruly and in all directions. His clothes are unwashed for days. For weeks. He has a smell to him like wet wood.

Mr. Shepherd, Walters says. I was under the impression we'd concluded our business.

Walters is a businessman. A city man. He smiles when he is thinking.

That rig you sold me won't work, Shepherd says. Not for nothing.

Mr. Shepherd, I believe I was very specific in the terms of our agreement. I sold to you a working rotary drill. Any post- sale deficiencies are your responsibility.

I can't get it to turn, our man says, as if he's not heard Walters speaking. It can't drill if it won't turn.

Walters sighs to signify his being inconvenienced. The others watch him.

Mr. Shepherd, are you trying to turn the rotary yourself? How the hell else does it turn?

The others chuckle.

Well, there's your problem, sir, Walters says. The drill bit alone weighs more than you. It's carbide steel for god's sake. The mechanism takes a horse. Or a strong mule. It can't be rotated by a man. Eugene Sandow, perhaps.

The other two men are laughing. Our hero does not know why. He is uncomfortable around them. Uncomfortable around anyone.

His forebears came to Texas from the hills and hollows of Appalachia and some died or cut loose along the way and those who settled in this new country did so with little means about them. Little possessions. They pulled what they could from the river—water and fish and paddies of rice—and they farmed cotton on small plots and tried their hand at cattle and tried their hand at rougher trades. A great uncle was knifed on a steamboat in Jefferson over a faro game. Another was hanged in Kilgore for stealing a horse.

There is no education in our hero's blood. Little in the way of socializing. He will not meet the eyes of these men at the table.

He looks instead at their shoes. They are shiny and black. So black they look wet. He has seen such blackness.

He has seen photographs of oil. But the photos do no justice. None.

I will be rich, he wants to tell the laughing men. I will buy the shoes from your feet and see you go barefoot, and should you acquire more shoes I will buy those too. I will buy every shoe on this earth before I see them on your callused, bleeding feet.

A mule, he says instead, and then leaves.

3

There has been talk o'er the years. Talk of a curse. Of a great-grandfather who deserted Sam Houston's army, took up with a gypsy in some traveling caravan of the mysterious and the absurd. When he deserted her too, she laid upon him a great malediction that would pass within his blood and the blood of his blood for all recorded time.

The curse, even when it is not spoken, is thought of at funerals for an aunt who is struck by lightning, a brother who drowns, and another brother who is killed in the Great War.

Utter nonsense, according to our man's mother. But his father was never so defiant. He denied it, the father, just less so. Less certain. As if perhaps it would give him such relief to know his own failed efforts were the work of some cosmic sorcery beyond his ability to comprehend, let alone control. That our successes belong to a higher power is a thought that offers comfort. That our failures are not our own is a thought that offers true salvation.

By this thinking our man has been selected. Chosen. Preordained. He goes forth from the hotel and in the thoroughfare he nods to no one. A proud nod.

He is off to the mule barn to strike a bargain if a bargain can indeed be struck, when swiftly he is set upon by sirens of the night. They call him baby. They call him daddy. They offer things they might do to him. Things they might allow to be done.

Surely Christ died because He knew we would on occasion fall into temptation, our man decides. Hell, if there weren't no sin, what would even be the point?

Our man has desires, you understand. And who can blame him? He has eyes, doesn't he? To see the women in their finery, the way their bodies move beneath their clothes, the way their chins dip down when they smile, embarrassed by their own loveliness.

Still, our man is penniless, so he passes by. He promises to return when he has made his fortune. He wants to tell them more. To have them touch his arms while he says he was only dipping water from the creek. But he won't speak of it. Not yet.

At the mule barn a boy is sitting on a stool and singing to himself. The mules stir in the pen beyond.

Are you the fella to see about a mule? Our man poses.

Nossir, the boy says. I'm the nightwatch. Mr. Renfro don't open 'til morning.

He ever barter? Towards the renting of a mule, I mean.

Sure. He'll let them go on loan, too. If'n you seem trustworthy.

You figure he might allow you to barter in his stead? Supposing I didn't want to wait until morning.

Nossir. I'm the nightwatch.

Right, but look here. Say Mr. Renfro gets here in the morning. He asks, how'd things go last night.

He don't ask that.

No, but supposing he does ask. And you're obliged to tell him there was a fella come by looking for a mule. You're obliged to tell him that, ain't you?

I reckon he'd want me to mention it.

Alright. So you mention it. And then ol' Renfro, he says, well, will he be back by this morning. And then, here you are with a sorry report that no, Mr. Renfro, the fella won't be back.

How come?

How co— because I don't want to wait until morning. I want the mule, now.

What for do you need a mule in the middle of the night?

It don't matter what for, I just don't want to come back here in the morning. Now, you could be telling Mr. Renfro that he lost out on a mule rental. Or, in a few hours time, you could be explaining to him how it is you got him a bit of business he was fixing to lose.

How'd I do that?

By renting me a goddamn mule.

Mr. Renfro don't allow.

I know he don't, son. You've done and told me he don't. But I'm telling you that it's my belief, in this here particular situation, that Mr. Renfro would want you to disobey his own rules in order to see my business done, lest I take it elsewhere.

The boy frowned.

There ain't no other mule barns close by.

Our champion closes his eyes. When he opens them he turns and looks back toward the lights of town. No one is about.

Do you know my name? He asks the boy. Nossir. I'm Jimmy.

Our man cracks Jimmy across the jaw and the boy goes down in a heap. He thought he may need to hit him a few times but it looks like the boy is out cold.

4

It was timber for our man's father. Years spent toiling in the turpentine camps until he could buy his own plot of mature, second-growth pines. The local timber industry had offered great economic opportunity for more than a century, and since the first saw mills were opened in Nacogdoches and Ironosa Creek the region had drawn to it destitute seekers of every order.

As trams and railroads stretched out across the country, the need for lumber increased and the proliferation of East Texas mills knew no equal. The growing nation called for pilings, telegraph poles, bridges and trestles, along with coal chutes, cattle guards, roofing and fencing. Company towns sprang up throughout the dense forestlands, with entire populations connected solely to the wellbeing of the mill. Timber was the future of wealth, his father said.

There is a photograph our man keeps with other totems and memorials in an old trunk. In the photo the father is standing with his arms crossed and squinting into the sun.

Behind him is a large tract of loblolly pines. Uncaptured in the image are the sawyer beetles and pinewood nematodes that will rot the trees from within, covering them with blue stain fungi and rendering them worthless.

5

He leads the mule away from town. They travel along dirt roads and game trails, paths marked by crushed rock or cut brush, and all of them winding through the thickets of like braided ribbons, crossing and recrossing in a matrix of tendons that hold together such perilous country.

He swings the lantern before him like a pale saber, slicing away layers of the dark only to have the dark return again, filling a void where the light has been but will not keep.

The homestead is three miles outside of town. A little cabin. Two bedrooms. A kitchen and a den separated by a wood burning stove. Our man ties the mule's lead rope to a porch slat and goes inside.

The place is dark and the air somehow thicker than the humidity without. The walls smell of soil and smoke from long ago fires. On the kitchen counter and the shelves above it there are glass jars full up with pickled vegetables and jams and a few substances our man cannot name. He has changed nothing since his mother's passing. Deer skins are strewn about the wood floor and hung on the walls and draped over windows like gothic curtains. On a table in the middle of the room and in various corners of the cabin, hardened wax has collected at the base of candles that he has not lit in years.

He sheds his clothing and goes naked onto the porch and pulls the ladle from its nail and scoops water from the bucket and drinks it and feels it running half-cool down his body. When he has finished he shoves the bucket toward the mule and nods and goes back inside.

Our man has always been a dreamer. On this night he dreams the earliest memory of his life. He sees acres of the forest engulfed in roaring flames like what the preacher says of hell. He sees animals–nature reacting to chaos. Deer fleeing the inferno with short hair afire. Screaming foxes. Squirrels dropping dead and charred from the burning branches. Smoking.

6

He awakes to a knocking at the door. He opens one eye and with it sees dust motes trapped and floating in rogue strips of sunlight come through cracks in the back bedroom wall.

Marion Shepherd, I need you to come on out. More knocking.

He pulls on the same clothes and is frowning before he opens the door.

It's a deputy. Barrel-chested fella that our man recognizes from around.

That kid tried to rob me, our man says in own defense.

The deputy appears confused. Only now does our hero see the other, more diminutive fella in the suit.

This is Leslie Roth, the deputy says. He's from First National. This land, and this here cabin, is now the property of the bank.

How's that? Hell, my Daddy built this house.

You owe property taxes, the bank man says. Your father also took two loans with us. Neither were repaid. You owe that too.

Our man turns back to the inside of the cabin as if there might be someone else to whom he can appeal. He is not familiar enough with taxes to argue. And he will be coming into his fortune within days. Hours even.

Alright. Well. Y'all just give me a couple weeks and I'll have you everything that's owed.

That time has come and gone, Mr. Shepherd. You've received three months prior notice.

Horseshit. When? Three months ago.

Alright, alright. Fine. Listen, our man leans in close now because he's going to tell them something extraordinary. He has told no one. Not Walters. Not the cooing girls. Not even the mule, whose purpose is directly aligned with what he has to tell. He leans closer still. He wants to be close enough to feel the power of their reaction.

There's oil on my land, he says. Neither a whisper, nor a shout. The words themselves are imbued with a certain regality that dictates a tone all its own.

The two men look to one another and then back to our hero.

As of this morning, the deputy says, it looks like there's oil on the bank's land. You have until sundown to vacate the property.

7

After he was forced to burn his timber, our man's father found work where he could. Mill work. Violent on the body. In those last days his father went about hunched and uncoordinated like an ill-constructed attempt of a man. One of god's early missteps.

So too our hero went into the mill. Papermaking. Cooking wood chips in a chemical mixture of sulfur and soda, smoothing their pulp into sheets with foundry presses and great mechanical rollers.

He liked the sound of the mill. Its roaring, pounding, deafening noise.

It overwhelmed his sorrows as they tried to surface. Drowned them out.

But when he returned home and sat alone on the porch the world was quiet and his mind left to wander. He tried listening for katydids and crickets and bullfrogs along the water's edge. He listened too for the howling of wolves though he knew such things are no more in this country—never will be again.

When the mill shuttered its doors and submitted to the Depression, our man found grunt work in the oil fields. Others did not.

While the men who employed him grew rich beyond measure, hundreds were forced to seek prospects in lands foreign to them. Many went without thought or motivation save that someplace else could not be worse than here.

He watched them pass by the derricks where he labored. They trudged barefoot or in weathered shoes, the dirt clinging to their tattered clothing and coating their faces in dark shades whereby their eyes seemed to glow white. They rode in the backs of wagons or on the backs of skinny animals and they rode with a distant look about them, as if they could see well beyond the horizon and were unsure of how to describe it.

There were old women and young children and there were proud, angry men and men who had already been broken. Men who walked by habit alone. Windup dolls of men who kept moving, kept breathing, but had been hollowed out long ago by a world that wouldn't stop taking.

8

Evicted from his familial home, our hero is now possessed by an urgency that holds no equal. He spends the better part of the day searching for Walters.

No, haven't seen him.

Saw him earlier, don't know where he's at now.

Who the hell is Walters?

And in his hour of need it is now that our man thinks of the gypsy and her curse. Thinks of vague relatives dying at the hands of some unseen sorcery. Thinks of burning timber. But no, our man is a man of faith. He's like Job, our man. And yet, he cannot help but think that even in the Sunday teachings there is no accounting of such things—no divine ledger wherein names are written and ordered purely by the tribulations they have endured. What is the prize for our own resiliency when the same is not asked of others? Hush now, he berates himself, for he knows the reward. He has touched the slick, wet godliness that awaits.

Here now Walters steps out of the barbershop and into the thoroughfare, trailed by the same two men from the cafe. Faith restored. Prayer answered.

Ah, Mr. Shepherd, Walters says before our hero can get a word in. I heard about your trouble with the bank.

I got a deal for you. Pardon?

A deal, our man says, his eyes with a crazed look about them. You buy me out of my land. Then let me stay on and work it for oil. The drill's already out there and ready to go. I got the mule too, right over yonder, just like you said. I'll pay you back whatever you gotta spend, then we can split everything else fifty-fifty from here until the end of time.

Walters knows our man is desperate. He can see it pulsing there on his face like the mark of Cain.

While I extend to you my deepest and most sincere sympathies, sir, I have no need to enter into such an agreement.

Our hero stares at him. Sizes him up. City man. Sales man. Somebody to blame.

He spits near Walters's shiny black shoes.

You wouldn't turn loose of a nickel to see the tits on the Virgin Mary would you? he says.

On the contrary. I am by no means a spendthrift. I am an investor. Why, just this morning I bought a foreclosed upon property a few miles outside of town.

It takes our man a few seconds but when he realizes the truth of things he launches himself at Walters. The two men intercede. Our hero takes a hard punch to the stomach. They grab him by either arm and drag him away and one of the men unholsters a pistol and holds it there against our man's head.

You bother Mr. Walters again, the man says and he doesn't finish the sentence because he doesn't need to. All things are understood through violence.

9

Two weeks prior our man strikes a deal with Preston Walters to have delivered a fully assembled, fully operational rotary drill. Into the purchase of this rotary drill he pours his life savings, such as they are. Oil is the future of wealth.

Now he is squatting behind his barn–it is still his barn for another hour–and taking stock of the rig. It sits, unmoving, atop the same sled on which it was delivered. He touches every part of its body. The drill string and swivel. The bit and base and platformed steel. Such strange alchemy. He hoists himself atop the apparatus and crouches there like some grotesque adornment. From this vantage he watches the sun in its setting. Blood orange. Falling away. Birds rise soundless against the evening sky.

Well I'll be goddamned if I'm gonna leave it here for that sonofabitch, he says to the mule.

But he will leave it. There is nothing else he can do.

He gathers up a few things in a canvas duffle and starts towards town. He stops and comes back for the mule.

10

In south county, a hundred yards off the ranch-to-market, is a rusted tin barn with dirt floors and big script-painted sign that reads: Grizzly Bar The trees that back it are towering, the structure dwarfed by their enormity. It is nestled at their feet like something that would be watched over. Something precious.

There are cars parked out front in no particular pattern and horses and wagons, too, though the majority of the patrons seem to have walked here, materializing up out of the woods like timber ghosts with vast unquenchable thirsts.

Enters our hero, bobbing and weaving through the smoke and the must of the place. Inside the barn is arranged like a long dance hall, with the bar on one end and tables scattered about, then a small empty space for dancing and then the short stage whereon a trio of men are plucking away at an Eddie Lang tune.

Here now are gathered every imaginable shade of the backwoods. Timbercutters, bootleggers, and part-time prostitutes waiting for a fool to marry. There are men who come only to this place and have not seen another vestige of the outside world for twenty years. For more. There are young girls who chance the night to sneak away from their snoring fathers. There are old drunks and young apprentices who will learn their ways. There are men who carry pistols and some who lean their rifles against the tables next to them. There are great bowie knives worn sheathed and unsheathed upon men's thighs. There are gamblers and tinkers. Musicians and mechanics. And there are volunteer firefighters who will set ablaze more acres than they will ever save.

Our hero moves among them, his eyes scanning the floor for loose change. Such a day, a life, cannot be survived sober. And the sin? What of it? Die again, if You need to. Just leave me out of it. Even if he has to beg, our man will have a goddamn drink.

Shep, a voice calls and our champion looks around this strange gathering of humanity until he sees a hand motioning for him.

Thomas, he says, squeezing up to the bar.

My old buddy, Shep, the man says, clearly drunk. Let me buy you a drink.

Shit, you can buy me two.

The man motions awkwardly at the barkeep who brings them whiskey.

I ain't seen you in… when's the last time I seen you? Thomas asks.

Your daddy's funeral.

Christ Almighty, has it been that long?

It has, our man says and downs his whiskey. Christ Almighty.

Our hero motions for another drink. On him, he tells the barkeep.

Thomas is briefly confused but another thought chases it away.

Shep, he is slurring. You know Momma passed on not three weeks ago. Sorry to hear it. Three weeks. Our man nods.

Couldn't even afford to bury her next to Daddy. Had to put her in the ground over in Rosedale.

That's a shame.

It is. It's a damn shame. But it ain't like I had no other options. Don't know what I would've done if they didn't have them burial permits so cheap.

The what? Our man asks. He is wondering how many drinks he can get away with before Thomas realizes what is happening.

Burial permits, Thomas repeats. That's how come me to put her in Rosedale. They don't sell you the plots. Just issue you a permit. It's still their land and everything.

Our conquering hero frowns. There is a mechanism in his brain which even at his most desperate hour cannot be shut off.

Whose land is it if you bought a plot? Thomas looks confused again.

Yours, of course.

Our champion is staggered. His knees weaken and he grabs hold of the man to keep himself upright.

Thomas laughs.

We ought to get together more, Shep, he says. You seem like a good time.

Thanks for the drinks, our man mutters and then he is gone into the crowd.

11

Three weeks prior our man has walked to the creek that runs along the edge of his property. It has been a hot day and he is fetching water for bathing. He rarely does this but he has dreamed so vividly of late about the touch of a woman that he hopes a good scrub might instill in him the confidence needed to approach someone sometime. The mere thought causes him to stiffen. His mouth goes dry. He scoops a handful from the creek and raises it to his lips. He stops. It feels strange in his hand. He sniffs at it and then lets it slide through his fingers.

My God, he says.

12

In the dead of night our hero has returned to the homestead that no
longer belongs to him. He leads the mule behind the cabin and out
to the old barn. He goes quietly, as if the bank man and the deputy
are on patrol somewhere nearby. One of Walters's men, waiting to
again press a pistol against his skull.

He emerges from the barn with a leather collar-harness and
lengths of chain.

As he affixes everything to the sled and then to the mule he
whispers in its ear, oil is the wealth of the future.

When all is secured to his liking, our man urges the mule
forward with a great shout.

13

Gracewood Cemetery is one and one-half miles away and though
there are uphill portions of the path the steadfast mule never breaks
its pace. Our man dances along beside it. Singing to it. Praising it.
Promising it everything its mule heart might wish. There are those
immaculate divinities of creation and then there is this mule,
standing there atop them. Unsullied. Unimpeachable. This mule is
endowed with the power of the holy spirit. The power of angels.
The power of Christ himself. God bless this beautiful animal.

The mule follows the road and the road follows the creek and
our man is watching them both and he knows where they lead. He
wonders at the geology of it all. He is hoping— praying with a
fervor known only to the most devout of votaries. Let it ever flow.
Let it not faulter.

14

In the early light of dawn they watch the towery pines give birth to
great shadows what reach out across a tideless sea of blooming
bunchgrass, its purpletop tridens put to a balletic bending by the first
wind of the coming fall.

They are gathered for the Sunday sermon but such pieties will have to wait as the crowd has now gathered to see something miraculous in its own right.

Just across the courtyard from the chapel is the lychgate and the cemetery beyond where stand elaborately fashioned headstones in fine rows like gothic soldiers awaiting some command. Further along are more simple markers, crosses and stone pilings, and the grass is thicker there, just above the creek, in the shade of a pecan tree, and the sacred cairns are scattered below like mutant fruit. And it is here that the crowd is looking. Staring. Gaping. For here is Marion Shepherd, our very own atman, walking a mule in circles o'er top the graves of his mother and father. And with each rotation the great drill digs further into the earth.

Our man senses their shock, their displeasure. He grins and waves.

What in God's name are you doing, Marion?

He looks around, our mischievous hero, as if there might be someone else to whom the question was addressed.

Just doing a little prospecting, he calls. You can't, someone cries.

Naw, see, that's where you're wrong. I paid Gracewood Baptist for both of these here plots, and seeing as how my drill and the path of the mule turning my drill don't never go outside the plots– well–I guess I can do as I please.

There are threats made. Legal action promised. But eventually the preacher gets the crowd inside the church. And in his sermon he teaches that no man can serve two masters, and he teaches the root of all evil, and he teaches of greed and idolatry and materialism, and he speaks these words as they are written: Everyone comes naked from their mother's womb and as everyone comes so they depart. They take nothing from their toil that they can carry in their hands. And as he speaks the Foundation of the Church begins to shake beneath them. Juddering vibrations that seem to encompass the whole of the world, as if the earth's anchor has itself been cut free– the mainspring of all creation recalled by a God ill content with his own handiwork, ready to clear the board and start anew.

Fear not, the preacher is calling. Fear not brothers and sisters and trust in the Lord our God. But what are words worth against such power?

15

And as the darkness comes spouting from punctured land it will usher in a future of raw material and rage and the world will tremble and our hero lets it wash over him. Baptized anew. And all that was done unto him he will do unto others. And hark, for here is our Lord and Savior, black with fortune.

THE CABIN ON CROOKED CREEK

Ashley Tunnell

The carriage lay on its side a short distance from the stone that cradled Tobias Fuller's head. One of the wheels moved lethargically, making a rough, scraping sound as it came to its final resting place and baptized the night in silence. After opening his eyes, he wearily pushed himself into a seated position. He winced as he touched his forehead, which he typically kept contained under a black felt bowler hat. Wiping something wet and sticky out of his eyes, he struggled to his feet. The moon was a discarded fingernail clipping, and Tobias used its thin light to scan his surroundings. He felt something warm seep down the side of his face, and he wrinkled his nose against the metallic smell of blood as he searched the densely wooded area for the horses; however, they were nowhere to be found.

The overgrown path was barely discernible in the dimly lit woods just east of the little town known as Crooked Creek. Stopping briefly at a cobblestone bridge, Tobias listened to the rush of the fast-moving creek after which the town was named. A thick layer of fog descended on the area and blanketed it in white and gray. The fog was too dense and the hour too late for travel. On the other side of the bridge, Tobias caught a glimpse of a small cabin in various stages of disrepair. He supposed that at one time the cabin may have been charming; however, it now stood in a state of melancholic decay. The walls were cracked and weather-worn, and ivy clung to the crumbling façade as though it were desperate to hold the remnants of the old cabin together. The fog rushed ahead with a mind of its own. Each particle of mist seemed determined to be the one to knock on the cabin's weathered door and announce Tobias's imminent arrival to its occupants.

The interior of the cabin was nearly as dilapidated as its exterior. Fragments of moonlight bled delicately through the gaps in the roof, and Tobias could see the ancient beams that sagged wearily above the remnants of the torn and faded wallpaper. The cabin drew a breath and watched as the scraps of wallpaper fluttered in its chilly breeze.

"Hello?" said Tobias. He was certain that he heard the walls of the cabin whisper his name as he entered; however, the only thing that answered his tentative greeting was the musty aroma of age and neglect. The outline of a wooden door was almost imperceptible on the opposite side of the room as Tobias began to cautiously make his way through the bowels of the cabin.

The moonlight reflected off a chandelier that stared glumly down from where it was bolted to the ceiling, illuminating a dining room table covered with a ragged tablecloth. It was set with tarnished silverware beside dusty plates for a long-forgotten meal. The fireplace, which had once been the heart of the living room, now stood cold and silent as its hearth embraced both dust and soot. A washstand stood at attention next to the wooden door. Its porcelain basin was cracked. The doorknob was rusted beneath Tobias's hand.

He opened the wooden door, and the bones of the little cabin settled and seemed to softly whisper his name. "Tobias." The bedroom was much darker than the rest of the cabin. Dim slivers of moonlight crept through the gaps in the roof, but there was not enough of it for Tobias to adequately navigate the cabin's small bedroom. He stumbled ineptly towards the center of the room where the four-poster bed appeared bulky and too big for the size of the room. Weary from his travels and carriage accident, he collapsed gratefully onto the dusty coverings.

Tobias peered at the wall across the room from the bed. "What a strange portrait," he said. The slivers of moonlight revealed a painting of a boy whom Tobias imagined to be the cabin owner's young son. The boy's heart-shaped face and flushed cheeks rested beneath a halo of wheat-colored hair, but it was the boy's eyes that Tobias found most striking. The artist had poured into them all the power and authority that his paintbrush could contain, and they gazed coolly out of the portrait until its stillness was moved by their realism. The image in the portrait bore an uncanny resemblance to the beggar Tobias had encountered during a visit with Crooked Creek's baker earlier that morning. The boy had clung to Tobias's freshly tailored coat with grimy fingernails as he gazed pleadingly through red-rimmed eyes masked in a thick layer of filth.

"Please. Just one loaf of bread," said the boy whose squalid, gray rags were steaming with a palpable odor.

"Let go of me, boy," Tobias said.

As his hands tightened on Tobias's coat in desperation, the boy pled again, "Please."

The flies had made their home in the boy's unkempt hair. Tobias was disgusted as he roughly shoved the boy back onto the sidewalk. The dull, gray wall of the baker's shop seemed to embrace the boy as he faded into it. Tobias tried to ignore the sinking feeling in the pit of his stomach. He did not wish misfortune upon the vagrants of Crooked Creek. He just preferred not to see them. "I am not an evil man," Tobias muttered to himself.

As Tobias removed his coat for the evening, the smudges of dirt left behind by the boy's dingy fingers lingered like a distant and unpleasant memory. Wincing at a pain in his shoulder from his mishap with the carriage, Tobias shifted his body weight to his uninjured side and fell into a restless sleep.

"Tobias." The voice was little more than a whisper. Tobias's eyes snapped open, and he scanned the room. He supposed he must have dozed off. The moonlight fell through the cracks in the ceiling and spilled precariously across the dusty bedding. His gaze came to rest on the portrait, and he frowned. The boy in the portrait no longer appeared to be rosy cheeked and smiling. The lifelike qualities that unnerved Tobias before had been replaced by sunken eyes staring vacantly into nothingness. His smile was more of a grimace. Were those flowers in his hands before? Tobias told himself that they must have been.

"It must be a trick of the moonlight," he said. His voice was no more than a whisper, but it seemed to echo hollowly throughout the drafty bedroom. The cold fog from his mouth chased the traces of moonlight in an ethereal race toward the wood paneling covering the walls. He wrapped his jacket tightly around his shoulders before lying back down on the grimy comforter and allowing sleep to take him.

"Tobias." Again, it was little more than a whisper that woke him from his restless sleep.

The moonlight fell across the walls now, rather than the comforter. His gaze fell on the portrait, and his heart began to beat uncomfortably against his ribcage. The color of the boy's skeletal eyes was no longer distinguishable, and his teeth were black with rot. The boy's thin, bony fingers still clasped the bouquet of flowers, but they were mostly wilted with a few dried-out petals hanging like condemned men. Tobias blinked rapidly and rubbed the sleep from his eyes as the fog that had permeated the musty bedroom slowly dissipated to reveal the portrait. The portrait of the boy with the flushed cheeks and unnerving gaze peered back at him, unchanged from the first time Tobias had laid eyes on it only a few hours prior. Shaking his head, Tobias turned away from the portrait. "Portraits do not change," he said.

Daylight could not be more than a few hours away, and Tobias wanted to leave the derelict cabin as early as possible. He told himself that he would waste no more time fretting over confounding portraits of strangers, and he fell into a restless sleep.

The moonlight had faded into a chilly sunrise. Tobias awakened slowly and peered blearily around the bedroom. Long abandoned cobwebs held the corners of the room together, and the air was heavy with dust particles. The hardwood floors were scratched and worn from the impression of countless footsteps. Time peeled the rust- colored wallpaper away from the walls in layers to reveal the intricate, graying designs of older wallpaper. The moth-eaten linens on the bed were the same rust color as the wallpaper. The pillows were lumpy and worn. The desk and the nightstand were elaborate and heavy. As Tobias took in the brightly lit room, the hairs on the back of his neck rose, and he ran from the home without taking the time to gather his freshly tailored jacket. The horses were tethered to a post by the cobblestone bridge. Tobias chanced a look over his shoulder at the cabin on Crooked Creek. It stood like a sepia-shaded soliloquy that would forever be whispered between the walls of a cabin that memorized the names and faces of forgotten people.

The horses knew the way to town, and Tobias found himself glancing curiously at the baker's shop as they trotted by its window display. The walls hid the beggar well, and Tobias tried to refocus his thoughts on the long day ahead of him. He was exhausted because sleep the night before had been scarce. Indeed, Tobias Fuller would find sleep to be an elusive companion for the rest of his days. For when he woke up in the cabin on Crooked Creek, there was no portrait of a young boy. Instead, he found himself gazing through a dew-frosted window at grass-covered hills, rolling gently into the trees of a darkened forest.

What Really Happened

John M. Williams

Tommy Edwards was the kind of new kid who got a pass from the first day. He was a well-built guy, for one thing—you would think twice before messing with him—and he would indeed prove to be a quick, powerful athlete, in three sports. Not basketball. Gravity kept him near the ground, and no one was a bigger disparager of his ineptness at shooting than himself. That's how he was—never calling attention to himself, most comfortable talking about things he couldn't do. Which wasn't much. Unless you counted things he wouldn't do—like drinking, smoking, cussing, or talking dirty about girls. His whole family—and they were a close family, the kindest, most decent people in the world—went to church three times a week—some church you had heard of but didn't know what it was. He resisted not evil and turned the other cheek. The only time anybody ever saw him mad was when somebody picked on somebody weaker than they were. He didn't go for that.

And even then it was just a red-faced, indignant, non-violent anger. You respected him and liked him because you couldn't not.

This is a story about the impossibility of knowing what happened, so I can't tell you what happened. But I'm the narrator and I can give you my version.

It was a group of seven or eight boys at Cooper's Lake that day, and it all happened so fast it was hard to say what really happened even while it was happening. And of course everybody just saw their piece of it.

Mark Thompson went under. That much was clear. Why he went under was not clear, since nobody was actually looking. True, he was only a fair swimmer, but he was only out a few yards from the shore, where the water was maybe eight feet deep, and nobody was tussling with him, he hadn't eaten within ninety minutes, he'd had maybe half a beer, and there was nothing there he might have snagged on, no dreaded undertow like at the beach—I mean, this was a lake where generations of kids, none of whom had any idea who Cooper was, had come to swim in the backwoods of Alabama. It was tempting to imagine some kind of 20,000 Leagues Under the Sea giant squid pulling him under, but there was nothing like that, no snake, no hundred pound catfish. Later, a possible leg cramp was mentioned, and that could have been a factor.

Three or four guys were farting around on the little strip of sandy beach, and Tommy, Brian Waller, and David Evans were out swimming in the vicinity of where Mark was, and of course later none of them remembered it quite the same way. Mark went under, when no one was looking, then resurfaced, flailing his arms and gurgling a cry, then went down again. That was as close to a consensus as they could manage.

Tommy and Brian were the closest and swam to the spot and dove down. David saw Brian come up before Tommy, treading water, wheezing in a panic, and for a few seconds the guys watching wondered if what had gotten Mark had gotten Tommy too—but then Tommy resurfaced with his arm under Mark's arms and around his chest, kicking his way toward the shallow water—at which point Brian, still half hysterical, came over to help and then everybody hurried to lend a hand pulling Mark up on the sand.

"Mark!" Tommy cried, holding his limp friend up and trying to shake him awake, unsuccessfully, then calmly said, "Help me lay him on his back." They did, and Tommy tilted Mark's head back, pinched his nose and gave him several mouth to mouth breaths. Mark didn't respond, and then Tommy started pushing his chest. Brian was kneeling in the sand beside him, looking desperate, as the others leaned over watching. After—who knows?—two? a hundred? minutes, Mark coughed, spit out some water, and then in a shocked gasp of inhalation got his breath back.

Everyone cried out in joy and relief. Brian looked around at their faces.

Mark opened his eyes, and from that moment was a different person. Maybe he had seen something he couldn't share. Whatever it was—you could say, he left something of himself in the lake that day.

And not just him.

By the time they got home there were several variations of the story, most of which, maybe because of their pulling him to shore together, featured some version of how "Tommy and Brian saved Mark."

That was what went into the newspaper, and of course Tommy never offered anything alternative.

Letting that stand was what changed Brian.

* * *

They all tried to return to their lives as they had been, and with the mercies of time mostly succeeded. Brian made it clear he didn't want to talk about the incident, and grew surly and withdrew if anyone brought it up around him. He began to avoid Tommy, nursing a seething competitiveness toward him, and taking subtle cheap shots at him behind his back. That didn't play well with anybody, and Brian began to grow aloof from his old friends. The next year he stopped playing sports altogether, broke off from the group, and changed crowds. He never really had another meaningful encounter with Tommy after that. When Brian did re-tell the story to his new friends—toked-up and responding with some heavy-duty "Wows"—there was a general migration of "I" into the territory of "We"—and who knows? maybe he had even come to believe it himself.

Belief being what it is.

The boys graduated and went their separate ways.

Brian, people said, went out to California and joined something.

* * *

Tommy went on to—well, I don't have to tell you—just say he

was a good provider and leave it at that. He married Patricia Thomas right out of high school and they had four perfect children. Two of them became doctors, one a therapeutic cellist, and the black sheep an academic.

Everybody else became what white southern kids from good families usually became.

Brian, of course, no one ever heard from again.

* * *

Everybody knows some close calls and tragic accidents from very young days. And then a classmate or two dies in high school, and after that the deaths pick up over the years, each with its own little shock, each one helping to solidify the case for our individual and collective mortality. But the news about Tommy's death, from cancer, in his early fifties, hit pretty hard. A man of no vices—good as gold through and through. The word "senseless" got worked to death.

At the funeral the pastor spoke of that day so many years ago when Tommy and his friend had saved their friend. Ironically, just how Tommy would have wanted it.

I guess.

* * *

The story would be remembered—and every now and then, if for whatever reason the subject was Cooper's Lake, where nobody went anymore, you'd still hear people mention in a somber tone the day that Thompson boy had drowned out there.

Even some who claimed to have been there.

Bones of Dead Man's Bluff

Robb Grindstaff

PROLOGUE
MARCH, FOUR MONTHS AFTER ELECTION

With the spring thaw delayed, the water levels on Lake of the Ozarks and Osage River remained low. If they waited until April, the lake would rise with snowmelt, the dam would release water, and the river would surge.

Lieutenant Charlene Ralls—Charlie—argued against it, but Major Taney insisted on one more check of the riverbank and rocks below the cliff while the water level was down. Just to check it off the list and put the case back in the cold files. They'd checked already, twice over the past few months, but the water had been higher then.

Charlie's team, including some sheriff's deputies and a group of volunteers, searched the banks of the Osage for the impossible. Again. A body that fell along the shoreline forty years ago would be long gone, one way or the other.

Perhaps at the bottom of the Missouri River by now, or the Mississippi, or buried in the sands under the Gulf of Mexico.

If it remained anywhere near here, it would be miles downstream, dissolved, any bits of bones scattered and buried under thirty feet of water and five feet of silt. But she had her orders. Mostly she sat in the van and took messages from the team, checking off sections of the map on the screen in front of her as they cleared each area.

They would only search the shoreline, searching underwater being useless. It was all beyond useless.

Charlie had been through this many times before. Needle in a haystack didn't even come close to describing it.

Her team had often discovered bodies—recent deaths, clothing still visible, hair still attached to the scalp. Dogs found the scent. Humans recoiled at a stench that alerted them they were close.

There would be no scent to catch from this one.

It broke Charlie's heart. Her little brother had never been found. Only his tricycle, six blocks from home, which sat in the middle of the sidewalk in an upper middle-class, suburban subdivision—nice homes with three-car garages, maybe a boat or an RV on a pad next to the garage, manicured lawns. They'd found the trike sitting right under a Neighborhood Watch sign.

She'd spent years searching with her parents. She'd continued the search after they'd given up and divorced, after her mother's overdose on pills prescribed by three different doctors.

Charlie had never given up. She'd redirected her search to help others. Fortunately, the highway patrol had dropped its minimum size requirements a few years before she'd applied. After six years as a trooper, she got her prized assignment to the Missing Persons Unit, which she soon discovered was all boring computer work to coordinate efforts between other law enforcement agencies. Managing databases. Reading and filing reports written by others. Two years of that before they assigned her to the IPC team: Interdiction for Protection of Children. She had a master's in forensics to go with her criminal justice degree, but she didn't protect any children.

She just tracked down their unprotected remains.

In five years, she'd moved up the ranks to supervising her own team, but had yet to reunite a missing child, alive, with the family. By the time cases got to her, it was too late to save one.

She couldn't take it any longer. Three months ago, she'd enrolled in night courses in real estate.

Another message. Another section checked off. They'd covered this section before, but when the water levels were up. Six more sections to search, two more to recheck.

Her radio buzzed. "Lieutenant, we've got a volunteer who thinks he sees something, but he can't get to it. Sending a deputy down to take a look."

Nothing. He's got nothing. We've checked that section twice already. "Go ahead. Let me know when it's cleared." They could wrap up this cold case before dark, search for something warmer, like the fifteen-year-old runaway in Springfield last month, or the nine-year-old who never got off the school bus in Columbia last week. They'd already given up on the missing girl in St. Louis, and that was only two years ago.

"Lieutenant, you might want to get down here. There's something . . . we're not sure what, but we can't reach it."

"Why do you need me?"

"Under a ledge. Too tight. You might be able to fit."

These guys might be more useful if they'd lose their beer bellies.

Charlie left the warmth of the van and traipsed carefully across the gravel parking lot, down a trail to the water's edge. She made her way along the slick, nearly frozen mud shoreline, flanked by trees, to where a rock outcropping made her footing even less secure. She climbed over on hands and feet, four-legged, before she could stand up and walk again.

Great place to break a leg.

The steep hill along the shoreline shifted to a cliff. The cliff. Dead Man's Bluff. The one they'd searched before—more than once—but the river was lower now, so there was a chance. Charlie pushed any optimistic thought out of her head.

"What do you have, Deputy?"

"That little shelf of rock sticking out there." He pointed. "Underneath."

Underneath would have been underwater the last time they'd looked here . . . and the time before that.

The deputy walked to the shelf, just big enough to stand on but maybe not thick enough to hold the weight of a couple of these fellows. Charlie followed until the deputy squatted down and aimed a flashlight underneath into a small crawlspace, maybe eighteen inches high, six to seven feet deep, about five feet wide. The whitewashed rocks were covered in dried silt and dead algae.

Charlie got down on all fours and looked. "What is it I'm supposed to be seeing? There's nothing here."

"On the left, way in the back." The deputy focused the beam. "That round rock."

"And?"

"Could that be a skull?"

Charlie remained silent, staring intently—just a rock, a round, slightly oval rock. Not jagged and broken like the other rocks, but the same color.

"Can you reach it with the grabbers?" Charlie asked.

"Nope, just out of reach. You think you can shimmy in there and see?"

The idea of shimmying in there did not appeal to her. At least it was too cold to run into any water moccasins . . . she hoped.

She stood and looked around at the more than half a dozen officers and volunteers who'd gathered. Not a single one of them would fit, most of them not in good enough shape to jog around the block without requiring medical intervention. One volunteer with a yellow safety vest pulled over his Carhartt coat looked like he might fit, but he had to be at least seventy years old.

"Fine."

She removed her hat, jacket, and gun belt and handed them to the deputy. The frigid breeze knifed right through her uniform as she pulled a scrunchy from her pocket and tied her hair back.

She lay down, then looked back. "Someone got a headlamp I can use?"

The headlamp interfered with the scrunchy, so she stuffed the hair tie back in her pocket and positioned the headlamp to keep the hair out of her eyes.

She crawled on her elbows and belly at first. When the space tightened, she could only slither like a snake, a wounded snake, her arms extended in front. If she raised her head to see where she was going, she bumped it against the ceiling. If she lowered her head, her chin scraped on the rocks. Her butt dragged across the underside of the ledge with each nudge forward. She dug her fingertips into the loose rock and silt to pull herself a few inches at a time.

She'd never really been claustrophobic before, but it kicked in out of nowhere. She stopped to control her breathing, calm her nerves. Only a couple more feet to go. It still looked like a round rock.

Waste of fucking time.

She hit the narrowest part and could go no farther, the rock—the skull, the old softball, whatever it was—still out of reach.

She tried to turn her head to look back. Worst case scenario, they could still reach her feet and drag her out. "Hey, can someone pass me the grabber?"

It took some maneuvering, and a solid knock on the head that would raise a lump, but she got the grabber in front of her and stretched it toward the object. One of those grabbers they sell at Target for old people to pick up things they drop but can no longer bend over to reach, or to retrieve the sock that fell behind the dryer.

The prongs wouldn't open wide enough to latch on. She tried to get the grabber to the side of the object, slightly behind, and inch it toward her a little at a time until she could get a better angle or drag it close enough to reach with her hand.

This is going to take hours.

Charlie slithered forward a little more, despite her brain screaming to get out. She repositioned the grabber and turned the rock. It didn't come any closer, but it shifted a little.

She tried again. Shifted a little more, maybe an inch or two closer.

This might work. Then I can get the fuck out of here.

With the grabber barely able to reach behind the rock, she tried once more to drag it toward her. It didn't come any closer, but it turned a little more. Turned just enough.

Just enough for Charlie to stare at an eye socket and a few teeth on the upper jaw.

CHAPTER 1
TWO YEARS EARLIER
20 MONTHS BEFORE THE ELECTION

Worth Sullivan sat at his desk, a large rectangle of solid blond oak, his attention bouncing from the fifty-five-inch flat screen on the wall to the two monitors on the desk. He'd muted the sound on all of them, but the same face appeared on all three screens, three different angles, three different news channels.

Senator Kirk Madison, media darling, retired four-star general, was officially announcing—due to millions of people begging him to, of course—his candidacy for president.

The chyrons at the bottoms of each screen displayed a different quote: save our democracy for future generations, heal our nation's divisive wounds, a leader who puts the people first. Yada-yada.

Worth's phone would ring soon. Every candidate, either party, coveted his endorsement, though he never gave one. He dreaded this call more than any of the previous ones.

Maybe he could talk Kirk out of running. Maybe it was too late for that. Why hadn't he called in advance? Why would he risk everything?

Worth knew why. Kirk knew better. Sometimes it's easier to ask forgiveness than permission, but sometimes not. Some things shouldn't be forgiven. Ever.

Every candidate had skeletons in their closets, but Kirk's run put more than his own reputation at risk. The truth, if discovered—a likelihood given the intense scrutiny of a presidential campaign—would destroy them both.

The press conference coverage ended, and the news reverted to Philadelphia. Worth turned up the volume.

The Philadelphia Incident, as the media had dubbed it, entered its third day. Day one had brought a peaceful gathering of a couple dozen protesters. On day two, nearly a hundred protesters camped in a nearby city park. The mayor didn't much care for that, so police in riot gear tried to send the growing group packing on day three.

Instead of scattering to the winds with the tear gas, more protesters arrived. Folks from the community and nearby neighborhoods brought food, water, and gas masks.

Worth muted the TV again when his assistant's voice piped over the intercom.

"Senator Madison is on the line." Marion had been his admin assistant for twenty years and performed the same duties the twenty years before that through a succession of his six predecessors.

"Thank you, Marion. Postpone that trustees meeting for half an hour, will ya?"

"Already did, Pastor."

"Worth, my good friend," the senator's voice boomed over the speakerphone. "Thanks for taking my call."

My good friend. That line always rankled Worth's last nerve. Yes, Worth and Kirk were friends, or had been, over several decades, but they'd spoken on the phone exactly twice in the past seven years, counting today. They hadn't seen each other in person in more than twenty years. They hadn't hung out since high school. Worth wasn't sure he'd ever been Kirk's *good friend.*

But all fell prey to Kirk's crutch phrase. He used the line in speeches from the Senate floor and TV interviews, often tossing it in when he vehemently disagreed with an opponent. It often sounded like, "My good friend, you're a total dick." Kirk could call someone a dick and make them feel good about it.

Worth wondered if Kirk used that line at home with his wife. *That was a great dinner, my good friend. No, my good friend, that dress does not make your butt look big.*

"I had a feeling you'd call." Worth clicked a pen and pulled the notepad closer, more to doodle than take notes.

"I take it you've heard the news."

"Watched you live. Good speech." Worth hadn't heard a word of it.

Worth had watched Kirk on TV often enough, like ten years ago when the president draped a Medal of Honor around then-Colonel Madison's neck. Kirk had personally led the mission to save three of his troops who'd been taken captive by a Colombian drug cartel during a joint military exercise. The news coverage of the daring raid drowned out the naysayers who asked if a failure of leadership had allowed their capture in the first place.

My good friend. GI Kirk.

"I'm surprised you're such a news junkie," Kirk said.

"Hard to avoid these days." Worth sketched a rectangle then added another, smaller rectangle inside.

"Yeah," Kirk said, "a lot of crazy going on right now. All the more reason to choose the right president before this shitstorm goes Cat-5."

Everything is a Cat-5 when Kirk is involved.

A year after the Colombia raid, newly promoted Brigadier

General Madison headed the evacuation of the Florida Keys in advance of a category-five hurricane, then the search, rescue, and recovery efforts that followed. He'd taken full advantage of the cameras and microphones by holding two press conferences a day for three weeks, making him a household name. Stories floated around the internet about leaving a grandmother sitting on her roof an extra hour so he could get the news crew in place before plucking her to safety in a basket connected to a helicopter—the chopper he happened to be riding in. The networks never reported those tidbits; they loved riding around in military vehicles just in time to get Pulitzer-prize winning footage.

My good friend. An American hero.

Worth stopped doodling. "And you think you're the right choice, I assume."

"Obviously." Kirk tried to laugh it off, but still sounded serious. "At least the American people deserve a choice, don't you think? Someone who's been battle-tested by something more intense than fundraising dinners."

Kirk's promotion to four-star general at forty-nine-years old, the youngest in decades and skipping one rank completely, came with a three-year assignment as the NATO commander, and more TV appearances. As that tour neared its end and the media speculated about his likely appointment as the next chairman of the joint chiefs, Kirk abruptly retired. He and his wife Morgan returned home to Missouri, to their new lake house.

Worth pulled his notepad closer. His doodle looked like an old TV, so he added a cable box on top, like his parents had when he was a kid. "Seems like you're on TV every time I turn it on."

"Ah-ha," Kirk said with a forced laugh. "I've never been able to keep up with you."

Worth doubted Kirk had ever watched him on TV, even though his Sunday morning sermons were carried by local affiliates in every major market in the country and live-streamed to more than a million weekly viewers. He'd been called the Millennial version of Billy Graham. The *Washington Post* had given him the title "America's Pastor."

Worth hated both of those titles. He didn't even much care for "Reverend."

He tore off his doodle, wadded it into a ball, and tossed it into the trash bin. It reminded him of his parents. "I assume you didn't call to make sure I saw you on TV." He had his practiced speech ready to launch as soon as Kirk asked for his endorsement.

"Ya know, for a preacher, you tend to get straight to the point, don't you?"

"Sorry. I guess I'm still talking to the military officer, not the politician. That's a whole new communication style for you, I'm sure."

"You know me well enough to know I'm no politician."

Worth didn't know that at all. Kirk had always been a political animal, ever since he was elected president of the student body as a freshman in high school.

But Kirk's politics had been the great unknown. Thirty years in the military after graduating from West Point, and no one knew if he was a Republican or a Democrat, a conservative or a liberal.

Not even two weeks into retirement, he stood on the steps of the state capitol in Jefferson City with the governor announcing Kirk's appointment to the US Senate. He'd serve the remaining months of the previous senator's term, who'd succumbed to a massive stroke the week before Kirk announced his retirement. The governor said the general was above party politics and that's what the country needed. A few months later, Kirk won a full six-year term as a Republican. It wasn't even close, even though he'd voted with the Dems about half the time and had negotiated compromises between the two warring parties.

Now, barely two years as a senator, he was running for president. Kirk Madison had always been a man in a hurry. "What I want to discuss with you," Kirk continued, "I don't want to talk about over the phone. Can we meet in person this week? Somewhere we won't be seen. Or heard."

"You want to come to St. Louis?" Worth asked. "Or we can meet in Jeff City." Worth had something to discuss with the good senator too, and not over the phone, but he wasn't sure they had the same topic in mind. Kirk would want his endorsement. Worth needed to talk about the one reason Kirk should immediately withdraw from the race—the one thing Kirk refused to discuss.

The X Factor.

"Why don't you come down to the lake?" Kirk said, more a statement than a question. "I got a boat. We can find a nice, quiet cove where reporters won't see us or hear us."

Worth hadn't been to the lake since his mother's funeral ten years ago. He didn't relish the idea. "Sure. Friday okay?"

"Let's make it tomorrow. I'll text you the address." Once a general, always a general. Kirk wasn't asking if tomorrow was convenient. He was detailing operational plans.

Worth saluted. "I can be there by noon."

When the call ended, Worth turned up the TV volume again. The protest downtown at the Gateway Arch, in solidarity with the Philadelphia crew, had grown overnight. At least it wouldn't interfere with his commute home this time. There had been an explosion at a Houston oil refinery, possibly intentional. Worth couldn't even pray again. His stomach burned with acid. His chest tightened. Tunnel vision threatened to close in. The combination of the spreading unrest and Kirk running for president might be more than he could bear. He turned off the TV.

"God damn him. May God damn us both."

***

The naked girl motions silently for him to come closer. He tries. His feet bog down with weight he can't explain. Each step slips. No matter how he struggles, he can't get any closer to the barely pubescent girl, her veins visible under blue skin, almost translucent in the moonlight. Hollow, blank eyes he can't bear to look at. A snake writhes around her waist like a belt. A wet leaf sticks to her cheek.

She waves him closer. "Come to me." He reaches for her.

She closes her eyes and leans back until she disappears.

Worth jolted awake and nearly kicked the terrier off the bed. He glanced at his wife, hoping he hadn't awakened her.

Gentry hadn't budged, still snoring softly beside him, her hair draped over her face.

He brushed the twig and leaf from the bed where the dog had been curled into a tight ball. "Stupid dog."

The nightmares had come every night for years, then weekly, then months between. Eventually, they had disappeared. Now they'd returned. She'd returned, standing right where she stood before—at the edge of the abyss.

THE EIGHT DIGITS

Stevie Lyon

The cotton gown hung like a sack on her slight frame. She fidgeted with a loose string on the seam and looked around, squinting in the fluorescent glare. She hummed sweetly to herself, a tune without a name. The doctor wondered if she knew she was being observed.

"She's the one." Juniper said. Her voice, usually still as the surface of Lake Powell, rippled just slightly as she looked through the windows into the surgical suite.

"But she's so ... young."

"The analysts have determined that's for the best."

"How the hell did they come to that conclusion?" The doctor's voice had the subdued snarl of a well-trained Doberman. He knew his objections were futile, but he couldn't conceal the depth of dismay.

"Doctor Pine, you know I can't answer any questions related to the details of Operation Evergreen. I've simply come to let you know that the patient has been prepped and you are to proceed immediately." She turned away from the wall of windows and began to stride down the corridor. The operating room lights at her back projected an elongated shadow on the floor, alien and emaciated. The clicking of her heels on the tile were a metronome. Just before she disappeared, he thought he heard her whisper the words "I'm sorry."

A young man stepped away from the wall and passed an envelope to the doctor. In handwritten cursive it read "Confidential: Patient Data." From it the doctor extracted a single sheet of paper.

Name: Jane Doe

Age: 3 years, 2 months Sex: Female

Race: White, Non-Hispanic

Notable History: Only child born to unmarried parents. Born at full gestational age, non-remarkable vaginal birth. Division of child and family services involvement triggered by positive toxicology screen at birth. Foster care placement initiated at six months. Biological mother, deceased (accidental overdose), age 23. Biological father, deceased (suicide by firearm), age 27. Currently in district custody after surrender by foster parents.

Diagnosis: Congenital aortic stenosis

The doctor noted the relevant details, folded the paper, and returned it to the envelope. It was swiftly retrieved by the young man who then disappeared into whatever lay behind the heavy looking door at the end of the hall.

—

Only the doctor had been informed about the eight digits. In this world where things were strictly "need to know", he supposed he was, in fact, the only member of the medical team who truly needed to know. He had been briefed shortly after his detention began, just after the terms of his arrangement had been agreed upon. It was the only time in his life he could remember learning something new and desperately wishing he could forget it.

He had considered his options, of course. There were really only two as he saw it—submit to their demand or refuse. A refusal would have meant a lifetime of imprisonment, torture, or death. And in the end they'd simply seek another doctor to execute the plan, would they not? Could he be sure that his replacement would possess the skills necessary for the complex procedure? Furthermore, he was promised that after the operation was complete, his debt to the nation would be considered paid and his record would be clear. His safety and the safety of his loved ones would be guaranteed, as long as he abided by the terms laid out for him. They could not promise this in any manner that was satisfactorily convincing, but he chose to take them at their word. Lastly, and perhaps most importantly, he did, for the most part at least, believe that concealing the eight digits as securely as possible was what was best for the world, as ethically dubious as he found the methodology to be.

When this ethical quandary transitioned from the realm of philosophical abstraction and took the form of a sweet-faced little girl in a too-big hospital gown and fuzzy socks, one who bore the most fleeting resemblance to his own lovely daughter when she'd been so small, his conviction calcified. There was no option. There was only the choice to proceed.

—

The eight digits were etched onto the inner surface of the replacement aortic valve. There had been whispers that a microchip was a possibility, but this analog method was deemed more secure. The doctor had practiced the operation daily—first in simulations, and then on cadavers, all under the probing watch of a gallery of nameless officers, their faces obscured behind balaclavas. At least some of them, he intimated, were fellow surgeons. Their questions were astute and exacting, revealing a shared expertise. In their presence the doctor felt himself become once again the over-eager medical student, delighted by their silent nods of approval and the eventual exhaustion of their questions. This delight was quickly overshadowed by a dense mist of shame.

They'd made it clear from the beginning that he could never, not once, not even for a millisecond, look within the valve. As much as the faceless officers were observing to confirm he could complete the operation skillfully, they were also there to ensure he could comply with this most important of edicts. Just one glance would compromise the security of the mission and therefore the security of the entire world, and he was reminded of this time and time again. They assured him that should any such indiscretion, intentional or otherwise, come to pass, he and all members of the team would be executed on site. No questions asked, no second chances.

Any fears he had of an unconscious or inadvertent look into the valve were eased with each day that passed and each successful practice run. He was confident that his hands knew where to go by feel and believed that his eyes would obey his intention to remain focused straight ahead at those most key of moments. He could perform his duties with the programmed automaticity of a robot, while maintaining the deft flexibility necessary to adapt should something unexpected happen. He'd felt ready for weeks, and he could tell that the analysts believed that he was ready too. All they needed was the patient.

But upon her arrival, the doubts began to creep back into his mind. He had never operated on a child so small. Could he still trust his hands? His eyes? His best intentions?

—

"Hi there, Sweetie."

He sat down beside her on the shimmering metal slab. The chill of the operating room pricked the exposed skin of his forearms. From inside the glass-walled suite the rest of the facility was an impenetrable shadow.

He extended his hand. "It's nice to meet you. I'm Dr. Pine." It felt comically awkward as it left his lips and he realized he had never before spoken it aloud, although it was all anyone had called him since he entered the facility. She smiled at him, an open, trusting smile, and he couldn't help feeling that she was glad to see him. Or at least she was glad to see someone. He looked at her and noticed the smallness of her teeth. The doll-like roundness of her cheeks. The wispy brown curls that hung down to her collarbone. He pondered her future and his role in it for just a moment before banishing the thought from his mind. "Did anyone explain to you what we are doing here today?"

She gave a barely visible shrug.

"Ok," he said, "You see, Sweetie, your heart has a booboo inside it that makes it not work as well as it is supposed to."

Her eyes widened, exposing the full expanse of her fractal-like irises, sparking with the colors of caramel and copper. "It's not your fault," he continued. "And we're gonna get you all fixed up today. My pal, Dr. Hemlock, is coming in soon. He's going to give you medicine that will make you sleepy, and you're going to take a nice long nap. And when you wake up it'll all be done. You'll need to rest in bed for a few days, but then you'll be good as new. New and improved actually! Does that make sense?"

She nodded and turned away, returning to her sweet melody.

—

The next hours passed in a flurry of synchronized activity. The bypass machine whirred and churned beside them, its rhythm becoming a chant. With each move of his hand, the doctor felt more alive than he had in months. More alive than he had since he'd last experienced freedom. The blood in his veins felt effervescent, and behind his surgical mask his cheeks pulled upward in a sort of smile. He couldn't let himself consciously label it as joy, or even pleasure, but he could at least acknowledge that he'd missed the controlled chaos in the operating room, and he knew that in his scrubs, with his scalpel, he felt like the truest version of himself.

When he held the valve in his hand, he paused. He imagined for a moment his eyes lowering. He imagined the digits as inverted particles of light hitting his retinas. He imagined committing them to memory. He imagined gunshots ringing out through the room. The shattering of glass. His blood mixing with their blood mixing with her blood. He imagined blackness.

But muscle memory did not fail him. His eyes did not betray. And the valve placement was executed with textbook exactitude.

—

There were sometimes months, maybe even whole years, when Operation Evergreen didn't cross his mind. Upon his return from the facility, the doctor rebuilt a quiet life. The life that he was promised. A life with an outpatient cardiology practice in the suburbs and a family he was allowed to grow old with. He'd taken photos of his daughter before the prom. He slept in on Sundays. He joined a garden club. And he laid each night beside his wife, who had known to never ask about what happened while he was away.

Whenever Operation Evergreen did make its way into his consciousness, his thoughts were of her. He thought of her when his own daughter announced she was pregnant by slipping a sonogram picture into his birthday card. He thought of her when the jingle that played through crackling speakers in the train station sounded familiar but unplaceable. He thought of her, of course, when the nation's grasp on democracy seemed slippery and the threats of totalitarians rang out with vehemence for all to hear.

And he thought of her when his granddaughter, eight years old and long-legged as a foal, snuggled beside him on the couch, a laptop balanced precariously on her knees.

"PopPop . . . wanna see the singer I'm going to see for my birthday?"

"Sure, Sweetie."

She pressed the spacebar, and a music video began to play. Even though pop songs all sounded practically interchangeable and desperately uninteresting to him, he watched and listened with all the focus he could muster seeing the hopeful expectancy painted across his granddaughter's face. In one scene the singer pushed a cart full of pineapples through an empty supermarket while bass hummed, and the kick drum pounded out like a heartbeat. In the next she was bikini clad on a jet ski, a cascade of mahogany hair blowing behind her as the sun sank towards the horizon. Then came an abrupt cut to a close up. Her eyes were lowered, and she sang with gauzy sweetness into a microphone as music swelled and careened toward a strident yet somber chorus. Her eyes lifted toward the camera and his breath caught in his throat. Behind long lashes, he saw the tiger-like swirl of her irises. Only once before had he seen eyes like that. Eyes he knew he would never forget.

He reached his hand out for his granddaughter's and grabbed it tight. "What do you know about her, Sweetie?"

"Oh PopPop! I can tell you everything!" She paused the video and angled her body towards his, wriggling her hand from his grasp. She hugged a throw pillow close to her stomach and bit her lip like she always did in moments of excitement.

"She's the biggest star on the planet, PopPop. She has like 300 million followers. Also . . . Um . . . " she paused, seeming to flit through a mental Rolodex of facts that weren't quite at the ready. ". . . she has a pet iguana! She loves to eat spaghetti with vegan meatballs! And her favorite color is purple! Just like me and Mommy!"

"Oh wow! That's so interesting." He nodded vigorously and hoped she couldn't hear the feigning in his voice. "Do you know anything else about her? About her family? About her childhood, maybe?"

He watched his granddaughter as she took a sip of water. It looped through a novelty straw on a rollercoaster-like trajectory between the glass and her lips. She put her cup down on the table and looked at him with seriousness in her eyes.

"PopPop . . . her life was really sad before she got famous. She's an orphan. Her parents died when she was a baby and then she lived in an orphanage. I didn't even know orphanages were a real thing! Did you?"

She didn't wait for a response.

"She had other problems too. See the scar on her chest?" Hannah navigated the video back to the jet ski scene and pointed at the screen. Between Jaylene's breasts there was the finest line, just a shade paler than her sun-kissed skin. "She had to have some operation on her heart when she was really little. She said that she would have died without it."

His mind flashed to the table. The glare of overhead light. The sound of his implements as they sliced through flesh. He felt split into countless tributaries, each with their own rushing current of thought. How did the analysts let this happen? Would it have been more ethical to thwart her success? How much does she know? Is it wrong for me to feel this proud of her?

"Should I tell you more?" she asked.

"Yes, Sweetie. Keep going. Tell me everything."

—

The phone rang. A restricted number. There was a voice he knew but could not instantly place.

"Dr. Pine?"

He hung in stunned silence until she asked again. "Dr. Pine? Are you there?"

"That's a name I haven't heard in a while," he eventually said.

"It's . . . Um . . . Juniper." Her tone was dry and serious.

"Yes, I'd figured that out. It took me a minute to clear the cobwebs, but I got there. And you can call me Teddy, by the way. Do you want to drop the pseudonym as well while we're at it?"

"It's actually not a pseudonym. Just a coincidence."

"Hmm, ok then. So, Juniper, to what do I owe the pleasure. It can't be anything good, so you might as well just get to the point."

"The eight digits," she said. "There's talk that they may be needed soon."

Teddy's muscles seized and for a moment his mind was a tunnel suspended in darkness. "You can't be serious," he eventually replied. "What's the threat? What's the target?" She paused. He recalled the last time he'd pressed her for information—how effortlessly she'd stonewalled him and toed the party line.

"There's talk of a preemptive strike."

Her words had been offered forth so freely, with the dry detachment that comes with years of governmental service. Yet he felt a grip around his torso, compressing his chest to the point that no breath could get in. His skin was near the point of igniting, and he felt acid rise into his esophagus.

"A preemptive strike? This is insanity. Does our goddamn fearless leader not understand the rules of engagement? Does he not understand the consequences? This cannot be happening. This cannot be what our nation has come to."

"We are working hard to buffer the public from the worst of it, but I'm telling you, things have gotten really scary behind closed doors, Teddy. There's in-fighting like I've never seen before.

Factions within factions. There's a contingent taking the whole 'stand by your man' approach. But there's another stance, one that I happen to align with. One that feels it is our duty to protect our citizens, and the citizens of the world, at all costs."

He felt his reality shifting on its axis. Everything that had seemed stable was beginning to tilt and slide.

"Does he know what would need to be done in order to obtain the digits?"

"He does," she said, her voice lowering. "The thing is . . . he doesn't care. Concealing them inside a human was meant to be a deterrent . . . an opportunity to reflect on the gravity of the choice . . . But . . . " She trailed off.

"So he knows the how. But does he know the who?"

"Who? No. Not even I know who. They kept her identity a secret from all of us who were there that day when you operated. And likewise, the team in charge of monitoring her whereabouts didn't know why they were monitoring her."

"Oh, ok. I see."

"What?"

"I know who she is, Juniper."

"You do?" There was a long pause before she spoke again. "Well, I suppose this changes things. Can I see you in person?"

—

They sat on a bench that looked out at the sea. Somewhere across that vast expanse of steely blue was landmass that once fit perfectly into their landmass. On that landmass there were orchids, and turtles, and humans who loved one another.

"It will probably be the end of everything," he said. "Will it not?" He looked directly ahead, choosing a single wave, and tracking it until it hit the shore. "I've thought about it from every possible angle. And I just can't puzzle out a scenario in which it isn't the absolute end of everything if he gets his hands on the digits."

"Neither can I." Juniper was solemn. Her forearm was bent across her chest and she fumbled with her shirt collar.

"I know we've considered the same options, you and I," he said. "And there isn't a clean one. Either way . . . she dies."

After a long pause he continued, half speaking to Juniper, half simply thinking aloud. "Even if we did get to her first, how would we make sure the information didn't end up in someone else's hands? The valve is titanium. It's not like we can toss it in the paper shredder or set it aflame with a Bic lighter."

Juniper responded without a moment of hesitation. "We dispose of it at sea."

"What's the point? It would take centuries to corrode."

"But also likely centuries for anyone to find it. Think about it, Teddy. A small piece of metal. A wide-open sea."

They sat in silence, Teddy imagining a scenario it was clear his companion had already imagined. Everything around him felt hazy and too far away. He rubbed his hands on the cracking wood of the bench, noticing each bump and ripple, reminding himself that he was real. That it was all real.

"This is madness, Juniper. I don't know. I just don't know if I can be involved."

"I get it. It wasn't supposed to be like this. She wasn't supposed to grow up and become someone."

They sat in silence again. Teddy had never had such trouble distilling his thoughts into words, but each one he tried to grab became vapor and his hand passed right through into nothingness.

"Would it have really made it any easier if she'd been a 'nobody'?" he eventually replied.

"Fair enough. An innocent life is an innocent life. But practically speaking? It would certainly be easier if she'd been a 'nobody'. Most people's lives are relatively invisible . . . Expendable . . . at least on a macro scale. But not her. Her resilience has defied all odds."

He nodded and returned to stillness. Eventually a new thought, like a droplet of condensation, made its way into his consciousness.

"Can I ask you something, Juniper?"

"Mmhmm."

"If you were her . . . would you rather know or not know."

They turned towards each other, eyes on eyes, for the first time that day.

"Know the reason? Before you kill me, you mean?"

"Yes."

"Honestly, Teddy, I think I'd rather know."

"I think that's the right answer."

—

His ears rang even though the encore had finished ten minutes prior, and his palms were cold with sweat inside his gloves. His granddaughter's new concert t-shirt hung past her knees as she tried to pry the envelope from his hand. He tightened his grip.

"I told you I'd hang on to it for safekeeping, Sweetie."

"But PopPop . . . we're next in line to meet her! And why'd you fold it up anyway?"

"It's safer that way. Nothing can happen to your beautiful artwork."

He hadn't let himself consider what it would feel like to be standing in front of her until it was too late to turn back.

"Hey," she said in a voice that dripped like snowmelt. "Thanks for being fans." She picked up a permanent marker, scrawled her name on glossy photo, and slid it across the table towards them. "It was really nice to meet you."

His granddaughter let out a high-pitched squeal and squeezed his hand.

"Actually," Teddy said, "we've met before. Long ago." The starlet looked at him, seemingly unconvinced.

"It was nearly 25 years ago. I wouldn't expect you to remember." He pointed to his chest. "But I'm Dr. Pine. I'm the one who performed your heart surgery."

A smile split her face as she sprung from her seat. She wrapped Teddy in the tightest embrace, and in his arms, her body felt warm. Soft. Fragile.

"My granddaughter made you a drawing," he said. "She'd love for you to have it."

He handed her the envelope with a trembling hand. As she opened it, Teddy pulled his granddaughter backward, despite knowing full well that the toxin could only be absorbed through the skin.

As soon as she hit the ground, he turned and passed his cell phone to his granddaughter.

"Call your mother to come pick you up," he said. "I love you both so much. Don't forget that."

—

Teddy had sailed so far from shore that that he could imagine the city lights were flickering stars if he cocked his head at just the right angle. There was blackness surrounding the small vessel on all sides, and in the darkness the bloodstains on this shirt looked simply like an extension of the sky and the sea. In his lap was an old coffee can stuffed with rusted nails and bolts, rocks, paperclips, and the titanium heart valve he'd extracted from the chest of his granddaughter's idol. How much easier it had been to remove the valve than to place it. But how much harder at the same time.

As the can splashed down into the inky sea, moonlight rippled on the surface. For a moment, the world felt beautiful. His secret felt beautiful. His ending felt beautiful. But then he thought of her. Of them. And he wondered . . . would they ever know the truth?

I did this for you, he thought. *For all of you.*

QUEEN OF THE SKY

Laura McHale Holland

Mommy says now that I'm eight years old I get to be queen all day. So early this morning, she put my queen costume from Halloween at the foot of my bed. I was so excited. I got out of my jammies and into that dress quick as a greyhound dog. It's this beautiful deep red with one of those accordion style collars that kinda makes me look like I don't have a neck, but Mommy says that's how the very first Queen Elizabeth used to look.

I put on my fancy black ankle boots, too. They're tight, but not too bad. I danced all around. Mommy gave me her sad, dented-can smile. It wasn't long before I knew why. She pulled out the bridal veil from my dress-up basket and said she'd looked and looked but couldn't find my golden crown anywhere.

I couldn't tell her I put it on at recess one day, and meanie Mindy ripped it off my head and ran away. I coulda caught up with her, but Mindy's Queen of the Playground, and if you want any teeny tiny bit of respect from anybody, even the squirrels that run along the fence, you can't cross Mindy. I made that mistake back in first grade, and nobody talked to me for a whole month. So at my humongous party today, I'll be wearing the queen costume minus the crown and with the veil instead. Mommy fastened it on my head with a tiara that came from a Happy Meal. Then she left and said she'd be right back with balloons and streamers and paper plates and favors and everything else we need for the party, which will be in the playground shared by everybody living in the five apartment buildings in our complex.

Sometimes Mommy goes out, and she's gone a long, long time.

On school days, I keep our key way down at the bottom of my Hello Kitty backpack, which Mommy found at a garage sale. I let myself in, do my homework, load the dishwasher, and watch TV. And once a week, ever since I turned seven a whole year ago, Mommy lets me take our laundry down three flights of stairs with change in a beaded purse she got me at GoodWill, and I get to wash and dry and fold like a grown up. But since today is my big queen day, not a laundry day, as soon as Mommy's back, we'll take all our stuff downstairs, and the party will begin.

Mommy says we'll put up a Happy Birthday banner on the play structure. She's getting a great big cake from Safeway, too. She's probably there right this minute. I don't know why it's taking her so long, though. She's been gone for hours and hours. I would be crazy bored if there weren't so many people to watch down below. I'm watching at the window, right this minute, looking for Mommy's zippy red Datsun.

There's Freddy and his dad throwing a football back and forth. Freddy's gonna be a big, NFL player one day. And there's this girl with a long black braid. She moved in last week. I'm not supposed to go anywhere except the laundry room when Mommy's gone. I'm never, ever supposed to go outside, but I do so want to invite that girl to my party. I don't think Mommy'll mind if I go downstairs just to see her. I'll be quick. It'll be like I never went out at all. Our elevator's broken, so I'm on the stairs. I go so fast that I'm forcing air out like a dragon, except minus the fire, by the time I reach the swings. But where is she? Gone already? I'll swing for a while and see if she comes back.

It's a beautiful day. I love the sunshine and all the people poking around. There's this boy, Stuart, over by the trash cans. Well, he's a teenager, not really a boy, and Mommy says he's up to no good and I should stay away. But he's walking a bicycle. A bicycle! It's got a big front wheel and a little back wheel. I bet the very first Queen Elizabeth rode something like that. Maybe he'll let me borrow it. Uh, oh, he's on the move. I run over, calling loud as I can, "Hey Stuart, can I borrow your bike?" He smirks at me like I'm some sort of court jester, not the queen that I am.

"You can have it if you trade something," he says, and I ask him, "but what do I have that you want?" and he says, "I'll take your boots. I'll sell them way quicker than this old thing."

So off my boots go, because who needs boots when you have a bike to ride, especially since the boots squeeze my toes. I'm sure glad I learned how to ride a two-wheeler last year. I fell down lots of times, but I got the hang of it. Riding this one's a little different with the giant front wheel and the tiny back wheel, but I'm managing. I really am.

It's the coolest thing ever, and the girl with that long braid is back, and she's waving at me, and Freddy and his dad are standing still, staring at me, and I'm confused because nobody notices me even when I'm all dressed up, but now more people are gathering, and Freddy calls out, pointing, he says I've grown wings, and I think that's crazy until I look over my shoulder, and it's true. I have gorgeous wings like a huge monarch butterfly coming right out of my back. And I'm off the ground. How can that be? I'm rising, rising into the sky. The new girl is screaming now, and Freddy's dad is on his cell phone, and the world below is a living, breathing game board, and my heart is beating like a captured bunny. Then I see Mommy's car.

I think at first she's heading home. I'd better figure out how to land, but the car's parked in front of The Last Stop Bar and Grill. I'm only eight years old, but even I know there's no grill inside. Mommy promised she'd stop going there. She promised to get everything we need for my party. She said it would be fantabulous. She promised, but it won't be. It'll be like every other day when I wait and wait for her, and she stumbles home with scraps from the trash bin behind some restaurant where people in clean clothes can't be bothered to clean their plates. I'm going higher and higher, and I don't care. The bar she loves better than bubble baths and kittens and ribbons and stories and stars and dreams we dream together is small as a speck of dust now. And I'm flapping my wings, and pedaling, and my dress is the best, and my veil is streaming behind me, and it doesn't matter that my feet are bare because I'm Queen of the Sky, and this is where I'm going to stay. Who cares what Mommy says?

THE CRYSTAL BALL

Saeed Ibrahim

Rohit's interest in star signs went back to his school days. His teacher, Professor Godbole, apart from being a Maths teacher, was also an amateur astrologer. It was from him that Rohit had learnt about the alignment and movement of the planets and their effect on a person's life and character.

Later on, with the pressures of his engineering studies and his subsequent employment as a software engineer, Rohit did not have the time to pursue a serious study of the subject. However, his faith in astrological predictions had remained.

Rohit was convinced that astrology provided an effective guide to steering one through life and planning one's future. He regularly followed the "What the Stars Foretell" column in the newspaper, and it was the first thing he looked at each week in the Sunday magazine section. Not that Rohit's current situation in life needed any particular guidance or reassurance. No dark clouds appeared to darken his horizon. For a twenty-six-year-old he was on a fairly good wicket and not doing too badly by most standards. His job was paying him well and living with his parents, he had few overheads. He liked his work and was popular amongst a small group of friends in whose company he enjoyed spending his free time.

Each Sunday he joined his buddies for a game of badminton at a sports centre near his home. The four of them would take turns to book a court in advance and after sweating it out on the court, they would get together for a round of beer followed by a game of carom in the games room. On one of these Sunday mornings Rohit and his friends had gathered together as usual in the clubhouse after their badminton game. His friends often pulled Rohit's leg about his penchant for the zodiac.

"Hey Rohit, have you checked your weekly forecast today? You can't afford to miss this one!" teased his friend Prakash.

Rohit had to take his elderly father for a morning blood test and for the first time in months, he had not had a chance to see the weekly horoscope column in the newspaper.

Prakash pulled out the Sunday paper from his backpack and, clearing his throat, he read out aloud the prediction for Rohit according to his birth sign:

"You may be required to make some tough decisions at work. Some of you may be walking on thin ice." Prakash paused for effect and looked up at Rohit.

A look of consternation appeared to cloud Rohit's face. He leaned forward to listen more attentively to what his friend was saying.

Prakash seemed to be enjoying the effect his words had had on Rohit. "Hold on folks - there's more to come!" he announced, as he continued to read from the newspaper:

"Avoid getting involved in any unnecessary conversations at work. There are hidden enemies who may be conspiring against you. The health of a parent may cause concern."

Rohit hastily grabbed the newspaper from Prakash, wanting to verify for himself what Prakash had announced. His face turned pale as he read the ominous prediction.

"Is everything alright, Rohit?" Sameer asked with concern.

Rohit did not answer. He looked troubled and disturbed by what he had just read.

Prakash, guilty at having upset his friend, offered: "Relax, Bro. Don't take it to heart. We know how utterly unreliable these forecasts can be."

"You shouldn't be taking this seriously. These words are not targeted at you. If anything, they could be applicable to a thousand others," Akbar tried to reassure Rohit.

But Rohit appeared distracted and preoccupied. He felt the need to be by himself and excused himself saying:

"Sorry guys I have to leave you. I have to check on my Dad who has not been keeping too well."

On reaching home, Rohit went up directly to his room, pensive and a bit shaken. He would not have given serious thought to the enigmatic warning in the week's forecast had it not been for the fact that it seemed to strike home with accuracy. At his software firm things had not been terribly favourable of late. The economic slowdown had had its impact on the IT industry as well. Many of the smaller firms had been badly hit and there had been job cuts and retrenchments. Had the recession caught up with his company as well?

What tough decisions were in store for him at work and what was the meaning of the words "walking on thin ice?" Was his job at risk? Was he likely to be fired on account of downsizing as some of his friends in the industry had been? The second part of the forecast was equally confusing and worrying. Who were the hidden enemies mentioned and was there a plot being hatched against him? Henceforth he would have to be on his guard all the time. And of course, as far as the health of a parent was concerned, it had hit the nail on the head. His father had been quite unwell recently and this had been a source of worry for both him and his mother.

With these disconcerting thoughts plaguing his mind, Rohit left for the office the following day. He had decided that he would try to be extra diligent in his work so as not to give rise to any complaints from his boss. Also, keeping in mind the warning from the horoscope, he would go about his activities keeping his ear to the ground, alert to any suspicious behavior around him.

Later that day, in the office corridor he saw a group of his co-workers huddled together in conversation and talking in whispers. As he passed by he noticed that they had stopped talking. Was there some conspiracy afoot and was this the group of hidden enemies that he had been cautioned against? Maybe it was just his imagination. He dismissed the thought and went ahead towards his work station. But the following day in the lunchroom, his doubts appeared to be confirmed when he saw the same group of colleagues sitting together at a table and looking meaningfully towards him. When they realised that he had noticed them, they quickly lowered their gaze and looked away in another direction. Rohit was now convinced that the group was plotting against him. But what was he to do? For the moment he had no proof to support his doubts. Maybe it was best that he bide his time until such time that he could furnish some concrete evidence.

However, his peace of mind had been destroyed and his sleep that night was troubled and disturbed. Try as he might, he could not get the words of the forecast out of his mind. The following Sunday he avoided meeting his friends and remained brooding at home. With uncertainty and self-doubt plaguing him, he needed some sort of reassurance that these forebodings would not come to pass and jeopardize his career in any way. He thought of consulting his astrologer friend, his former Maths teacher Mr. Godbole, but found out to his dismay that his old mentor had passed away only a few months earlier.

He had almost given up in despair, when on going through the classifieds, his eye was caught by the following ad:

"Worried about your future? Get your fortune told and find out what destiny holds for you. Contact psychic reader Madame Aishwarya".

There was a phone number given beside the name and Rohit hurriedly noted it down before returning the newspaper to its usual place in the living room. His parents normally took a nap after the family's Sunday lunch and Rohit decided to use this opportunity to make the call. He nervously dialed the number and with a beating heart he waited for the phone to be connected.

On the fifth ring, the phone was picked up and a tired, gravelly voice at the other end announced:

"Yes, who is this?"

"Good afternoon, Ma'am. Is this a good time to talk to you?" Rohit asked tentatively.

"Well, not exactly. But go ahead. Tell me who you are and why you are calling"

This is not going to be easy, Rohit thought to himself, as he braced himself and stammered back:

"I am Rohit and . . . I . . . err . . . saw your ad in the paper today, and . . . err . . . I was wondering if I could have a consultation with you this evening."

"Is this for yourself? If that is the case you can come today at 6 pm. Call this number and ask for directions. I charge Rs. 1,000 for a fifteen-minute consultation." A number was called out and the call was ended abruptly.

Rohit just about managed to jot down the given number. He felt a bit unsettled by the strangeness of his telephonic interaction and the mystery that seemed to surround Madame Aishwarya. Why hadn't she explained the address herself and what was this other number he had been asked to call? He was in two minds about whether to pursue the matter and make the follow up call or just forget about the whole thing. He finally decided that having come this far, he may as well continue. He picked up the phone and dialed the given number.

"Royal Lodge, good afternoon," a male receptionist's voice answered.

Rohit was taken aback. He thought maybe he had dialed the wrong number. He had half expected to be put through to Madame Aishwarya's secretary. But . . . Royal Lodge? The mystery seemed to deepen.

"Royal Lodge, good afternoon," the voice repeated.

"I was given this number by Madame Aishwarya," blurted out Rohit. "I have an appointment with her at 6 pm this evening."

"Yes Sir. Madame Aishwarya is a long-staying guest at our lodge. Would you like me to explain the address to you?"

The Royal Lodge, as it turned out, was a modest-looking guesthouse located in the centre of the city, close to the railway station and the main bus terminal. It was one of several reasonably priced lodgings opposite the city's transport hub that catered mainly to budget conscious travelers, itinerant traders and salesmen and young employees entering the job market.

Rohit arrived early and was told to wait as Madame Aishwarya would only see him at the appointed time of 6 p.m. Striking up a conversation with the receptionist, Rohit learnt that Madame Aishwarya was a clairvoyant who had once been sought after by princes and prime ministers alike for her amazing psychic powers and her ability to foretell the future. She had fallen upon hard times and was practically abandoned by her high-flying clientele. She now lived as a long-staying guest at the Royal Lodge. She slept for most of the day, saw clients by appointment in the evenings, and did a weekly horoscope column for a daily newspaper.

When it was time, Rohit was led up a narrow staircase and ushered to a guest room on the second floor. His discreet knock received a brief "Come in" in the same raspy voice. Rohit entered a small, darkened room lit by a single blue electric bulb that suffused the interior with an eerie half-light. One wall of the room was hung with a single, large portrait of a long- haired god man with a sandalwood garland adorning the frame. A strong aroma of incense pervaded the entire room and added to the other-worldly aura of the small, confined space. In the middle of the room was a rectangular table and hunched over it was the figure of a rather large woman in her mid-sixties, dressed in a black, ankle length kaftan and a spotted blue head scarf worn over a striking, though heavily made-up face, which could have once been described as handsome. Apart from a heavy, beaded necklace and large earrings, Madame Aishwarya wore no other jewelry.

"Take a seat, young man. You are allowed a consultation of fifteen minutes with three questions that you would like answered."

In the centre of the table was a quartz crystal ball, of a size somewhere between a cricket ball and a football. The crystal ball was mounted on a small metallic stand and next to it was a lighted candle whose flame illuminated a number of tiny crack-like imperfections in the crystal, throwing up sparkling rainbow-type images. Rohit sat transfixed, totally mesmerized by the sight in front of him. The lady now closed her eyes in concentration and after a few minutes she re-opened them, placed her hands over the orb and gazed intently into its depths.

Rohit had come with the idea that he would unburden himself of all that had been troubling his mind, but totally awed by the lady's persona and the fascinating object that she held between her hands, he appeared to have lost his tongue. Forgetting about the three questions, Rohit, with some difficulty, managed to get across in a few words his concerns relating to his workplace and his fears about losing his job.

"Dark shadows are hovering over you at your place of work. Evil forces are at play to thwart you in your career. I hear whispers and see an open pit lying in front of you," intoned Madame Aishwarya as if in a trance.

Rohit gripped his chair and broke into a cold sweat.

"But fear not, young man. You will ward off your enemies if you wear a moonstone close to your skin. The moonstone is your birthstone, is it not? It will keep the evil forces away and draw only good vibrations towards you. Health-wise, don't be afraid of sickness in your family. If a person you are close to is ill, he will soon be healthy again. Romance and marriage are in the air for you. Your parents will arrange your marriage and it will be a perfect match. I see several children."

With these words, she rose from her seat, blew out the candle and covered the crystal ball with a square of cloth, indicating by her actions that the consultation was over.

"You may place the fees on the table here. I think you know your way out," she informed Rohit in a tone suggesting that he was dismissed.

Rohit was speechless and stunned by the clairvoyant's words. He put the money down on the table and stumbled out of the room confused and bewildered. He had expected some comforting words of reassurance, but the lady's sinister words had only served to reinforce his misgivings. His father was already well on the road to recovery and his health was no longer a matter of concern. As for marriage, it was the last thing on his mind right now.

Dejected and disillusioned, he trudged to the office the following morning. He had not got over his dark and depressing frame of mind and he found it difficult to concentrate on his work. Mid-morning he was summoned to the manager's office. This was what he had feared all along. It was only a matter of time before the death knell would sound, and this was it. Today he was going to be given the dreaded pink slip.

On entering the manager's office, he was surprised to see that he was not alone. There was his immediate supervisor, the manager and the CEO of the company, all of them seated in a row. He would have preferred to be given the bad news by just his supervisor, instead of being humiliated in front of the entire senior management team.

"Good morning, Rohit. Do take a seat," the CEO called out in a cheery voice. Why did he have to sound so cheerful? If only he knew how nervous it made him having to face all three of them together.

Rohit barely managed to return his greeting and with a weak smile, he sat down in the chair in front of the manager's large desk.

"Your supervisor and manager have been telling me," the CEO began. Rohit swallowed hard and lowered his head, waiting for the axe to fall.

"They have been telling me how happy they have been with your work and the additional responsibilities that you have undertaken. It has also been a year since you have joined the company. It is now time for you to get a promotion and an increase in your emoluments. Congratulations, Rohit! You have been made a team leader and you will henceforth report directly to your manager."

Rohit could hardly believe his ears. The three stood up to shake hands with him, and the manager informed him that the HR department would give him his new terms of appointment sometime later in the day. Rohit struggled to his feet, mumbled his thanks to the trio and left the room in a daze. It took several minutes for reality to sink in and before he could breathe a sigh of relief. When finally, the impact of what he had just been told dawned on him, a cry of joy escaped his lips as he pumped his fist in triumph. With a spring to his step, he returned to his desk, barely holding back the temptation to immediately call his family and friends to announce the good news to them.

With renewed self-confidence and a restored belief in himself, Rohit returned home that evening with the realization that his fears and misgivings had after all been totally irrational and unfounded. So much for crystal balls and astrological predictions!

Voltus Electricalus and Strata Illuminata

Ramey Channell

They were married. The Wedding March ushered them briskly out of the candle-lit church into the ecstatic sunlight. Rice and birdseed were thrown. Brown sparrows and gray doves skittered along the warm sidewalk amid the feet of exuberant guests. A solitary squirrel ventured down the trunk of a massive oak tree to peer at the festive crowd, as Albert Slater led his bride to the car parked at the curb.

That was on Saturday. Now it was Wednesday. Marissa was still trying to get used to the fact that she was now Mrs. Albert Slater. She thought she might never get used to the fact that she was Mrs. Albert Anybody. Albert was such a difficult name to get used to: so old fashioned and stiff. She would have preferred a Daniel, a Greg, or a Jason. Albert was a stuffy, dusty sounding name.

But, here he was. Thank goodness he didn't look like an Albert.

They stood together on the hotel balcony overlooking the endless view of mountains piled one over another into the blue distance. Sun struck his clean thin face, causing him to squint as he smiled at her. She could see scattered prisms of refracted sunlight in his hair. Suddenly the thought struck her that he actually seemed to emanate light.

That's it, she thought. He looks electrical!

She continued to watch him, the sunlight firing off his face, his eyes, his red hair; then she had to explain why she laughed.

"It's because you look electrical, Albert, like a volt of electricity! Like a hundred watts. Like a thousand watts. Like a bolt of lightning tearing across the sky, like the king of all lightning and electrical impulses."

Albert had no objection to being the King of Electrical Impulses, and since it amused her, he let her fashion a costume for him out of coat-hangers, plastic dry-cleaning bags, shoulder pads snipped from articles of clothing, a clear plastic belt strapped diagonally across his chest.

"Wild King of Electricity," she addressed him that night inside their institutionally impersonal honeymoon suite. "Your name henceforth shall be Miraculus Voltus Electricalus." And she laughed and laughed.

And he laughed too, watching his new bride apply red lipstick lightning streaks to her fresh just-married face and along both arms from shoulder to wrist. He pranced about the room, uninhibited for the first time in his life, striking poses he deemed to be thoroughly electrical, as she continued drawing red zig-zags of lightning from her thighs to her ankles and from her breasts, downward across her stomach and abdomen. She moussed her blonde hair into two huge spikes that actually looked quite like horns, and she sprayed them with hair spray until they radiated stiffly from her head. Then she fashioned a costume for herself, folding many sheets of white writing paper into fans which she tucked into her bra and under the straps and around the elastic of her bikini panties. Then she encircled herself with a long, heavy-duty extension cord which she ripped from the lamps on each side of the king-sized nuptial bed. From this, she dangled her curling iron, her hair dryer, his electric razor.

"My electrical darling!" he exclaimed, as if he had recognized her for the first time.

"Yes," she answered. "I am known as Strata Illuminata." And she danced for him: a frantic, twitching pavane with many starts and stops, like an electric light switch flipped on and off.

Thus, when they came back from their honeymoon, they possessed a private world, inhabited entirely by electrical lovers of wattage. No one else guessed that there was such a world, and that, of course, made it all the more amusing. When in the company of relatives and friends, often they looked shyly at each other when anyone mentioned power surges, or they winked furtively across the table when someone predicted an electrical storm.

They felt, even more than most young married couples, special, set apart, conspirators. Mythological.

They had a nice little home, a renovated 1940s bungalow on the Southside. There were tall trees in the back and thick, luxurious green grass in the front. The young couple enjoyed lying on their backs on that verdant green carpet at night, watching the stars and talking of the distant electric galaxy from which they came. Soon they began wrapping themselves in long strings of Christmas lights, augmenting their electrical costumes with thousands of tiny luminous bulbs. His were multicolored; hers were clear.

They purchased more and more extension cords, stringing them end-to-end, so that the two glowing, frolicsome beings of enlightenment could run about across the lawn each night, sparkling and volatile, dancing dances of astonishing incandescence on the dark summer grass.

Strata Illuminata teased and tempted her mythological hero, Voltus Electricalus, as she romped across the dew covered lawn. The fescue glittered under her feet, reflecting brilliant beams cast by the thousands of tiny lights adorning her otherwise naked body. V.E. laughed lustily, and gave chase.

"Come to me, my flashy seductress!" he called, pursuing his flickering loved one. "Illuminata! Illuminata!"

She squealed and threw herself into his arms, giving little thought to the crackling of tiny bulbs. They bought only the kind that would continue to burn if one burned out.

The thunder of the approaching storm was muffled by the shouts and laughter of the radiant lovers who were now entangled in their multiple extension cords as they thrashed about in fervent embrace. The immense bolt of lightning ripped out of the turbulent sky and made contact with their many-lighted bodies.

And that was the end of that marriage.

EULOGY

Janet L Oakley

When I think of Rolf I think of rivers:
Long rivers, skinny rivers,
Rivers with boulders and pebbly beaches,

Rivers flowing swift at high water,
Rivers slow but clear as glass showing where the Dolly
Varden hide.

Rivers of salmon and steelhead going to the sea.

Before I met Rolf the only rivers I knew were the Allegheny
and Monongahela,
the Ohio and Shenandoah, Sluggish rivers, brown and old.

Rolf showed me wild rivers
With eagles and ancient spruce bottoms, king fishers and heron
And elk dipping their heads into the water.

Stillaguamish, Nooksack, Lyre and Hoh,
Skagit, Samish, Queets and Sauk
Rivers of legend, rivers of dreams.

May he always be there along them casting, casting until I come
to him.

Wrapped in Grief and Relief

Nancy Julien Kopp

The new story of my life began
when my father died leaving me
wrapped in both grief and relief.

Grief that a father who loved
me deeply had disappeared
like early morning fog,
softly, silently.

Relief that never again would I
suffer his verbal abuse,
his emotional blackmail,
his ranting hatred of those
different from himself.

Grief let me dwell on the love.
Relief made my heart swell
with deepening gratitude.

The Hearing

Julie Green

Blair stood on the bridge. The city rose in front of her reflected in the mirrored surface of Lake Clara Meer, the buildings and newly greened trees reversed—her life upside down. She studied the reflection, the still water holding it in perfect balance for a nano second before a breeze nudged the edges and the landscape seeped into a soft watercolor. The analogy suited her. Blair is an artist.

The last time she'd been here was when Jack was having some good days. Like now, it was spring, the warm light a counterweight to the chilled morning breeze. It was so clear, today's reflection of the cityscape and her memory of that day.

She pushed the big silver cuff up her arm, took hold of the metal rail and let her weight go as she leaned back and looked up at the sky. She breathed in the honeysuckle and freshly mowed grass and turned back to the car thinking, we are mirrors that reflect it all . . . the wild orchids and ostriches, cyclones, and the lemon fragrance of the magnolia. She turned her attention to today and the work she had to do for the Arts Council. She was in the city to report to the General Assembly appropriations committee. There was movement to axe the budget, leaving artists and small organizations treading water.

She'd caught a flight from Savannah to be here, then would go on to Charlotte for her opening. Three years of drawings and paintings. She'd worked hard. It would be a big night. But whenever she was away from home, she felt at odds with her internal rhythm. Shellman's Bluff was her loadstone and the source of much of her work the past five years. The salt marsh and light . . . last week she'd taken the boat to Blackbeard Island and collected driftwood, shell fragments, lichen; natural forms that contained energy and structure. The critics refer to her work as abstract. She believes people absorb what they need from art, what speaks to their own inner mirror of experience. Her work is based in the objective world; her world of deep stars, dirt roads, rusted road signs and the generative marsh grass that sustains a world beyond the temporal. What drives her to create is the need to reveal that which doesn't quite exist; to uncover the mystery hidden for our overly stimulated urban eyes. That is the sad futility in artmaking, to animate the inanimate. Yet she works toward forms that are hyper revealed and embody as much air and energy as the mullet that leap in the marsh.

The car dropped her off at Liberty Plaza. She could hear the traffic from I85 beyond the groups of homeless gathered in the pocket park. Blair hadn't been downtown since her residency at the college two years ago. She turned toward the direction of CNN and thought of Jack, his brilliant investigative journalism and work as a correspondent. Sometimes, his loss shifts her off balance.

She turned up Capitol Avenue to the appropriations building where an aid to Stanley Espada, Director of the state Council for the Arts stood on the stairs, waving. Blair crossed the street between press trucks and pedestrians.

"Ms. McKenna, thank you so much for coming. Your presence and support of the councils' work is so welcome now."

"I'm glad to be of help. Stan and I go way back to high school. He was editor of the lit journal and regularly rejected my overly dramatic poetry." Blair's laugh joined the warning beeps of a truck backing up in the street. "I have about an hour before I need to leave for the airport. I just sent him a text that I'm so sorry I can't stay for lunch."

"Yes, he knows about tonight's opening and is grateful for your time. Follow me to the hearing room. You'll be seated at the table with a mic. The committee members are in front, press behind and on the side. I'll sit behind you if you need anything. The committee chair will welcome you and invite you to share your remarks. We have a lineup of celebrities going to bat for us today. Janelle Monae will be in this afternoon." The aid almost danced. Blair turned and looked at the street.

"I hope the press trucks mean you'll get airtime."

"That's the plan. Big names translate to 6 o'clock news. The budget for the Council has never faced such big cuts." The assistant motioned toward the crowded hallway. "I doubt the committee members will have questions, so you'll be excused after your report, and I'll get you back to the Uber for the flight."

Blair walked into the paneled room lit with brass sconces flanking the state seal. It was a sober room with polished wood that had witnessed political schemes and plenty of smoke danced over decades to lead the state forward or propel an inflated ego into the public eye. The committee members were seated in a semi-circle on a dais in front of her, well above everyone else in the room. The press was moving and shooting as she took a seat and placed her notes on the table alongside a tray of glasses and pitcher of water shedding condensation onto a white linen napkin.

The chair gaveled the room to order. "Ladies and gentlemen, this committee will hear testimony regarding the budget for the Georgia Council for the Arts 2025-26. Our first guest is Ms. Blair McKenna, artist, recipient of a McArthur Fellowship, and noted art's advocate. Ms. McKenna, the committee has your written report, you have five minutes."

"Thank you, Mr. Chairman. The Georgia Council for the Arts is a strategic arm of the Georgia Department of Economic Development whose mission is to cultivate the growth of vibrant communities through the arts. That, as you know, is the mission statement. Last year sixty-seven organizations in 50 counties received $600,000 in funding." Blair looked up into the eyes of the representatives. "Art touches lives and changes people. Art has the capacity to bring people together and make better human beings. I believe that the arts are essential. I'm going to give you a couple of examples.

"Jenkins is the poorest county in Georgia. The county was awarded a grant of $6,000 to send the Lark String Quartet, and Rising Ozark Bluegrass Ensemble to three county middle schools for six public concerts this past year. The program served over 1,200 residents of the county and employed eighteen musicians and arts administrators." She glanced up to see most legislators were listening. There's much more that she'd like to say but won't.

"The Education Grant supports arts in schools throughout the state. Woodley Elementary received a grant for the fifth graders to explore theater. They worked with actors and a tech team. All 68 students wrote their own monologue coached by local actors. They teamed with a high school student and with the guidance of a resident teaching artist, collaborated to create a visual to support the monologue. An exhibition of the pieces along with the printed monologue was installed in the Moultrie Arts Center. The building was open every day for the community to come and enjoy the exhibits at no charge." Blair paused and with an expressively elevated eyebrow continued. "Each afternoon, students flash mobbed and presented a dramatic monologue in the gallery space. The center saw the largest turn out post-covid.

"Bartow county used a program grant to send dancers into four elementary kindergartens to teach literacy. This innovative program introduced in South Carolina has the students move to the sounds the letters make and create the letters with their bodies. Studies have shown that combining kinesthetic pedagogy with standard reading fundamentals increases literacy by 34%. The program will continue for three years, and the students will be tracked throughout grade school to compare their outcomes to their peers."

Blair rested the notes on the table and surveyed the room, then went off script. "This is three programs out of the Council's over 200 performances and exhibitions. Some of them may not be your cup of tea. An agency with a diverse task by nature produces a wide-ranging wash of offerings.

"But if five kids from Moultrie are swept up in the process of making art or theater and become employed in the arts, or three kids in Tift begin to study the cello or piano, or an entire grade level surpasses their peers in reading ability, it's worth it. The arts change lives, not only for the participating children, but in the ripples circulating to their families and friends who watch them as they grow into more complete human beings." Blair pushed her readers on the top of her head like a headband and sat back.

"Thank you, Ms. McKenna for your report and your lifelong advocacy for the arts. Do any members of the committee have a comment or question for Ms. McKenna?"

The Arts Council director had prepped Blair and the ranking minority member to bring out the salient statistics. "Ms. McKenna, can you tell us if the study of art in grade school and college is an investment in the state's economic vitality?"

"Yes, Representative Holland. A recent study by Boston College has shown that individuals who consider themselves entrepreneurs and whose work led to patent rights were more likely to have reported an educational background in the visual arts."

"And could you tell us, overall, the economic impact of the arts in Georgia?"

"In 2020, Georgia's arts industries employed 134,217 workers. The state budgeted 1.8% to the Georgia Council. Despite unprecedented challenges during Covid, the industry contributed $23.8 billion, or 4.2% GDP to the state's economy."

Blair sat back and pushed the silver cuff up her arm. She had gotten her stats in. The last one, illustrating the staggeringly low amount budgeted to the arts each year by the state government would be repeated by each of the guest artists to make sure it was picked up by the media. She was thinking about getting to the airport when Dewey Pruitt, the congressman from Appling County flicked a finger to speak. He was thin and angular with a pallid complexion and the feral baring of a rodent. The progressive members of the committee shifted in their seats and the director's aid pushed a note into Blair' hand. *'He will try to deflect from your report. He wants the spotlight. Ignore him.'* Blair looked out at the committee members while the press turned mics and cameras to the congressman.

"Ms. McKenna, we thank you for your presence with us today. I just want to clarify if I may. Is the Blair McKenna here today lecturing us on spending taxpayer's money on banjos in swamp East Georgia, the same Blair McKenna who was implicated in the mysterious death of the journalist, Jack Dickinson?"

Blair felt the weight of rage begin to mount and weld her to the chair. She'd come too far since Jack's death to let this snake rattle her or sabotage the focus of this meeting. She locked eyes with Kitty Holland, the ranking minority member who lowered her chin, her steady gaze a ballast.

Blair exhaled slowly and leaned forward toward the microphone; her fingers laced together in a taut fist. She raised her eyes and looked directly at Mr. Pruitt. "I believe the congressman is referring to the suicide of Mr. Dickinson, a tragic loss for the country and a painful, personal loss for me. Mr. Dickinson was a brilliant journalist and the kindest of human beings. He would be reluctant to point out that the discussion of his death bears about as much relevance to the GCA budget as the congressman caught on video surveillance fucking an intern in a janitor's closet. I however have no such reservations."

There was an explosion of camera clicks, a 'whoop' from the gallery and scattered applause. The congressman's pasty complexion bloomed an odd shade of purple. The ranking minority member stifled a laugh and the Chair gaveled for order. "If there are no further questions the committee will recess for a break and continue with our next guest at 10:45. Ms. McKenna, you are excused, and we thank you for your time with us today."

Congresswoman Holland gave her a subtle thumbs up and slowly nodded her head as Blair gathered her things.

She rose and was escorted from the hall by the aid toward the exit and awaiting car. Press and photographers followed her shouting questions: *"You weren't implicated in Jack Dickinson's death, is that correct?" "When Mr. Dickinson died, how long had you been together?" "Do you include his image or notable stories in your artwork?"*

Blair was both emptied and seething. She looked around at the gathering press and small crowd in the lobby, steadied herself, and walked past them to the car. The devastation of Jack's suicide had been completely disorienting in its scale of loss. Jack—beautiful, sweet poet, revered journalist, had been the love of her life, her champion, and the most compelling man she'd ever met. It was shattering to know that even her love couldn't overcome the depression. Blair looked out the window as the dome on the Capitol reflected a stark shaft of gold. Grief delayed reality. It took a year and a half for her to hold the fact of Jack's suicide alongside her work as an artist; to feel she could be a friend, a family member, a functioning human being. The air in the car felt stale. She would get on the plane for the opening and summon the energy to be present and attentive. But for the moment, she dropped her head to her hands and cursed the cosmos for pain, loss, and the unkindness in the world that is never necessary. She wished she could postpone the opening and go back to Shellman's Bluff. She and Jack had built their lodge at the Bluff as a retreat. Now it was home, source of her work and vessel for a lifetime of images and memories. She sat up and reclaimed herself, ready for the trip to Charlotte and the intensity of the opening. Then she'd head for home and would be back at the bluff by mid-afternoon. Tomorrow night she would spend some time floating in the kayak and wait for the silent, shooting stars as the shrimp click open the night.

THE KINGDOM

DeLane Phillips

The Sunday School teacher asked the class what the kingdom of heaven was. I got excited because I knew the answer. In last week's class I didn't know the answer and I don't like it when I don't know the answer.

Last week, I got confused on Paul's missionary journal travel's lesson. I couldn't remember where he was half the time like Eliza Jane. Eliza Jane knows everything. That's because her daddy is the preacher. Eliza Jane was an expert on Paul and knew where he was the entire class. None of us did. This time no one was going to outsmart me, not even Eliza. She doesn't like it because I leave off the "Jane" part of her name.

The teacher asked, "Don't you want to be in the kingdom when you die Eliiizugh Jane?" Eliza is her favorite student.

"Yes, Miz Saw-rulls," replied Eliza, smiling like Miss America.

I raised my hand. Miss Sorrells sighed. She always does that when I raise my hand. I think it's because I'm not as pretty or smart as Eliza. Maybe it's because my Daddy's not the preacher. Or, it's because my mother teaches the five year olds. Nobody wants to teach the five year olds. Jesus wouldn't even take 'um. They are just plain awful.

Momma teaches the five year olds because she says Jesus loves the little children. I asked Momma if she was sure about that because last month one of the five year olds escaped from class, ran downstairs, out the back kitchen door, across the street, and into the graveyard before Momma caught him. I asked Momma if she whooped him with a Privet switch like she did me when I misbehave. Momma replied, "Of course not, Jesus loves the little children."

Miss Sorrells knows that I will go home and tell Momma she would not let me answer a question. It's impolite not to let me answer and that's not what Jesus would want her to do in front of the class. Especially being a Sunday school teacher and all. That's why I have all of her attention. And, I know the answer.

Miss Sorrells peered down at me through her diamond-edged reading glasses, smiling like a Miss America through her carnation-pink lips.

"Yes, Hun?" asked Miss Sorrells. She had that carnation-pink lipstick stuck to her left front eye tooth. I wonder if she knew that.

"Miss Sorrells, the kingdom of heaven is my Granny's table!" I shouted. All eyes in the class were on me. Bobby Hanley, whose daddy is the superintendent of the Sunday School, giggled from behind me. I would get him after church.

"Come again?" questioned Miss Sorrells, looking confused through the twinkly glasses. Maybe she didn't hear me. She still had lipstick on her tooth.

"Miss Sorrells, I said the kingdom . . . "

"Hun, I heard you the first time," replied Miss Sorrells in her firmest Sunday School teacher voice. "Now, why don't you eeelaborate on the kingdom to our little class?" Eeelaborate. She wants me to eeelaborate. I think that's the same thing as preaching.

I hate it when she calls me "Hun." That's the special name my aunt calls me when she wants me to paint her fingernails. She always uses the same color, "Berries," by Revlon. She buys it at the Revco in town. I don't like Miss Sorrells using my special name. Anyhow, I was not going to let Eliza outshine me after last week's missionary travels disaster. I was an expert on the kingdom and I was going to eeelaborate. I began to eeelaborate on the kingdom. You know, just like the preacher does.

"Miss Sorrells, the kingdom of heaven is just like my Granny's table! You see, my Granny don't go to church on Sunday like regular folks. She stays home. But my grandaddy does. Granny and grandaddy are members of the Good Hope Congregational

Holiness Church. They like him at the church 'cause he gave them all the land for the outbuildings and such. They built this big ol' building where everybody can eat dinner after the funerals."

"What does that have to do with your Granny's table, Hun?" inquired Miss Sorrells. I knew she was listening.

"Miss Sorrells, after church my Grandaddy brings everybody home to eat dinner. Most Sundays we go down there to eat too, unless Momma's worn out from teaching the five year olds." Miss Sorrells was nodding her up and down.

"Granny stays home from the services so she can cook everything. First she goes out to the garden and pulls the corn, cuts it off, and fries it up in a skillet. Wait, before that, she has to kill the chickens. She goes out to the yard, rings a few chicken necks and . . ."

"Yuck" screamed Eliza. Bobby Hanley giggled again.

Miss Sorrells patted Eliza's head and said, "It's alright, Hun."

Miss Sorrells frowned at me. I decided to keep going, regardless of Eliza's sensitivity. I figured I wouldn't eeelaborate on the yucky parts since Eliza had apparently never witnessed chickens having feathers boiled off. But, knowing how much Eliza's daddy ate at church dinners, I'd say he had a chicken or two.

"Granny fries up them chickens. She might even serve a roast on the side, or ham. While the chickens are a'fryin' in the iron skillets, Granny's rolling out pans of biscuits. While that's going, she'll have a pan o'cornbread in the oven." Once I mentioned biscuits, I had Bobby Hanley's full attention. Bobby loves biscuits.

"She bakes the day before." I named them off one-by-one. "Pound, coconut, plain white, plantation, apple, chocolate, white, lemon strawberry . . . " The list was endless. I sighed, thinking of all those cakes. The room was silent. I continued to eeelaborate. "There will be a good assortment of pies . . . say, chocolate, pecan, buttermilk, egg custard, coconut, peach, peanut butter, blackberry, and cobblers! Granny will have pot o'green beans simmering on the stove in the kitchen . . . she tops off the beans with pieces of quartered white potatoes, sprinkled with black pepper. Sometimes I sneak in the kitchen, lift off the top of the pot, and reach down inside for a tater or two." All eyes were on me. I bet the preacher never had this much attention when he eeelaborates. In my opinion, if he'd talk a little bit more about eatin' and less about dyin', folks might act interested.

"The family shows up to help out. Some will bring a dish, but they don't have to. It's okay with Granny if you show up empty-handed. Granny just loves to feed folks. My aunt always brings "Blueberry Fluff." Now, there's a dish even Jesus would love." All eyes were still on me, even Miss Sorrells. I thought I saw her lick the carnation-pink lips. I wondered if that lipstick was still on her tooth. Maybe, I should take her to the side later and tell her, you know, just to be all Jesus-like and nice.

"Go ahead, Hun," said Miss Sorrells, the twinkly glasses nodding up and down. Her voice sounded just like she was talking to Eliza Jane.

"Yes Ma'am," I replied. I raised my arms and spread out my hands just like the preacher when he eeelaborated on Sundays.

"All them folks my Grandaddy invites from the Congregational Holiness church come driving up in the yard. They get out of their cars and stand out in the yard talking about the service and the preacher. All the family is driving up at the same time and ever'body gets excited when they see each other, like it's been years or something. The men are dressed in their Sunday suits and smell like my Daddy's Old Spice cologne. The ladies are still in their Sunday best dresses. Well, except for Momma. She usually sneaks to the bathroom and takes off her pantyhose because they hurt by that time." Miss Sorrells' carnation-pink lips turned down.

"Oops." I forgot I was standing in the presence of boys. I changed the subject. "Everyone comes in through the front porch screen door, into the kitchen. There's so many folks and food, the table can't hold them all! Granny starts putting dishes on top of whatever space she can find. She spreads food onto the top of the freezer and even the dryer. That's three tables of food! Sometimes, we have to set the desserts in the kitchen by the stove because we run out of room on the freezer and the dryer. Next, the men folk all sit down at the big aluminum kitchen table with the red vinyl chairs. Their wives fix their plates and set them down on the table before them. By that time, the kids have come in and washed up. We all gather 'round, so Grandaddy can ask the blessing."

Grandaddy prays, "Good Lord, bless this food to the nourishment of our bodies and our hands to greater service . . ."

Half way through the blessing my mind wanders because of the macaroni-and-cheese. I always get distracted by the macaroni-and-cheese. Miss Sorrells was nodding at me again. I could tell she wanted to know more about that macaroni. "Granny makes her macaroni with spaghetti noodles. She don't buy no store bought. It's all homemade. She throws in an egg and some canned milk. But, the best part is the hoop cheese slices she lays on top of the dish. She sprinkles black pepper over the top, just like the taters."

Bobby Hanley yelled. "Yummy!" That was as good as an amen to me.

"Grandaddy finally gets to the 'amen' part of the blessing. The men dig into their plates. The mommas are getting children plates of food and sending them out to the porch to eat. Finally, the women get to eat. They sit in the den together, that way they can talk about women things.

"Once the men finish their first round, they start passin' dishes for the second. Granny helps hand them the dishes from the tables, so they don't have to reach. They pass the meats, then the vegetables: creamed corn, green beans, collards, mashed taters, macaroni and cheese, sweet potatoes, peas, potato salad, cabbage, pinto beans, fried okra " I shook my head thinking of what was to come after church was over. I couldn't wait to get out of there.

"Granny walks around asking, 'More tea?' She waits on everybody. She passes the bread baskets full of biscuits and cornbread. Then she passes her homemade jams and butter. The men all smile at Granny, nod politely, and brag on her food. They tell her to sit down and eat, but they don't really want her to. They like the pettin' she gives them. We all eat until we can't hold another bite, completely satisfied. And, just when we can't eat another bite, guess what?"

"What!" everyone yelled, even Eliza Jane.

"Granny goes in the kitchen and stirs up chocolate gravy." I eeelaborated.

"Oh!" yelled Miss Sorrells, her eyes closed dreamily behind the twinkly glasses. She had licked off the carnation-pink.

"Miss Sorrells, that's the kingdom of heaven! Everybody's invited. It's okay to show up empty-handed. And, when you can't eat another bite, God's in the kitchen stirring up chocolate gravy!"

"Amen, Hun, amen!" yelled Miss Sorrells.

I think I like her calling me that.

THE OLD MAN OF VISTA VIEW

Shayla Dodge

The old man of Vista View kept the grounds of a building in the Mediterranean town of Saranda, Albania. With pearly long hair, and a few teeth peeking from his cavernous smile, his lumbering belly couldn't be contained by the dingy painters' shirts he wore. On his swollen feet, his shoes were tattered, and he moved with a patient gait, as he hauled rocks from one end of the complex to the hill below. God would have been able to tell you of his toil. His life of laborious work, his wife at home griping because of his inability to provide for his family. But the old man of Vista View was not educated, his parents never had the means to send him to school, and at 17 he had to fight in a civil war which he didn't side with. After 8 long years of shimmying belly down in the dust and heat with an AK47 he really didn't use, he was finally discharged, and the war was declared over. Under the next dictatorship of twenty years, he worked as a laborer in the spring and summer, and mainly as a meagerly paid cleanup personnel for the city each winter.

His wife, who bore him three, grew more disenchanted with each kid. Angry that the old man of Vista View had impregnated her, saddened by her aging skin and weathered features, and embittered by the expectations for women without a present man. She would tax him with her distress daily. Nagging and complaining, weaponizing her sex, painfully pointing to all his shortcomings when he was going about his work about the house. "Why have I not been built the villa you promised?", she would growl. "When are you going to fix the roof", and "Why would I want sex when you cannot afford the children we have?" And who could blame her, the old man would think. He was not a wealthy man, many of the previous neighbors had already moved into new houses, or nicer buildings. Though most had taken up black market activity to stay wealthy, they were still able to send their kids to nice schools in the capital.

His kids had remained ignorant. He had no ability to send them to private tutors to learn English, Spanish, or Italian. He had nothing but a life of toil to offer them, and yet he was patient and kind to them. And each day after school he would take his kids out in his dungy and teach them how to fish or have them help him in their little garden and he would explain the principles of life. Patiently, he would tell them the importance of always being compassionate and kind, no matter what life brought your way. Of how Karma works, and what each stage of life will bring.

When his kids would come home with red slips for missing homework, or pink slips because of a disciplinary intervention, instead of yelling he would spread his arms and wrap them in his love. Because of this, the old man was at ease with how his children were developing. And he was as proud as any other father who would show up to the school in their fancy cars with their loud and arrogant ways. The old man knew that good was in store for his children, if not now, then eventually.

The next day when the old man woke up and went to work, it was only to find his boss was gone. It was Friday, and the old man was supposed to get his paycheck. But this was not the first time that his boss had forgotten to pay him. In fact, if there was a truth about it, the problem was more endemic than this. The old man's boss would also not buy the materials he agreed to or end up cutting corners in other ways. This fact could have made the old man angry, but instead he simply would remind his boss of his missing paycheck and continue on his way.

So, on this day, as any other, the old man started by going in the back behind the building to begin by getting out his wheelbarrow, and the meager tools he had. He ended up mainly using his bare hands, sifting through the larger rocks to find the biggest ones to set aside, and the medium ones to be thrown over the side. It was just about noon, the old man knew because the sound of the call to prayer was just over, when down came the young couple who lived upstairs. Instead of following the path down into the city, they turned to him, bringing a little package, and what looked to be a plastic bag filled with some dark looking cakes. Though he could not understand what the couple said, being of a different nationality, he gathered that they had brought him this gift because of his service to them during the previous days. He saw, and thought he heard them say these were chocolate cakes. And he was pleased they had thought of him, so he thanked them loudly, and gave them a wide generous smile.

It was not until they were gone, that the man began to examine the package. He thought to himself, he would have one cake now, and save the rest for his family. But there was something in the package which he hadn't seen. Oh, it was a blue napkin, and when he took it out, $1,000 fell out. At first, he was so startled he didn't know what to do. But then he thought of running after the young couple to give it back, for he had not done them bidding to receive anything in return. Then he realized that this gift was given to him in this way for a reason. It was not a challenge to his honor; it was a gift of compassion. This he could accept, he finally decided.

As soon as he began to realize this a large black bird swooped down and snatched up the bills from the ground. There must have been some cake on the bills, for the bird would not have wanted it otherwise. But before the old man could do anything, the bird was up so far in the air, there was no way he would be able to catch it. Instead of crying out in despair or even feeling blue about losing such a prized gift, the old man shook his shinny hair and laughed, took out a chocolate cake and took a big bite. Life is suffering, he knew. To have something taken away before its prize was realized was nothing new. So, for this old man, it was not a burden. He thought to himself, what a nice young couple. Then he picked up his rake and began to sift rocks again, and when he went home though he didn't say to his wife that the bird had stolen his prize, his wife was pleased to eat a cake or two.

She finally admitted loudly "That young couple must have thought you were a nice man."

Fallen into Oblivion

Edilson Afonso Ferreira

No more
  guys and girls happily driving
  open-air convertible cars on weekends, free of seat belts
  tethering their bodies, sweet winds swaying, fighting, and
  playing with their loose hairs.

No more
  children walking on the streets to school,
  carrying notebooks in their arms,
  not in backpacks, not on buses.

No more
  young boys playing marbles in holes they had dug on vacant
  lots near home, their mates flying kites heavens above.

No more
  bicycling around only for pleasure,
  without protective helmets and gloves.

No more
  family sitting on the front porch after dinner,
  sharing the latest neighborhood news.

No more
  walking in the fields by night,
  under tender and puissant moonlight.

No more
   people greeting each other and sending good vibes,
   even if they were unknown.

No more
   fresh milk bottles delivered home by the morning,
   but milk boxes at immense supermarkets,
   with sleepless cameras furtively watching over us.

No more
   letters, no business letters,
   no love letters, only emails to be lost in cyberspace.

No more
   couples who face the difficulties of everyday life,
   profess mutual and sincere forgiveness,
   respect the common oath once made,
   so engendering true and honest love.

No more
   parents, sons, and daughters going out together at night,
   carrying in common dreams, dramas, and desires,
   like a pack of wolves who have not learned to segregate.

No more
   growing, assembling, and sharing rooms and lives together,
   indifferent to some strange customs of those who never
   knew to love and like themselves,
   our children becoming children of all of us.

THE COLOR OF GRIEF

Chris Wood

The sun sets in hues of fuchsia and misty rose
as shades of my favorite color
flood my mind — my pastel pink prom dress,
shirts, scarves, and pants I wear daily,
the blush tie my husband wore on our wedding day,
and my mother, her urn wrapped in pink satin.

I embrace summer, limp through the hot days
remembering the color that ignites passion
and calms my spirit. Though this year, the dazzle
of azaleas, butterflies, and rose quartz paled
as Mom slipped away, her soft, coral lips no longer
drawing in the fragrance of life.

HOMELAND

Jasna Gugić

By the power of love,
relax my wills
and burn the hate
in the root of ancient oaks
from my homeland
because I am not the root
lands of shame.
I do not belong
to a small tradition.
With the power of love
to silence
and be a grain of wheat
among the vast fields
of my plains.
To Be strong
in the childhood
and don't go further
of what one thinks to want.

The Painted Porch

Fhen M.

at the side of the street of Campoyong
a space between the ligneous living room
& cacophony of the outside world
I sit here in the painted porch
watching the public crowd pass by

on the glass table on the tiled deck
reads a journal on realist painter
in his oil on canvas *El Kundiman*
a man plays a 1930s piano
& a maiden sings a love song
now mute indeed are tongue and heart

Krebs watches townspeople walk by
yet he remains on the periphery.

A Christmas Purchase

Celia Miles

We were young, silly, and naïve beyond belief; had new jobs as teacher and Christian Education director, and Christmas was coming. My husband and Jackie's boyfriend were out of town. We had a couple of days to ourselves. We would celebrate.

We decided on spaghetti for supper and hot buttered rum to go with it. Spaghetti we had, but neither of us had ever bought liquor. Our parents didn't have it in the house; our colleges allowed no alcohol on campus. In fact, our counties were "dry:" no beer or wine in grocery stores and no retail liquor outlets. To find hard liquor, off we went, some thirty miles to Asheville, with Jackie driving her first (badly used) car and me holding on to the dashboard as she tried to control the vehicle.

At a brick-faced structure with lots of glass, we stuttered to a triumphant stop. I waited for Jackie to get out. She was typically the leader, the one who sang loudest and best, who flirted easily and laughed sweetly.

"Well," I said. "Go on in."

"I'm not going in there," she replied. "What if I see somebody from home? Or heaven forbid, some church member."

In the almost deserted parking lot, two men walked to their car, not a glance in our direction. We looked at the store. No customers visible.

"Go on," I urged.

"I drove," she declared. "You go."

I knew that determined tone. I'd go in or we'd drink Pepsi

with our spaghetti. I squirmed a bit as she laid her hands on the steering wheel and waited.

"Okay, okay, I'm going. What kind?"

"Huh?"

"What, uh, brand do you want?"

"Do I want? You said we'd have hot buttered rum if I made spaghetti." She sounded antsy, probably thinking about driving back. But she was right. In some magazine for new wives, I'd read about the joys of hot buttered rum on wintery nights. My suggestion. My turn.

She handed me a twenty-dollar bill. "We'll split it."

"I'm gone." I hopped out.

Pushing the "Enter" door, looking neither to the right nor left, I went straight toward the rows and rows of bottles of all colors, prices, and sizes, clear, dark, amber, even green. I saw signs for Bourbon, Gin, Scotch, Vodka. Hmm. I was a bit overwhelmed by the possibilities. Maybe I'd get something else. I knew Hemingway drank . . . what was it? My mind went blank. Rum it would be.

After I'd gazed, entranced by all the options, the clerk, an older man, drawled, "Help you find something, young lady?"

Oh no. Would he ask for identification? I'd left my purse in the car, having been warned by Jackie's dad that purse snatchers loved parking lots and single females. I glanced at him; he looked vaguely familiar. But not my kin. Maybe he was one of Jakie's cousins and uncles. But he didn't identify himself.

"Rum," I managed. "I'm looking for rum."

"Third aisle." He waved toward the back of the store. "Not a big selection, not much demand."

Being absolutely ignorant of quality, taste, or country of origin, I grabbed a bottle that the twenty would cover with some left over. Whew.

I set the bottle on the counter and said, as if the clerk cared, "Found it." Almost proudly, I handed over the twenty. It seemed to take forever for him to place the rum in one brown bag and then into another.

"Don't want to risk breaking it." He handed me my change: a

five, four ones and some coins. My hands felt a little clammy but I smiled and thanked him.

"Hope you like it," he said. "My wife uses it in some fancy cakes she bakes."

Baking? This was not for baking or wifely stuff! I had a sudden surge of confidence. We were going to drink this—not make muffins. I stood straighter and turned toward the door.

There, perched on a high stool, just outside the turnstile, sat a girl-child in a Salvation Army uniform. Pretty, pale, and smiling at me, she was the perfect picture of innocence—and I was surely the opposite. I felt myself shrinking. Could I just slip by the Madonna in prim blouse and longish blue skirt? Could I ignore the fact that I was spending "good money" on something trivial, frivolous, downright sinful, that I expected an adult evening of sipping hot buttered rum on this Christmas break, eating spaghetti without a thought of calories or essays to grade? Could I ignore the difference between my selfish self and Miss Salvation Army's selfless giving of her time for the benefit of others? Could I possibly return the rum?

Not exactly an option. I was stuck between the arms of the exit turnstile.

"Hi," the perfect girl murmured gently, a beatific smile on her no-lipstick face.

"Merry Christmas," I muttered, hastily dropping the handful of dollars into her little red bucket. I heard a soft, "Thank you" and "God bless," as I headed for the car. Breathing deeply, I thought, okay, the worst is over.

Jackie lied with aplomb after a siren pulled us over and a uniformed trooper approached. I dropped my Christmas scarf over the bottle at my feet as he pointed out a broken tail light and a muffler barely hanging on. Jackie charmed him with her patter about being late for the church's children's program. He tipped his hat.

"Just a warning, ladies, but get those things attended to." He grinned. "You don't want to spend any time in the slammer." We thanked him, and he gave us a cheerful wave. We seemed quietly guilt-ridden on the way back to her apartment. When I placed the double-bagged bottle on the kitchen table, she said, "Any change?"

"Gone to the Salvation Army." I busily warmed a couple of cupfuls of rum on the stove. At my tale of remorse, she shrugged and put on the pot for spaghetti. With a cup of rum, a pat of butter on each, we sipped and wondered what the heck was so good about it. The spaghetti was boiling as we sipped and sighed, sipped again. No use. I emptied my cup into the sink and poured a small glass straight from the bottle. Much better.

"I read somewhere," Jackie stirred the pot and kept sipping her warm drink, "that you know spaghetti's done when it sticks to the wall when you throw it."

She took another gulp and then with a great "splat" a glob of spaghetti hit the wall above my head.

"Sorry about that." Jackie giggled. "Darn. I meant to throw just a strand or two."

I stared at the strings of spaghetti sliding down the wall, white on blue. She giggled again. "Guess it's not done yet." She finished her cup, pointed to the bottle. "I'll have what you're having." She pursed her lips, slurred her words. "Did Spencer Tracy say that in *Northwest Passage* or *Casablanca?*"

Ultimately, we enjoyed all the spaghetti but not all the rum. Weeks later, I asked Jackie what happened to it when her mother visited.

"Heck," she said. "I knew she'd rummage around here while I was at work. So I poured it down the toilet and put the bottle in Mr. Ramsey's trash can."

"Next time you're buying," and I vowed, "but no more rum for me."

"Next time I'll get Scotch. That's what my pastor drinks."

THE CHRISTMAS WELL

J. L. Oakley

When the city pipes broke at four above zero, the water spread out across our road like the thick roots of a crystal Banyan tree and froze. We all came out to stare, our boots slipping on the remains of last week's snow.

It was three days before Christmas. Our trees and lights were up, our cookies in the canisters, and stockings on the mantle, but we had no water.

"Not until the twenty-eight," the Forest Hills Water Department said and would have left it at that until someone got the brilliant idea of hauling up a water tank and putting it at the top of the hill.

"At least it's something," a neighbor said and went to organize her pots.

Others weren't so sure and said that the season was ruined.

Our community well arrived that afternoon. An old World War II water tankard bristling with spigots, its camouflage shell looked odd against the neat pre-war brick homes lined with hedges and crusted with old snow. Curious children and their parents watched a brief demonstration, and then were left to their imaginations how they would actually do it.

I heard about the tankard after I came home from junior high school. Mom, Dad, and my brothers, John and Bruce, had already carried enough pots of water into the kitchen to make it look like a battlefield after a major roof leak. (There was a leak of some sort, a family member later recalled. A pipe had snapped from the cold.) We had water in stew pots, canning pots, sauce pans, and even a few tin cans for the powder room. A large boiler was on the stove for doing dishes and washing hands.

In the living room behind the swinging kitchen doors, Handel played on the radio. The windows were painted with angels and snowflakes. The tree was ready to trim. Christmas was not going to be delayed.

Winters are cold and often snowy in Pittsburgh. Except for the hordes of children with whom I sledded in the open field below the alley, neighbors only glimpsed and waved at one another as they communally scrapped ice or snow off windshields on the way to work or to shop. Snowman-worthy snow might bring out a few townspeople for a moment's divertissement, but that was usually reserved for the younger crowd. Most folks kept to their calendar of baking, Christmas card writing, and package sending-off.

Visiting applied only to a few close friends and often it was by telephone to catch up on the day's news. In winter we just stayed inside.

The Christmas well changed that.

From morning to night we bundled up in our bright wool coats and scarves and rubber over-boots and trudged up the hill to the tankard with our pails and pots in hand, like ants making lines to a picnic. Neighbors that we hadn't seen since summer or hardly knew at all tiptoed down their steep stairs or off their brick porches to go to the well. As we gathered at the spigots, conversations blossomed in the frigid air, puffing out like little smoke signals.

"What's news, Mrs. Hanna? Did you get your tree?"

"My car didn't start again."

"My grandkids are coming for Christmas Eve."

The pots and pans were filled, but so were the spaces between neighbors. Older times were recalled and strategies on hauling water offered.

"When I was growing up on the farm we had a pump. Had to prime it every time. Mother always kept a can of water next to it just for that."

"We had a well in Italy. The whole village used it."

We stopped and listened to the stories. We filled and hauled and laughed at our communal inconvenience. Our own village was born right there in our neighborhood.

Anything with a handle was employed. My family preferred our aluminum camping equipment, pots with wire handles that nestled together in the cellar when they weren't in use. But neighbors ran the gambit of tin and copper pails to saucepans. Someone arrived with a wagon full of number five cans.

Techniques on catching water varied. Some hung the handle on the spigot and let the container fill until it looked too heavy to lift. Sometimes it was. Others held the handle of their pots until they began to tilt. All day and night we came, the water spilling on our boots and onto the bare pavement of the road. It was so cold that the water froze, leaving icy blobs around the tankard. At night under the street light, they gleamed like diamond cow pies.

On Christmas Eve day, the morning broke clear and cold, but by noon the sky had begun to grow flat. The wind stung our cheeks like a sharp wet kiss. We scurried for last-minute presents and lingered over the evening meal wondering if it would snow. Would we get to church? Or would we have to stay home? Service at eleven o'clock in the evening was always an adventure.

Dark fell at four o'clock. We turned on the lights on our tree and in the windows. Outside, it began to snow. Invisible first to the eye, the flakes grew from pinpoint to apple blossom size, sashaying down to the frozen ground. Bit by bit, snow crystal by show crystal, the snow covered the street, the cars, the knobby roots of the oak tree in front of our house with a tenuous mesh of white velvet fuzz.

Then as gently as it started, the snowfall suddenly exploded, throwing out snowflakes like the contents of a huge featherbed. In a silent rush, it covered everything and piled up, mutating the street into a close, distant world. By 5:30, it rose four inches deep with more to come.

"Janie, girl, will you go out and get water for dinner?"

I pulled back from the window and smiled at my mother, who stood at the swinging door leading from the long living room to the kitchen. She wore a Christmas apron with ruffles and her hands were covered in flour. Behind her wafted the smell of cinnamon.

"Sure."

I went into the kitchen and down to the side door landing where coats and boots collected. My mother handed me some pails. I opened the door and stepped out onto virgin snow.

In my life there are scenes that have stayed with me always. They are hallowed memories, forever magical in my mind.

Going to get water from the community well that Christmas Eve is one of them.

The world beyond was still and silent, and a strange pale blue light reflected off hillocks of snow that looked for all their worth like confectioner's sugar.

My neighborhood had undergone a remarkable change.

It not longer seemed an average residential street in a big city, but rather, a country lane in a long-ago time. The streets and yards had become one vast empty field, its hedges hidden somewhere under the snow. Candles flickered in windows. The trees overhead formed a tunnel whose roof was made of mist and falling snow. Far off, a street lamp beckoned like a muted star.

I tightened my mittened grip around the handles of the pails, and like a character from "A Christmas Carol," went out to get water from the well.

When I reached the top of the street I stopped. Under a street lamp, the Christmas well stood, its cylinder shape topped off with several inches of snow, its tongue and wheels hidden. The bright yellow light of the lamp played over it and gave it a curious glow-like the manger in the Nativity scene under the star. It was impossible to see into the gloom around it. There was only the well and the snow rushing down from the sky. I felt utterly alone and at peace.

I put down my pails.

"Merry Christmas," a neighbor said as she peered around the other side of the well.

"And a Happy New Year," said another. "What a beautiful night."

From beyond the well, a line of scarves, hats, and coats dusted with downy snowflakes stepped forward with their pots and pails to say hello.

My neighbors' faces were red with cold but each had that

particular smile of good will and humor that had brought us to the well.

Christmas had come. A broken water pipe had not delayed it. We would gather our water and carry on with our lives as if nothing had happened. Except that something had. With each pot and pail of water we carried away, we also took a new sense of community and resourcefulness-and perhaps the true meaning of Christmas.

I live in the Northwest now where we rarely get snow at Christmas. But each Christmas Eve, I think of that snowy night when I went to gather water at the Christmas well. As I turn on the lights in my windows and on the Christmas tree, I look outside at my tree-lined street to where a city light stands guard above the hedges. I don't even have to close my eyes to see the Christmas well glowing there under its light, the snow falling down on its cylindrical shape and the neighbors gathered around.

It is etched forever in my mind.

Let us always be neighbors to one another, not only during the holiday season, but throughout the year.

Plain Girl From Mazeppa

Hubert Blair Bonds

Funny how a whole world can wash away, and life goes on. My world changed—forever—one hot August morning, in the year of our Lord, 1858. I was only fourteen.

Mama and I were picking cucumbers. It was one of those mornings where you can see the heat before you feel it.

"You're slower today, Mama."

"I can't get going today. Don't know why."

"Go sit in the shade for a bit and get some water. I'll finish up this row."

"I believe I will, Addy. Maybe get some water."

I finished the row, filling the bushel basket almost to the rim. I expected to see Mama at the well house, but she wasn't there.

I climbed the back steps, "Mama? You inside?"

The spring on the old screen door squawked as it opened. I came around the corner, and Mama was there, lying in the middle of the kitchen floor. Her skin was blue, and cold to the touch.

I ran to the back porch and rang the bell that Mama used to called Papa for dinner. Clang. Clang. CLANG.

Time stopped until Papa grabbed my wrist to stop the ringing. "What's wrong? Where's your Mama?"

I cut my stare toward the kitchen. Papa rushed by me. "Oh my God. Naomi. NAOMI!"

Afterwards, I took over the work of the house and looking after Papa. It was expected and I had no choice. I started to understand how Mama must have felt about being a slave to a house and a man.

"These biscuits are as hard as a rock."

"I had to get the wash pot started this morning, Papa. I ran out of time. These are from supper."

I could see the fire in Papa's eyes. "I don't expect a lot. But I do expect three fresh-cooked meals a day. Your mama used to do it. Why can't you?"

"I'm sorry. I'll do better. I'll start getting up earlier."

"See that you do."

Too soon after Mama's death, Papa started keeping company with Sallyann Parson. Her father was a wealthy landowner, including the farm we rented. He had the only cotton gin in this part of eastern Iredell County, and that alone gave him a lot of clout with folks.

I had first seen Papa and Sallyann talking at the Talbert's barn raising. At noon, all the womenfolk were getting the dinner ready. But not Sallyann. She sat under the scuppernong arbor, doing her embroidery. All the neighbor ladies also saw.

Mrs. Talbert's sister was the first to say something, "Look at her. Hasn't lifted a finger to do a thing, except hold that needle."

Amanda Peacock tried to shush her. "Josephine Allred—you know better than to criticize a Parson. Your husband's cotton won't get ginned."

"Well, it's the truth and you all know it."

I watched Sallyann, all fancy and smelling faintly like the lavender powder Mama used to wear.

That evening, I said to Papa, "I saw you talking with Sallyann under the shade tree."

"Yes. Why?"

"The other women were talking about her not helping to get dinner."

"Old peahens. They don't know everything. She's sickly. She can't do work like that. And it ain't no business of yours. What you need to know, I'll tell you."

"Yes, Papa." I was angry, but I didn't cry. But, that anger settled on my soul.

One morning not so long after the barn raising, Papa said "You may as well know that I'm fixin' to ask Sallyann to marry me. Her father is going to make me his farm foreman. We'll all be living over there. Mr. Parson has offered to let you work in their kitchen, provided you know how to cook. I'm inviting them to dinner soon so you can show them. With your food. If you can't impress them with your cooking, you can be a housemaid."

His words stung, worse than any slap would have. I knew right then that I would be the one deciding my own fate. Not Papa. Not Sallyann. Not Mr. Parson. Mama had raised me to be proud, even though we were poor.

After supper on Saturday night, I pulled the hot water and filled the bathtub. "I'm going to take a bath. I want to go to church tomorrow."

"Why are you going to church?" Papa asked. "I'm not going, so you will be walking."

"I can walk."

The next morning, I used some of Mama's lavender powder, braided my plain brown hair and put it up. In my best dress and Mama's hat, I headed to the front door.

"You look more like your Mama every day." It was the nicest thing Papa had said to me in months.

"There's food in the warming oven, if you get hungry before I get home."

"I'll probably wait on you and hear what the preacher sermonized about."

I had barely set foot onto the road when I heard a wagon.

I turned and saw that it was William and Amanda Peacock and their family, headed to church. Mr. Peacock stopped and tipped his hat, "Howdy do Miss Addy?"

"Good morning Mr. and Mrs. Peacock."

Amanda smiled. "Ain't no need for you to walk to church and muss up your dress and straw hat. You can ride with us."

"Don't want to be a bother."

"Not a bit." Turning her head toward the rear of the wagon, she spoke to her son. "Will—get down and help Addy in."

With his typical goofy grin on his face, Will did as he was told. "How are you this fine Sabbath?"

He reached for my hand. I didn't use much effort to get in the wagon because Will's strength propelled me up. The warmth of his fingers in mine shot all the way up my arm and straight to my chest.

I had barely noticed Will's little sister. "Hey Maudie. You look pretty. I like your dress."

"I like yours too, Addy. Will thinks that you're pretty." His face turned three shades. "Stop that Maudie. I'll tell Addy that she's pretty on my own. Don't need your help with it."

The Peacocks insisted that I sit with them during the service. Will and I shared a hymnal, and our hands touched as we sang 'Fairest Lord Jesus'. It was my turn to blush three shades of crimson, embarrassed that somebody else would see.

That evening, Papa was loading up a biscuit with molasses. "It's set. Sallyann and her folks are coming for dinner on Saturday."

"I've been thinking about what to cook."

Papa nodded, "Fix chicken and dumplings. That's the best thing you make."

"Yes Papa."

Saturday morning, I was up before daylight. I had enough of Mama's good china for everyone and I had worked all week polishing the silver. Mama would have been proud of the table.

"It looks good. I'm proud of you." Two nice things from Papa was unheard of. I barely had time to say thank you before there was a knock at the front door.

Papa hurried to answer it. As I was checking on the dumplings, he yelled out my name. I moved the pot to the side and took off my apron. I checked myself in the mirror, between the kitchen windows, as I had seen Mama do hundreds of times.

I exchanged pleasantries with the Parsons and then excused myself back to the kitchen. Mrs. Parson said, "If you need any help, come and get me."

"It would be best for her not to ask me. I don't know about kitchen work," Sallyann giggled.

Papa chuckled. "You don't need to be there in that hot kitchen. She can handle it."

My head spun. It's all well and good with Papa that I'm slaving away in the heat. But poor Sallyann can't be expected to do that. Was this going to be my life? My hands shook too bad to touch the stove. I ran out the back door, planning to run until I couldn't run no more. But I had no place to go. My father controlled me until I was married. They would bring me right back if I left. My temples began to pound. I wet my handkerchief at the well and wrapped it around the back of my neck to relieve that awful throbbing. The screen door opened.

"What the hellfire are you doing? Don't you know you've got a house full of hungry people to feed?" Papa's face was red.

If a tongue could be bit in two to keep it from saying what it wanted to say, mine would have been in pieces. "I'm coming. Get everybody ready. Show them where the washstand is. The water is fresh. I put new soap and towels out. I'll be right there."

Walking to church the next day, I once again heard the Peacock's wagon behind me. They picked me up and carried me to church. Papa created a stir in the congregation by showing up for services with all of the Parsons in tow. His hand was entwined with Sallyann's. Sometimes, he moved it to the small of her back, guiding her along like she was Queen Victoria. The whole congregation noticed. Mrs. Peacock noticed. After church let out, she took me by the arm, and practically drug me over to where Papa and Sallyann were standing. "Howdy do, Mr. McNeely. Sallyann. I just wanted you to know that we've invited Addy home with us for dinner. We'll get her home before dark."

"Well, thank you so much, Mrs. Peacock. That will be like a tonic for Addy. She needs a restful day."

Sallyann was smiling at me. "Addy, I've been telling everybody what a fine meal you had for us yesterday. Everyone at home is excited about you coming to work with them in the kitchen."

What a thing for the Peacocks to hear that my own father thought so little of me. "Thank you Sallyann. I do appreciate your kind words, but I only know what Mama taught me. I'm just a plain girl from Mazeppa. Never been places like you have; nothing like your schooling at the Normal School in Salisbury."

She reached out and touched my arm. "I think you're a whole

lot more than a plain girl from Mazeppa. I have a lot to learn from you after your Papa and I are married."

Mrs. Peacock interrupted. "We best be getting along before my dinner is ruined. Don't worry about her Mr. McNeely."

Amanda Peacock asked me to sit on the front seat on the ride from church. About fifteen minutes in, she said "Addy, dear, this isn't any of my business, but your Papa expects you to work in the Parson's kitchen?"

"Yes'm. I cooked dinner for them yesterday to show them that I know how."

She looked toward her husband. "That's about the most God-awful thing I've heard in many a day. Expecting his daughter to be a servant for his new wife's family. It's bad enough to be keeping company so soon, and with a girl Sallyann's age . . . "

Mr. Peacock interrupted and shook his head, "Mandy, it's not for us to judge."

"I still think it's awful."

After Mrs. Peacock's wonderful dinner, I read Bible stories aloud from their family Bible. Maudie got scared with the Jonah and the whale story. Will didn't make it any easier, teasing, "You know there's a great big fish out there in our pond. I've only seen it at night, but it's big as a whale. You'd best be careful out there, Maudie."

About half past three, Mr. Peacock said it was time to be getting me home. "Will, you take Maudie along and get Addy back home. The night air will be setting in soon."

Maudie sat in between Will and me. He put his right arm around her, but I could still feel the warmth from his hand when it came near my shoulder. "Yessiree, I want my own farm someday. I want to work it, and watch things grow. Maybe my own cotton gin and make my own cottonseed oil."

I looked over the top of Maudie's head and caught Will's eye. "Sounds wonderful. I want to be a farm wife, I think. Like my Mama was. Maybe have some children."

"That sounds like a female version of my own story. I like the sound of it. We're sayin' the same thing, aren't we?"

"I think we are."

Will turned the team onto the familiar ruts of the road down to our place. I said, "You know, this farm will be for rent when Papa marries Sallyann."

Will's grin returned. "Is he renting this farm from Mr. Parson?"

"Yes. Who else?"

Maudie had been watching us, her eyes going from my face to Will's. "You two should get married and rent this place yourselves. Addy knows the garden, the orchard and the animals. Mama always says this has the best springhouse in the county."

"What do you think Addy?" Will's face was that shade of crimson again.

"Maudie said what I was thinking. You get your farm. I get to be the farm wife I'm hankering to be. We're young and strong and can do it."

As Will stopped the wagon, I could see the tenderness in his eyes. "We have a plan. I'll tell my folks tonight and Papa and I can go see Mr. Parson in the morning. And I'll ask your father for your hand."

I could only smile back at him.

He got down off the buckboard and beckoned me down. His hands on my waist lingered a bit longer. His smile was a bit broader. His eyes sparkled a bit more. He said, "Maudie, take the horse to the trough for water while I take Addy the rest of the way to our front door." Will took my hand in his and we walked to the front door. I stood on the second step to be face-to-face with him.

"I don't have a ring or nothin' right now. But no man has ever wanted a girl to say yes more than I do. Will you marry me?"

"Yes, Will. And you don't have to worry about a ring."

Will said, "Oh, you'll have a ring, Addy McNeely. You can bank on that," smiling that wonderful goofy grin.

Inheritance

Ellen Birkett Morris

Some people are born to sin; others inherit it. I didn't know which of these I was until I crossed paths with the Cabots.

The room smelled of lemons and vinegar. Alma Cabot lay stiff across her cherry Duncan Phyfe table. A tall woman, her legs almost reached the end of the table. Her face was slack where it was usually stern, but still, there was no trace of softness.

The table had a high shine. We didn't own a mirror. When I looked down, my reflection startled me. My hair hung in wild tendrils around my face. My eyes were hard. I'd been sitting with the dead woman for fifteen minutes according to the grandfather clock in the corner.

Mrs. Cabot wore her best dress, purple brocade with pearl buttons and matching earrings. I was sure her son Daniel would relieve her of these before her body went into the ground. I heard pearls came from a grain of sand that irritated the oyster. I wasn't surprised that this was Mrs. Cabot's jewelry of choice.

Though she had absented her body, I half expected Mrs. Cabot to pop up and start talking about the fine wood finish, turned edges, and four-legged base of the table. She loved ownership and often spoke about the "fine pieces" her grandmother had brought over from England. She told these stories to anyone who would listen, including my Mama, who spent years mopping the Cabot's floors and cooking their dinner—and then went home to a bed of straw ticking. If I had been my mother, I would have spit in the Cabot's food—or worse, but my mother played by the rules, ones that were set and broken by the Cabots. Because the Cabots had money, nobody said a thing. Mama believed in God's final judgment, but I wasn't sure it was wise to leave it up to Him, what with his reputation for mercy and all.

Mrs. Cabot would have squirmed at the thought of being laid out on her elegant table, though that was the custom around these parts. I wouldn't be seated at this table if she hadn't passed.

I was here for one reason, to take away her sins. My granny had been a sin eater, as her granny was before her, a custom from England that came with her across the ocean along with the family's meager belongings. Part of me thought the ritual was foolishness, though I never said so.

The other part of me feared it was real and wondered about the weight of my granny's soul.

Before she died, Granny wrapped up her black cloak and left instructions with Mamma that it was to be passed on to me. I liked to believe she thought I was tough enough to handle the job and smart enough not to take it too seriously. Either way, I'd been bearing the sins of the Cabots for a while now.

I was born on the wrong side of the river, in the elbow, a patch of land by the bend, prone to flooding. It was the kind of place people with no sense, or no money, lived. It took my family several generations before Daddy finally built the house up off the ground. So then, when it rained, we were on a dirtier version of Noah's Ark, one with nearly as many inhabitants (Mama, Daddy, me, the twins, four feral cats, three dogs, a chicken and two songbirds). With less food, of course.

Daniel Cabot had crossed the creek to fetch me that morning. It wasn't his first visit. That was shortly after I turned 16, the summer that it flooded and our crops washed out. We almost starved that summer. Daddy let Daniel in and sent him to my room. I didn't know what was happening, but Daddy stood in my doorway and told me to make Daniel welcome; then he closed the door. Daniel stood still, looking at me. I saw his lust, but also a look like he was judging cattle. For all his looking, I don't think he saw me at all. Then he lifted my gown over my head and carried me to the bed.

He was his mother's son, greedy and prideful. He panted as he took me from behind. I stared at the water stain on the wall. It was big and yellowed with ragged brown edges in the shape of a dog. When I was little, I pretended it was real and called it Yeller, which always made my Mama laugh. While Daniel labored, I imagined running through a wide field with Yeller, someplace far away from the elbow.

Daniel pressed his finger against my teeth until I figured I was meant to suck on it, which I did, though I fantasized about biting it off and feeding it to Yeller. At first, I gagged, but then I pretended it was a piece of ice melting in my mouth until it disappeared into nothing.

The Cabots owned the coal mine, but Daniel's finger was as soft as a baby's, unstained by labor. The nail was clean, though raggedy from his chewing it. He smelled of expensive soap, a sharp citrus smell that would come to signal danger to me. I said nothing while he spent his energy on me. I barely moved, hoping he'd get bored and move on. That night, and every visit after, he left fifty cents on my dresser. I never touched the money, but it always disappeared.

I was proud of myself for not crying out that night—or the many nights after. He would have wanted me to whimper and moan. But I didn't want to wake the little ones and stain their first memories with sounds of suffering. When he left, I rinsed my mouth at the washbasin and ran wet rags across my thighs. The rags came back bloody. The next morning Ma washed the stains from my sheets without a word.

This morning, Daniel had stood in the doorway and said, "Mama's dead. The corpse cakes are in the oven, and we need you down at the house."

I dressed quickly in my cloak and took a fine linen handkerchief from Ma's drawer. When we got to the house, I placed the handkerchief on the doorstep. I would retrieve it and the money when my work was done.

Daniel had pushed me roughly in the direction of the dining room and left me alone with her, while he went to fetch his brother. I knew Abraham by reputation only. He had been away at school and then opened a law practice in Charleston.

I walked around the room, running my finger across the scrolls and leaves of the carved sideboard. I slid open a drawer to find linens embroidered with sprigs of lavender. A small sachet of lavender was in the corner of the drawer. I held it to my nose; the sharp, fresh scent reminded me that just outside these walls, the fields were bursting with life. I went back to the table and sat across from Mrs. Cabot, where I could see her face as it slowly turned to stone.

I had been a sin eater before, but that family was strangers to me, folks who had come into the mining camps from Pittsburgh and lost their daughter to the flu. I wondered how much sin she could have accumulated in her five years, not much I would reckon, but the family was superstitious and wanted to send her off to the afterlife with a clean slate. The girl had taken up only a small portion of the table. A corpse cake had laid on her small chest. I said the words, and the mother handed me the cake. The cake had raisins and currants inside and crumbled in my mouth. The family watched as I ate every crumb. When I got outside, two dollars sat on my handkerchief.

I waited until I got into the woods to stick my finger down my throat. A volcano of sweet cake and fruit left a mess in the grass. It was no time at all before the bees came buzzing around it. I figured I'd only taken in a little of the sin, nothing mortal, nothing that would keep me from heaven.

I was jumpy today, my stomach a strange mix of nausea and hunger. I was used to hunger, but the nausea was a more recent development. I had been waking up with my stomach roiling around. I kept a few peppermint leaves inside my pillow and chewed on them when things got bad. I ran my hand around the smooth edge of the table. I could do anything now—carve my initials into the underside with my pocket knife, slide the silver sugar shell into my pocket, take a piece of the old woman's hair for some kind of hex. But instead, I touched my stomach and whispered in the dead woman's ear, "I'm carrying your grandchild."

Nobody could tell yet. The small swell in my belly was hidden by my dress. But my state would reveal itself soon—and there would be hell to pay. I looked out the window at the tall oak standing in front of the house. It was a huge old tree with a gnarled trunk. The thick branches came out like tentacles spreading toward the sun, taking up space against the sky. I saw a strong, low branch, a perfect place to perch and watch the world, and I took in the sturdy branches just beyond, footholds to the sky. My son would never play there.

I heard the back door close, and I sat back quickly and raised the hood of my cloak to cover my face. Daniel pushed the door open, a plate of cakes in his hand, and he held it for another man. Abraham was tall and resembled Daniel around the nose and forehead, but he had much kinder eyes.

He reached his hand out toward me.

"Don't bother," said Daniel.

The man raised his eyebrows. I held back a smile.

Abraham looked at his mother. "She's not here. There is no trace of her," he said, quietly.

"Only death could still the likes of her," said Daniel.

"What is this?" asked Abraham, nodding at me.

"A local burial custom of the rabble, some malarkey about eating the sins of the deceased. Mother insisted we do it if she should die."

If she should die! Did the Cabots think immortality was theirs for a price, like everything else?

Daniel laid the plate of cakes on his mother's still chest.

The cakes were round and small and black around the edges.

The brothers looked at me expectantly.

I picked up a cake and held it to my mouth. When my teeth bit down, I felt like a vulture feasting on the entrails of some small, soft animal that had gotten in the way, but I knew I was that small, soft animal and Daniel wouldn't quit visiting me at night until nothing was left of me but a crimson stain on the floor. I chewed and swallowed, felt the hard cake scrape down my throat.

I heard myself speak, though in my mind, I was far above the house, circling, waiting for my chance to pounce. My voice was loud and strong.

"I pledge my soul for your sins and ask that God Almighty

remove those sins from you and place them up on me, and I eat this food to show that I have taken your sins upon me. If I lie, may God strike me dead."

I looked at the brothers, whose eyes were closed. It was done. I walked to the door. I could see the coins shining on my handkerchief. I bent down to scoop them up. I felt a presence behind me. Abraham stepped forward and pressed five dollars into my hands. I looked him in the face, wondering if my son would look like him.

It was enough money for the train east. I could be alone with my sins. I'd find a place somewhere, get a dog, and take in sewing. I would be free. My son would live unencumbered by legacy, free in a way I could only imagine. I walked quickly through the woods, stopping only to put my finger down my throat.

I rushed home and began to pack. I took my two dresses, crochet hook, and knitting needles and the skein of yarn I had been saving to make mittens for the twins. I stopped to touch the stain on the wall, which, in the light of day, looked like nothing but a dirty spot.

Mama stood in my doorway. "Don't," she said.

"I've got to." My hand wandered to the five dollars folded in my pockets. I looked into her face and noticed the lines worn into its surface, the hollows of her checks.

"We'll starve."

If I stayed, I would become her, more indebted to the Cabots with each passing day, for whatever table scraps they decided to throw my way, like a dog—worse than a dog, since I was more than my appetites.

I pushed past her and ran out the door. I ran all the way to town and bought a ticket to Richmond. I barely had time to sit down before the train pulled up. It was my first time on a train. The seats were covered in leather, and the interior was trimmed in wood. I knew I stood out in my simple dress and mended shawl. I took a seat near the door. It wasn't long before the rocking of the cars lulled me to sleep. It was a dreamless sleep, not like my dreams at home, where I was forever trying to escape from some unknown pursuer.

I woke up as a man made his way down the aisle with a trolley that carried a teakettle and cake. "Refreshment, Miss?"

I had a cup of tea with cream and sugar. I sipped it slowly. When I got settled, this would be my new ritual—a cup of tea in the quiet of the afternoon while the baby slept. Prince, West Virginia, its hunger and fear, would be far behind me. I got off in Charleston, searching for the way to my connecting train. I had only taken a few steps when I felt a hand grab my arm and smelled the citrus scent of Daniel's soap.

I pulled my arm away, and he reached forward and held me tight. I struggled to break free and stomped on his foot. He pushed my face close to his and spoke through gritted teeth. "I'll tell them you robbed me. They'll find the rest of Abe's money on you, and you will go to jail."

I stopped struggling and looked beyond Daniel to see my train pulling out of the station. "How did you find me?"

"Your mother told me you were running away. I knew you wouldn't get far on foot. I saw Abe hand you the money and figured you'd go to the train station."

My mother was foolish enough to see the Cabots as benefactors.

***

I was silent on the train ride home. Daniel stared at me, his mouth twisted into a smirk. "You're hardly worth the trouble. Your bloom is fading, and you're getting fat."

He was ignorant as well as mean. I had nothing now, no family, no allies, just the hint of possibility in my womb that I was sure Daniel would take from me the minute he was born.

When I got home, I hugged Mama and smiled at Daddy. Let them think I was content to stay. I waited until the middle of the night to leave my bed and put on my black cloak. I touched the wall to say goodbye to Yeller.

***

The rope hung on a nail on the wall of the barn. It wasn't heavy. I made it to the oak before the moon had emerged from the clouds.

I climbed to a high branch. The face of the Cabot's house was silent. How surprised Daniel would be in the morning. How quickly word would spread among the neighbors. I'd seen my father hang pigs upside down to drain the blood plenty of times. I secured the rope, fashioned a noose, and placed it around my neck.

I imagined my body swaying in the wind, a spectral figure in my dark cloak. The bees would still buzz, the river would flood, girls would get visited in the night, and the Cabots would sit counting their money, polishing their silver, with no idea of what had been taken from them. I let myself fall.

The Victorian Dandenongs

Margaret Pearce

The Victorian Dandenongs, a unique and hilly area shaped by an upheaval of ancient volcanoes, is both impressive and inspirational in its beauty.

A lot of its unique character and environment has been much changed by settlement and clearances. Daniel Defoe who wrote Robinson Crusoe said that the first thing man did on settling an alien environment was to attempt to change it into a copy of his home environment.

This is a proven fact. New inhabitants import their culture, patterns of thinking and flora and fauna. They surround themselves with familiar things, build homes that are familiar, and plant their familiar gardens around them. Only then, homesickness eased, they settle in to the business of putting down roots.

In the Dandenongs, as everywhere else in Australia this custom of changing the environment through flora and fauna is well in evidence. There are cleared paddocks for grazing, food and flower crops that make the countryside look like a direct transplant from other countries.

The camellias, rhododendrons, magnolias, cedrillas, and other blossoming trees, azaleas, bulbs and other alien flowers decorate, enhance and enrich the Dandenongs both aesthetically and economically. However these change the basic timeless and primeval character of the hills as little as lace curtains around flying saucer portholes.

The less decorative flora was often brought in or sneaked in uninvited to ease the newcomer's homesickness. With its successful invasion now well entrenched it turned feral. Buttercups, onion weed, blackberries, jasmine, honeysuckle, foxes, rabbits, cats, dogs and deer are now equally well in evidence. Only the feelings they arouse in local inhabitants are no longer homesickness. These invaders and intruders are now recognised and discouraged through the changing views of the inhabitants as to what they are, unwanted, ugly and destructive aliens.

Dedicated friends and lovers of the Dandenong's clear waterways and bushland from the alien weeds choking them, replant the native vegetation and pursue the feral flora and fauna with unflagging and deadly enthusiasm. This is not a recent or late-come attitude to conservation. Since the beginning of settlement in the hills, the original greenies have argued and fought for conservation of the unique fern clad beauty of the gullies and tree covered hills to be preserved.

It is very much against Daniel Defoe's view, but in an interesting reversal, it is the environment that is causing subtle but far reaching changes to the culture, character and nature of its inhabitants.

The survivors of the waves of settlers who moved into the Dandenong's and coped with the harsh natural rhythms of flood, fire, drought, landslip, and other less natural disasters have been shaped by their experiences. To survive they had to adapt to the long series of hardship years and the occasional productive year. They have had to evolve a tenacity as deep rooted as the tap roots of the trees, a cheerful optimism as green as the new growth after fires and an endless patience and acceptance of life in the hills.

Charles Darwin wrote learnedly of flora and fauna in isolated places developing along its own unique lines. The Dandenong's, shouldering itself above the tamed suburbs still gives that impression of isolation, as if it is some Robinson Crusoe type of island. Visitors and other pilgrims sense the difference between the Dandenongs and its encroaching suburbs as eons in time and in distance rather than a twenty minute drive.

The isolation, more imaginary than real in these days of good roads and tamed bushland, still subtly works and changes the attitudes and characters of the inhabitants.

First there is acceptance, as the hills become home and no longer an alien world and then the fanatic growth of the loyalty and love that the remaining corners of original environment inspire. Returning the bush environment and its inhabitants to at least a portion of its original self has become and continues to become an absorbing, satisfying and continuing crusade.

Secondly there is the growth of what might be called the cult of individualism. The Dandenongs could become one of the last bastions of that oddity in conventional society, the eccentric. This is often as marked as the architecture as it is in some of the dwellers.

Thirdly, the Dandenong's also nurtures another facet of its inhabitants. Does the isolation and dreamtime primeval timelessness present in the hills and gullies encourage the growth of creativity in the crafts? Or are painters, writers, potters, sculptors and other craft workers attracted to the hills for their inspiration?

There is something about the atmosphere and character of the Dandenongs that makes the protective up swell in green and conservation movements seen as a natural progression. Things happen and keep on happening in the Dandenong's. If you stand apart and look at it objectively it is oddly puzzling.

Community protests and other movements to protect and restore native environments rise and fall with apathy and disinterest. In the hills you only have to walk through the natural parks and their beauty spots to be aware of the long term and continuing determination to protect, preserve and restore.

The culmination of all dreams is the restoration of original flora and fauna. It is like a tantalising holy grail to restore the once-upon-a-time paradise of the Dandenongs before mining, logging settlement, clearances, land developers, even some businesses and the criminally careless mistakes tainted it.

Daniel Defoe's statement doesn't fit all situations. Although it is natural that the first desire of a new inhabitant is to alter an alien environment into a home environment, in the Dandenongs it is the other way around. It is the environment that works on the inhabitants. Their character, their attitudes, their culture and their definition of a home environment all subtly but permanently change to one which fits the hills themselves more comfortably.

And all benefit from the Dandenong's loyal inhabitants and their definition of progress, to continue conserving and restoring the Dandenongs to as much of its original dreamtime self as it is possible.

Life After Death by Thesaurus: A Bug's Legacy

Ellen Notbohm

My day began as many do, with a writing prompt: Describe the last creature you killed.

Unless we're a stockyard worker, a hunter or fisher, or a euthanistic veterinarian, perhaps the only thing some of us ever kill is a bug. Or a garden slug. Or the occasional gut-twisting road kill, the Darwinian squirrel who ran toward our car rather than away.

The bug who crossed my path was merely in the wrong place at the wrong time. In the moment, I couldn't understand why I killed him. (How do I know it was a him?) He wasn't eating my crops or plants, wasn't threatening to sting or otherwise poison me or my food. He was just there. In the hindsight that came within seconds, I knew I'd killed him out of instinct. The primal, perfectly irrational strain of fear, the elephant-and-mouse kind, the sense of being ambushed by an alien.

I don't know what kind of bug he was, and it happened so fast that I don't remember much of what he looked like.

He was dark, perhaps charcoal gray, his body perhaps three-eighths of an inch, diaphanous wings above it, filament legs below. While I strung beautiful words together in a writer's cottage in the woods, he came in through an unscreened window and landed near the top of a page of my Oxford Writer's Thesaurus, splayed open to where I was searching out synonyms for something starting with g. Good? Great? Gross?

He landed near the binding, the cleft where two pages meet. He never knew what hit him. I snapped the book shut, sniper-decisive.

He took the full weight of 700 pages of the Oxford Writer's Thesaurus, with the force of an overreactive full-grown human author behind it.

Not a particle of time elapsed between the slamming of the tome and the wondering why. Why hadn't I gently lifted the book to the window over the desk and with a gentle puff of breath, shown him the way out? I couldn't deflect the bald truth, that I was a guest in his environment. An invasive species. The cottage was one of six nestled in forty-eight acres of farm and woods on an island in Puget Sound. Having critters for neighbors was part of living in those woods. Every day I met up with bunnies and frogs and owls. At the beach I meandered among live sand dollars, crabs, gulls, herons, and an array of crustaceans. Never would I have dreamed of harming any of them. Why did I subject this insect to such a brutal judgment? I could not justify it, could not write it off to some deeply embedded generic ick factor.

The days tumbled by, each one slipping in the east window of the cottage and casting its beam on the thesaurus calmly poised to assist with the next sentence, paragraph, chapter. I knew my gossamer-winged victim was in my book somewhere, squashed flat as the proverbial bug. It was a large book, yes, but I couldn't avoid him forever. A faint dread, guilt-tinged, tingled in my fingers when I turned the pages, looking for better words for pretty, large, simple. When my time in the cottage came to an end, he traveled home with me, snug in his wordy tomb, where the same sun slipped into a different east window. And still I didn't allow myself to lookup for words starting with g.

The first time I saw him, months later, two-dimensional, almost mistaken for an illustration on the page of all those g words, I flicked on by as if my hands were on fire. The second time, after yet more months of avoiding g words, I did what I should have done the first time—lifted the book, took it to the door, and brushed him gently back into his world.

That bug haunted me for eight years, until a moment of secondhand clemency came to me through my son. Working in the back room of a large thrift store, he spotted a butterfly that had somehow made its way into the building and now perched unmoving atop a bin of donated goods. A white butterfly, perhaps tan, hard to tell in the dusty light. He also couldn't tell if the butterfly was alive, but he knew it couldn't survive indoors, so he slid his hand underneath it and gently cupped it, still motionless, while he walked quietly to the swinging back doors. Outside, he slowly unfurled his fingers to the summer sky. The butterfly flexed its wings and soared majestically into the breeze. "Bryce!" a nearby co-worker exclaimed in his melodic Kenyan cadence. "You saved a life!"

A few more years went by, our family welcomed the next generation, and finally I found some peace in my atonement.

Everything about the day was classically autumn, the vivid crimson, amber, and auburn of the trees against a dazzling sky in sparkling air just cool enough to require jackets. The woods offered up a wonderland of a walk through bucolic childhood pleasures with our sons and granddaughter. Barely two, she talked in single words and short phrases but she knew how to lead a nature walk. We followed her runs through the leaves, meticulously stacked fir cones into artful sculptures, sorted pebbles by size and color, tossed sticks in the creek from a footbridge, called to the ducks. It never entered my thoughts that anything might mar such perfect joie de vivre, this joy of discovery for a toddler and the joy of reliving it for the adults.

A few yards short of our outing's end, a ladybug crawled across the sidewalk in front of us. We all bent to admire it, the red shell, the delicate spots. Our grandie knew it was a ladybug and cooed over it endearingly until suddenly and inexplicably, she raised her boot and stomped it flat.

My son the butterfly rescuer and I gasped in horror. My husband shrugged it off with "Kids step on bugs." We glared at him while our granddaughter's father gently explained to her why this wasn't okay. We straggled back to our cars, our exuberant fall mood injected with a note of melancholy.

We'd said our goodbyes and see-you-soons when our subdued toddler abruptly climbed into our car, into my lap, and uttered the first full sentence she'd ever spoken to me.

"I'm sad about the ladybug."

Her eyes were steady and brave. She wanted an honest conversation.

"I'm sad about the ladybug too," I said, without drama or accusation.

"She broke."

"Yes. Sometimes when things are broken they can be fixed, but not this time. All she wanted was to fly home and now she can never do that again."

"I'm sad."

"I'm glad that you're sad. It shows what a kind heart you have. You'll never step on a ladybug again, will you?"

"No."

Later I'd open my old thesaurus, dusty with disuse since being nudged aside by speedier online searches. There, in the section of g words, I would at long last find peace in the many synonyms for grace [noun]: a reprieve, an absolution, a kindness, a blessing.

SLEEPING SICKNESS

Kimberly Parish Davis

1971—It's difficult to say precisely where I was in 1971. It was a bleak time. My mother was driving back and forth to Wyoming marrying and divorcing an asshole who abused my dog. Superdog was only 12 pounds, but every ounce of him was fighting fit. Even when the bad man put him in the freezer, or on top of the china cabinet to see if he'd try to jump off and break his little neck. I think Mom and that guy married each other twice—each time only for about six months. Superdog and I just got dragged along for the ride. I had no choice but to change schools 5 times between fourth and sixth grades.

It's interesting when I remember that the two horses Mom kept when she and Dad divorced didn't have any trouble traveling out of the state of Texas, at least, not that I recall. There was that Venezuelan Equine Encephalomyalitis going on in Texas, and for a time, 24 states actually banned Texas horses from entering their borders. (Like you can stop mosquitos at man made borders.) It made sense at the time, though, because it could infect humans too. I have vague recollections of people being afraid to go to the barn. My mind shows me the barn on Brittmoore Road, so I know that for at least part of that time I was in Texas, but the regime had changed. I was a stranger in that place I'd roamed as my own when I was younger. My new step brother and sister rode their bikes to the barn to feed horses and clean stalls. That terrified me—crossing the Katy freeway on a bicycle. My other grandmother was a great hypochondriac, and I know I stayed with her part of the time I was in Texas, and I know she talked to me about sleeping sickness. No doubt her fears colored my view of that place I'd once loved. That summer, 1971, more than 1500 equines died in South Texas. There were no human deaths, but 110 cases were reported.[1] So, yeah, people were afraid, just like they were afraid of the Corona Virus coming from China in 2020.

I was in Texas on summer vacation, since Mom and I had gone to Wyoming towing four horses behind her lilac Sedan deVille. Not King Like Star, Mom's special favorite. Daddy kept him out of spite, and it broke her heart because Daddy had King Like gelded almost immediately. In the divorce settlement, Daddy'd made Mom choose Triple Hope or King Like, and she'd kept the filly, who was worth more money. It had been an impossible choice. She loved them both. There'd been no contest over me or the house. As soon as Mom found another man with a barn to put her horses in, we headed out. And me? Daddy already had a new woman with a ready-made family to slot right into the space we'd just vacated. But the horses? They fought bitterly over the horses, both crystal clear about where their priorities lay.

I can't remember the name of that colt of Bo's that we took with us, but he set the tone with the Wyoming husband immediately. It happened the day we arrived when they went to unload the horses at their new barn. Mom's horses never responded well to manhandling, and when the jerk tried to force the colt to do something, it went wrong in a hurry. Mr. Wyoming wore a scar on his face for the rest of his days.

Texans weren't very popular in Wyoming. I can recall my first day in the fourth-grade classroom of my new elementary school. The building was old with dusty wooden floors that creaked and radiators that hissed. It smelled of damp, and I was cold. I didn't yet have the right clothes for the frigid playground. The second semester was already underway, and since I had been having some difficulty in school back in Houston, it seemed like changing schools would be a good thing. Then I sat down in that cold classroom in

---

[1] https://www.ncbi.nlm.nih.gov/pubmed/235212

Cheyenne. During the Wyoming History section the day I arrived, there was a lesson about Wyoming's cattle boom, I think, because the topic somehow turned to Texas, where for twenty or thirty years immediately following the Civil War, Texas had a surplus of cattle, and men being men, always on the lookout for a way to make a buck, started moving massive herds north. When the "cattle bubble" burst, the cattle ranchers got nasty and started attacking sheep camps.[1] Don't quote me, but I think this is what was known as the Range Wars. So, as the teacher, a shriveled up old prune of a thing with cat-eye glasses and grey smoker's teeth and skin and a phlemy cough, glared at me, she said, "We know someone from Texas, don't we, boys and girls?" All thirty of those children turned in their seats to glare with the same contempt on their faces that their teacher wore. So, right off I didn't feel welcome in Wyoming.

Our short lived home in Wyoming, though, was sublime. The sky and the land were so big, so open, so blue. The not- nice husband had 1500 acres with a house and barns set way back off the highway. A railroad ran through it, and I was scared when he and Mom went out at night. I'd bring the big dogs in from outside to keep me and Superdog company, and I imagined hobos jumping off the train and coming to slit my throat.

We must have barely missed the ban on Texas equines moving across borders. We'd never have gotten them through Colorado, but we had no trouble bringing them back to Texas.

---

[1] https://www.wyohistory.org/encyclopedia/spring-creek-raid-last-murderous-sheep-raid-big-horn-basin

The Last Time

J. B. Hogan

I saw the night sky with
  no light pollution was long
  ago in the mountains
from the front porch of
a small cabin tucked away
  beside a small lake in late
November and the air
was crisp, clean, and
clear and there were no
clouds and no moon and
the stars came down to
the horizon and there
were so many stars you
could barely make out
constellations and the
stars were so bright
it was overwhelming,
  it felt like a celestial
wind was passing through
me and I was becoming
  smaller and smaller and
yet at the same time
part of some enormous
  magnificent, awe-inspiring,
  even terrifying existence
  that I did not understand
but gave me immense joy
to be the tiniest part of.

Visitation

Royal Rhodes

You told me you were an angel, the
first night I met you on the balcony
overlooking the city's carpet of lights.

Later in my room you shyly revealed the
elliptical scars marking your back where
once were wings in rainbow hues.

Their absence caused me much wonder like the
Y-shaped scar on your torso -- but there were
things we never mentioned.

You kept changing -- the green like jade in
your eyes, and your crown of dark hair cut
short to look like a boy's at times.

When you were angry your fingers felt
as cold as the frozen lake deep in hell as you
said: Cross your heart and hope to die.

You said the smell of blood repelled you. When
you took me into the silent wards you stopped
outside several doors and wept.

The last night you stayed, you blindfolded me as
we fluffed the sheets like snow angels with your
cold hand set on my colder heart.

A Wynter's Tail

Patricia Feinberg Stoner

Crispin de Beaufort Wynter flounced through the outer office, muttering under his breath. Angelica looked up from her keyboard in surprise. This wasn't the Crispin they all knew and loved at the agency. The Crispin who always rolled up with a fresh green carnation in his immaculate sports coat, the Crispin who always had a kind word and a suggestive wink for the bedraggled troupe of actors waiting to see Cynthia March, the formidable head casting agent.

'What's the matter, Cris?' Angelica asked sympathetically.

'Nothing! Absolutely nothing! That's what La March told me. I know for a fact that they're casting the *Dream* for the Barbican this week, and everyone knows I am famous for my Bottom.'

Angelica bit her lip, but the waiting group were less tactful. Titters, some stifled, some not, ran round the room and someone was heard to remark, *sotto voce*, that Crispin's bottom was, indeed, well known to some.

'But oh, no,' the indignant actor went on, 'La March says she has nothing for me.'

Three days later, it was a transformed Crispin who bounced into the waiting room.

'I've had a call-back,' he crowed. 'From La March herself. A most intriguing phone call. She wanted to know if I'm any good with horses. It's got to be that new historical epic of Spielberg's. I'd heard they were casting for the battle scenes. Better brush up my equestrian skills.'

At that moment a discreet light lit up by Angelica's desk, and she said, 'You can go in now; Cynthia is ready to see you.'

Crispin emerged some ten minutes later, looking bewildered.

'Well, that was very mysterious,' he said. 'Apparently it's all very hush hush and Cynthia couldn't tell me very much. She said when she heard horses were involved, she thought of me immediately. I've got riding listed as one of my skills in *Spotlight,* you know—an actor has to have quite a few strings to his bow, especially nowadays when there are so many *reality TV stars* and *soap actors* competing for parts with real actors.' He cast a contemptuous glance round the waiting room.

'Oh, and she did say, Cynthia that is, that my comedic skills would come in handy. Don't say they're considering me for Falstaff? Anyway, they're doing the final casting in Brighton—Cynthia said I've to go down there on Wednesday and meet up with 'Steve' in the Pavilion.' He tapped the side of his nose and winked knowingly.

'Well, we all know who Steve is, don't we? Well, if she wants to be all cloak and dagger about it, who am I to say *neigghhhh*?'

And with that he tapped himself vigorously on the celebrated bottom with an imaginary riding crop and cantered out of the office.

Crispin de Beaufort Wynter was *not* good with horses. In fact, they terrified him. It was, coincidentally, in Brighton that an eight-year-old Crispin had had his first encounter with the equine species. A thrilling entry in the Donkey Derby had come to an inglorious end when the donkey he was riding suddenly stopped dead. Crispin did not. His howls and wails drew anxious glances from nearby families, who suspected murder at the very least, and he had to be consoled with several ice cream cones.

Still, steady the Buffs, Crispin told himself sternly. He made an appointment at a local riding stables, where a kindly groom and the gentlest of trots on the smallest of ponies reassured him that he could handle anything Spielberg asked of him. It was, after all, mainly CGI these days, he reasoned.

Come Wednesday, Crispin reported to the Brighton Pavilion at the appointed time. He had chosen his attire carefully: a tweed jacket and fawn trousers with just a hint of fullness at the thigh, a whisper of tightness at the calf which, when worn over well-shined brown boots, suggested—but did not shout—jodhpurs.

His experienced eye took in the familiar scene of the casting call: the tables askew, strewn with dog-eared scripts and abandoned paper cups half full of cold coffee, the production assistant bustling about with her inevitable clipboard, the producer sitting apart, scribbling in a dog- eared notebook. No sign of Steven Spielberg, but that was only to be expected at this stage of the game.

'*Crispin*!' The shout rang out across the room, and a small, energetic person threw himself into the startled actor's arms.

'Crispin, it's so *good* to *see* you! When I heard we were *getting* you, I couldn't *believe* our luck! You'll be the *star* of the *show*, just see if you're not! I'm Steve, by the way, but of course you knew that.'

'Er...' Crispin began, but the small person steamrollered on.

'Naughty, *naughty* Cynthia, expecting you to come and *audition*! Of course the part is yours, it was practically *written* for you. Now *trot* along and see Marcie, she's got some *wardrobe* questions to go over with you.'

At the far end of the room a space was screened off. This, Crispin assumed, was the wardrobe department. Marcie, the wardrobe mistress, was tall and angular with a pronounced mustache and a no-nonsense manner.

'Hello, there, Crispin,' she said. 'Oh good, you're not too tall. You'll match well with Derek. We have to get this business sorted quick sharp, or there'll be no end of ructions. Let's see if this will suit.'

She was holding up one half of a pantomime horse's costume. It wasn't the head.

About the Authors

Candice Marley Conner is a haint at The Haunted Bookshop in Downtown Mobile and an officer for her local writer's guild. Her poems and stories are in various anthologies and magazines including *Well Read, Wild: An Anthology of Poetry, Woolgathering, Chicken Soup for the Soul,* and more. She is the author of three picture books and a YA Southern mystery.

Kaye Wilkinson Barley, is the author of one womens fiction novel, WHIMSEY; several published essays and short stories, including a contribution (VOODOO AT THE JITTERBUG) to the Anthony award winning anthology BLOOD ON THE BAYOU, and co-author, along with her husband Don, of two photo essay books, including the most recent CAROUSELS OF PARIS.

Mike Ross has written professionally and privately for decades, published in newspapers previously. He received his BA at University of Munich (Germany), and two MAs in the US. Ross taught German for thirty-five years and in summers was a professional tour guide, which he still is. Ross decided to write permanently to share his experiences with others who might not have the same opportunities to experiences them for themselves.

Will Maguire is a songwriter and writer living in Nashville. His work has appeared in a variety of magazines and journals most recently *Salvation South, The Memoirist* and the *WELL READ* Collected Anthology

AJ Concannon is originally from Glasgow, Scotland, but has lived in Japan for more than three decades. Writing both fiction and non-fiction, his work has appeared in such publications as *Scottish PEN* and *The Japan Times*. He is an award-winning screenwriter and his films have played at various international festivals.

Patricia Feinberg Stoner is an award-winning British writer, a former journalist, copywriter and publicist. She is the author of three humorous books set in the Languedoc, in the south of France, *At Home in the Pays d'Oc, Tales from the Pays d'Oc* and *Murder in the Pays d'Oc*, and also three books of comic verse: *Paw Prints in the Butter, Pelicans Can't Read* and *The Little Book of Rude Limericks*. A Londoner to her fingertips, she now lives in West Sussex, on the south coast of the UK.

Gregg Norman lives in Manitoba, Canada. His work has been accepted by numerous poetry journals and literary magazines, including *Lothlorien Poetry Journal, Dark Winter Literary Magazine, Borderless Journal, Synchronized Chaos, Book of Matches Literary Journal, Medusa's Kitchen, Horror Sleaze Trash, The Littoral Magazine, MasticadoresUSA, The Piker Press, Academy of the Heart and Mind, Raconteur Magazine*, and *Suburban Witchcraft*.

Robin Prince Monroe delights in writing for children; and has authored seven picture books, a middle grade novel, and a chapter book. Recently released titles for grownups include, *Ridiculously Easy Crockpot Recipes, Ridiculously Easy Creative Problem Solving, Time Trees and Grandpa's Knees*, and *Loss of a Loved One*. Her work has also appeared in *Guideposts*, and *Money Matters*.

Ramey Channell is the author of three novels: *Sweet Music on Moonlight Ridge, The Witches of Moonlight Ridge*, and *The Treasure of Moonlight Ridge*, and children's picture book, *Mice from the Planet Zimlac*. Ramey's poems and stories have been published by *Aura Literary Arts Review, ASPS, Birmingham Arts Journal, Ordinary and Sacred as Blood: Alabama Women Speak, Belles Letters 2, Well Read Magazine*, and many other collections.

April Mae M. Berza is the author of *Confession ng isang Bob Ong Fan* (Flipside, 2014) and *Berso de Berza* (Charging Ram, 2012.) Her poems and short stories appeared in numerous publications in America,

France, Canada, Belgium, Romania, India, Japan, Great Britain, and the Philippines. She received an Honorable Mention in the 19th HIAHaiku Contest and the 7th Akita Russia-Japan Haiku Contest. She currently resides in Taguig, Philippines.

Anne Leigh Parrish's new novel, *The Hedgerow*, appears in July 2024 from Unsolicited Press. *Diary of a False Assassin*, her next poetry collection, will arrive in December 2024, also from Unsolicited Press. She lives in Olympia, Washington.

Born and raised in the grittiness of New York City, Brittingham spent a large segment of her adult years in the blue skies and humidity of South Florida. Today she resides along the magnificent (and sometimes tumultuous) shores of Lake Michigan.

Michael Austin is a short story writer living in Madison, Wisconsin. He won the Eudora Welty Award for his collection of stories, "Under the Circumstances." He is currently at work on a novel set in rural Wisconsin during Prohibition.

Sara Evelyne is a poet, researcher, and brain injury survivor. She writes to remind others to 'never forget how far you've come just by waking up today.' Sara's poem "Written in the Stones" is forthcoming in *Letting Grief Speak: Writing Portals for Life After Loss*, a writing craft book by Columbia University Press. C

Jennifer Susan Smith is a retired speech-language pathologist, residing in northwest Georgia. Her work appears in *WELL READ Magazine, The Bluebird Word, San Antonio Review, First Literary Review East*, and more. Jennifer is chairman of Alpha Delta Kappa Pages and Pearls Book Club and is a member of Chattanooga Writer's Guild. When not writing, she enjoys walking and audiobooks.

Loretta Fairley is a native of south Mississippi and has been writing since 1978. She has freelanced for various publications and has published two volumes of poetry at Amazon. In addition to writing, she enjoys reading, nature, photography and computers.

Award-winning author, J.L. Oakley, writes historical fiction that spans the mid-19 th century to WW II with characters standing up for something in their own time and place. She also writes the occasional personal essay. *Dry Wall in the Time of Grief* won the 2016 grand prize at Surrey Writers. Recent awards have been the 2020 Hemingway Grand Prize award for 20th century war time fiction and an Honorable Mention Writer Digest Self-pubbed Ebooks for *The Quisling Factor*.

Kris Faatz's short fiction has appeared or is forthcoming in journals including *Atticus Review* and *Rappahannock Review*, and was longlisted for Wigleaf's 2024 Top 50 stories. Her second novel, *Fourteen Stones*, was released in June 2024 by Highlander Press. Her third novel, *Line Magic*, was shortlisted for the Santa Fe Writers Project's 2023 awards. Kris teaches creative writing and is a performing pianist.

Ed Nichols lives in Clarkesville, Georgia. He is a graduate of the School of Journalism at the University of Georgia. He has had many short stories and prose poems published in magazines. Below is a list of his published books. I Wish I Could Laugh – A chapbook of prose poems, Perfect Land – A collection of prose poems, The Boy In The Book – Flash fiction and prose poems, We'll Talk Some More – A collection of short stories, The Professor And Confederate Gold – Novel.

Linda Imbler is the author of nine paperback poetry collections and four e-book collections (Soma Publishing.) This writer lives in Wichita, Kansas with her husband, Mike the Luthier, several quite intelligent saltwater fish, and an ever-growing family of gorgeous guitars.

Annie McDonnell is a lifelong literary advocate. High Point University, NC '91. Best-selling and award-winning author of *Annie's Song: Dandelions, Dreams & Dogs*. It was acquired by Pandamoon Publishing and set to be re-released in the Spring, 2025. She is the founder of The Write Review Literary Community, podcaster, book reviewer, author consultant, and matchmaker. Annie has been introducing us to books and authors since 2006, when she began reviewing books for *Elle Magazine*. She is also a Proud Stiff Person Syndrome Warrior.

Mike Turner retired to the Alabama Gulf Coast after more than 25 years as a Federal law enforcement executive. An adult ed ukulele class opened the world of music and songwriting to Mike; with more than 200 original songs to his credit, he was featured on the "15 Minutes of Fame" stage at the 2020 Monroeville Literary Festival. Mike has had more than 300 poems published in more than 65 literary journals and anthologies. His poetry book, *Visions and Memories*, is available on Amazon. His poem, "A Sense of Peace," was awarded the Alabama Writers Cooperative's 2023 Roger Williams Peace Award for Writing. When not writing and recording, Mike explores the backwaters of the Northern Gulf with his wife, Pamela Caudill, on their recreational trawler.

Micah Ward is a retiree who lives in central Tennessee. His fiction has been recognized with three Honorable Mentions at the Lorian Hemingway Short Story Competition. Micah has been published in numerous regional and national running publications and won the Road Runners Club of America award for Club Writer of the Year in 2012.

James Wade is the award-winning author of *Beasts of the Earth, All Things Left Wild*, and *River, Sing Out*. He is the youngest novelist to win two Spur Awards from the Western Writers of America, and the recipient of the MPIBA's prestigious Reading the West Award. James's work has appeared in *Southern Literary Magazine, The Bitter Oleander, Writers' Digest*, and numerous additional publications. James lives and writes in the Texas Hill Country with his wife and children.

Ashley Tunnell, a writer from Blairsville, GA, is completing a bachelor's degree in English from UNG, and she intends to pursue her master's degree in the same field with a concentration in creative writing. Her work has been published in UNG's literary magazine as well as the Southern Literary Festival's anthology of poetry and short stories.

John M. Williams is a mentor in the Reinhardt University MFA Creative Writing program. His latest publication is his novel *End Times* (Sartoris Literary Group 2023). Other publications can be found on his website at johnmwilliams.net , which hosts his blog, johnmwilliams.net/blog . He lives in LaGrange, Georgia.

Robb Grindstaff's journalism career took him from Phoenix to North Carolina, Texas, Wisconsin, DC, and Tokyo. Robb has five novels published along with a couple dozen short stories. He is a fiction editor, having edited more than 200 books in seventeen years. He now writes, edits, and teaches fiction full time from his home in Lake of the Ozarks, Missouri.

Stevie Lyon (she/they) is a long-time lover of all things suspenseful, surreal and spooky. Her fiction often looks at the world through a slanted psychological lens, focused on the shadowy side of all things. Stevie is a practicing clinical psychologist, professor, and fronts the dream pop band Project Trustfall.

Laura McHale Holland writes stories long, short, true and untrue that tend to bend reality—often with characters (including herself) whose lives have gone terribly wrong but are ultimately redeemable. She has won several indie publishing awards and tells tales on stage occasionally.

Saeed Ibrahim is the author of two books - "Twin Tales from Kutcch," a family saga set in Colonial India, and a short story collection entitled "The Missing Tile and Other Stories." His short stories have appeared in "The Deccan Herald," "The Week," "The Blue Lotus Magazine," "Borderless Journal," "Muse India," "Outlook India," "Different Truths" "Lothlorien Poetry Journal" and "Setu Bilingual Journal."

Nancy Julien Kopp lives and writes in the Flint Hills of Kansas. She has been published in 24 *Chicken Soup for the Soul* anthologies, many other anthologies, ezines and magazines. Her writing includes poetry, fiction for children, creative nonfiction, short memoir, and articles on the craft of writing.

Julie Green is a retired museum curator, wife, mom, lifelong choral singer, and radical arts advocate. She writes in her living room with her dog Tashi who rarely provides inspiration and sleeps a lot. She is currently finishing a novel and putting together a chapbook. Her work has appeared in several journals including *Slant, The Reach of Song, Circle of Women* (Emory University), and *Naugatuck River Review.* She is the 2023 and 2024 recipient of the Herbert Shippey Award for Excellence in Southern Poetry, and the Low Country Award for Short Story given by the Southeastern Writers Association.

DeLane Phillips is a Southern voice. She is a mom, a daughter, caregiver, dog mom, writer, and teacher. Many characters and settings featured are from her childhood in Monroe, Georgia. Later in her life, DeLane attended Emmanuel College in Franklin Springs, Georgia, where she was featured in Emmanuel's annual "Montage," receiving first place in prose. A few years later, after the passing of her mother, DeLane returned to the muse of much of her writing, her homeplace in Walton County. She continues to write and supports her 83 year old father, as he battles Alzheimers' disease.

As a multilingual & multicultural, Shayla Dodge grew up in the backwoods of the Smoky Mountains of North Carolina. She completed her BA in the Czech Republic and pursued her master's degree in public policy in India and the Czech Republic, completing it in 2011. Shayla then moved to the US and worked for 10 years in the fields of mental health and education. She served as the chief editor of Herland Newsletter from 2013-15, and her writing has appeared in *The Shift Newsletter, Plato's Caves Online, The Pinecone Review, All Your Stories*, and *Well Read Magazine.* She is currently based in Oklahoma City, Oklahoma.

Mr. Ferreira, 80 years old, is a Brazilian poet who writes in English rather than Portuguese. Has launched two Poetry books, *Lonely Sailor* and *Joie de Vivre*; has 200 poems published in 300 different publications, in international Literary Journals. Has, also, been nominated for the Pushcart Prize. He began writing at the age 67 after retirement from a bank.

Chris Wood manages numbers by day, spends evenings cleaning up dog hair from the abundance of love from her fur-babies, and writes in between to balance her right brain from her left. Her work appears in several publications, including *Salvation South* and *Poetry Quarterly*.

Jasna Gugić is the Vice-President for public relations of the Association of Artists and Writers of the World SAPS; She is a co-editor of the anthology, *Compassion—Save the World, one poem written by 130 world poets*. Jasna is a multiple winner of many international awards for poetry and literature, and her work has been translated into several world languages. Her first independent collection of poetry was published in 2021, a bilingual English-Croatian edition, entitled *Song of Silence*. She lives and works in Zagreb, Croatia.

Fhen M. studied the academic subjects Writing in the Discipline, The Literature of the Phillipines, and The Literature of the World at Eastern Visayas State University. The Waray poem "Uyasan" ("Toy" in English") written by Fhen M. was published in a collection of literary works entitled *Pinili: 15 Years of Lamiraw*. His English verses "Lighthouse," "Seaport," "Barbeque Stalls along Boulevard," and "Tetrapod" appeared in *Poetica* anthology series published by Clarendon House. In 2024, Red Penguin Books' *About Time: A Coming of Age Poetry Anthology* will publish his piece "Outside the Block Universe". One of his poems will also be included in *Flora/Fauna Anthology* by Open Shutter Press. Fhen M. submitted verses in Waray for the 5th Lamiraw Creative Writing Workshop, including the siday "Duha nga mga pagtug-an" (translated in English as "Two confessions"). David Genotiva, Merlie Alunan, and Victor Sugbo were some of the distinguished panelists of this writing workshop held from the 5th to the 7th of November 2008.

Long time retired community college instructor, Celia Miles has twelve novels to her credit, a textbook, and two short story collections. Her favorite topics are old grist mills and the neolithic sites in the British Isles. She lives and writes from Asheville.

Hubert Blair Bonds, a native of Kannapolis, NC, has lived in Atlanta, GA for more than 30 years. He is retired from the federal government with 34 years of service. Currently acting Treasurer at the East Point Historical Society, his hobbies include gardening, film history, and writing.

Ellen Birkett Morris's debut novel *Beware the Tall Grass* won the Donald L. Jordan Award for Literary Excellence, judged by Lan Samantha Chang. She is the author of *Lost Girls: Short Stories*, winner of the Pencraft Award. Her fiction has appeared in *Shenandoah, Antioch Review, Notre Dame Review,* and *South Carolina Review*, among other journals. Morris is a recipient of an Al Smith Fellowship for her fiction from the Kentucky Arts Council.

Launched on an unsuspecting commercial world, Margaret Pearce, ended up copywriting in an advertising department and took to writing instead of drink when raising children. Margaret completed an Arts Degree at Monash University as a mature age student, and has primary and teenage novels published as listed on Amazon, Book Depository, Kindle, and writers-exchange.com

Ellen Notbohm's work touches millions in more than twenty-five languages. She is author of the award-winning novel *The River by Starlight* and the nonfiction classic *Ten Things Every Child with Autism Wishes You Knew.* Her short fiction and creative nonfiction appears in many literary journals including *Eclectica, Brevity, Halfway Down the Stairs, Fabula Argentea, Eunoia Review, Bookends Review, Does It Have Pockets?,* and in anthologies in the US and abroad. Her books and short prose have won more than 40 awards.

Kimberly Parish Davis is the director and founder of Madville Publishing. She sometimes teaches English Composition, Creative Writing, and Technical writing. She spent five years on the editorial staff of Texas Review Press. She has a new short story collection forthcoming with Cornerstone Press, fall 2025. The title is *Trust Issues*. Find her on the web at kpdavis.com.

J. B. Hogan has been published in a number of journals including the *Blue Lake Review, Crack the Spine, Copperfield Review, Lothlorien Poetry Journal, Well Read Magazine*, and *Aphelion*. His eleven books include *Bar Harbor, Mexican Skies, Living Behind Time, Losing Cotton*, and *The Apostate*. He lives in Fayetteville, Arkansas.

Royal Rhodes is a poet and essayist who lives in a small village in central Ohio. His poems have appeared in a number of literary journals in the U.S., U.K., and Canada. He especially loves to read the works of the ancient Greek and Roman authors.

Lindsay Carraway's artwork reflects social, cultural, and political issues mixed with dreams and visions of her schizophrenic mind. Moving through from the past to the future she uses a series of images, symbols, and numbers, that she sees or hears from her visions or dreams to form the stories she wants to convey.

These stories are usually ideas that are on her mind or subconsciously pulling at her.

Showing symbolism of the south, sexuality, family, and religious nods, along with peeks into the future, and remembrance of the past, together the painting and collages showcase a glimpse into her mind as she sketches with paper and paints the ideas she has from within.

WELL READ is always on the lookout for submissions from writers and artists who have stories to tell. We combine new and established voices from diverse backgrounds and celebrate different perspectives. We want people who aren't afraid to shake things up, speak their mind, and share their humanity.

No prompts or themes - no boundaries

www.wellreadmagazine.com

www.ingramcontent.com/pod-product-compliance
Lightning Source LLC
Chambersburg PA
CBHW020729210626
46807CB00016B/511